LAST STOP ON THE WINTER WONDERLAND EXPRESS

REBECCA RAISIN

B
Boldwood

First published in Great Britain in 2025 by Boldwood Books Ltd.

Copyright © Rebecca Raisin, 2025

Cover Design by Alexandra Allden

Cover Images: Shutterstock

The moral right of Rebecca Raisin to be identified as the author of this work has been asserted in accordance with the Copyright, Designs and Patents Act 1988.

All rights reserved. No part of this book may be reproduced in any form or by any electronic or mechanical means, including information storage and retrieval systems, without written permission from the author, except for the use of brief quotations in a book review. This book is a work of fiction and, except in the case of historical fact, any resemblance to actual persons, living or dead, is purely coincidental.

Every effort has been made to obtain the necessary permissions with reference to copyright material, both illustrative and quoted. We apologise for any omissions in this respect and will be pleased to make the appropriate acknowledgements in any future edition.

A CIP catalogue record for this book is available from the British Library.

Paperback ISBN 978-1-83533-530-7

Large Print ISBN 978-1-83533-531-4

Hardback ISBN 978-1-83533-529-1

Ebook ISBN 978-1-83533-532-1

Kindle ISBN 978-1-83533-533-8

Audio CD ISBN 978-1-83533-524-6

MP3 CD ISBN 978-1-83533-525-3

Digital audio download ISBN 978-1-83533-526-0

This book is printed on certified sustainable paper. Boldwood Books is dedicated to putting sustainability at the heart of our business. For more information please visit https://www.boldwoodbooks.com/about-us/sustainability/

Boldwood Books Ltd, 23 Bowerdean Street, London, SW6 3TN

www.boldwoodbooks.com

For Jason Stevens

1

16 DECEMBER, KENT, ENGLAND

Wedding Day

I have the sudden urge to run.

That would be OK if: a) I was the running type and b) it wasn't my wedding day.

No one mentions wedding jitters are this intense, do they? My bridal party excitedly chatter ten to the dozen, while I lock a rictus smile into place that hides my inner angst. It takes a surprising amount of effort to get facial muscles to cooperate. My laissez-faire expression can't be fooling anyone because my make-up artist, Rox, says, 'Blink twice if you need help.'

A burst of hysterical laughter escapes me. 'Whaaat...? I'm fine. I'm good! I'm great.' Her eyes narrow. Have I overdone it? I dig myself in deeper. 'I'm marrying the man of my dreams in a Christmassy winter wonderland wedding. What's not to like?'

Rox narrows her eyes but doesn't probe further. Phew.

Truth be told, my fiancé Miles has been a little distant in the lead-up to the wedding, but then so have I. Life's been chaotic helping clients with their last-minute Christmas travel itineraries, while tying up loose ends for our wedding and dream honeymoon. Miles hasn't involved himself with any of the planning, until a month ago when he insisted on changing our intimate wedding into an extravaganza of epic proportions, so now I'll be walking down the aisle with a lot more eyeballs on me than I'm comfortable with.

Miles is the type who likes the spotlight. I'm the other type. Opposites attract though, and isn't marriage all about compromise?

There was a point I thought I'd remain single forever, because travelling the globe working remotely for years made it hard to find a soulmate. A summer fling here and there, sure, but those were only seasonal.

It's not as if I didn't want to find true love, it just never found me.

Until it did. In the shape of handsome, athletic Miles, an old high school crush, who blindsided me with his confident swagger and high-octane energy after I'd returned home for a 'quick' visit to see my family. Here I am, a year and a half later, having said yes to the dress! Putting down roots, of all things. Although I quietly worry that the travel bug will bite once more – staying put has never been my thing but Miles assures me we can deal with any forks in the road together as a team. A team of two!

'I can handle a nervous bride,' Rox says. 'It's the criers I find difficult.'

'The criers?' So it's not just me? Do all brides feel this same seesaw of conflicting emotions on their wedding day? A mix of excitement and trepidation. Why doesn't anyone mention this? It seems rather pertinent to know.

'The criers are the worst and won't be told, y'know? Mascara is the bane of every make-up artist's life. Even waterproof isn't infallible and once the eyes are bloodshot, there's not a lot I can do. I'm not a miracle worker, am I?' Rox shakes her head and continues with a litany of complaints about brides who've ruined her cosmetic artistry.

Right now, bloodshot eyes are the least of my concerns. It's my escalated heart rate I'm worried about. Just how long can it beat double time before it gives up the ghost completely? It's strange that I can confidently explore a foreign country where I don't speak the language or know a single soul, but just the thought of a church full of hometown locals is enough to send me spiralling.

'Like, why are they so overwrought? You've got the blubbering mess type...' As Rox rambles on denigrating former clients, I picture holding my hand over her mouth until she runs out of breath and her face goes blue. Probably an overreaction but here we are. At least I know this panicked feeling is not unique to me.

'I suppose they're happy tears though?' my mum interjects as she sits beside me getting her make-up done by a much less bitter make-up artist, the lucky thing.

'Yes, tears of *joy*.' Rox emphasises the word as if it tastes sour. 'Be warned, once the mother of the bride starts, it all kicks off.' She shoots Mum a withering glare in the reflection of the mirror. It's all rather threatening but I bite my tongue against a retort because that would not be fitting under the circumstances.

Rox locks her gaze back on mine. 'You do not want puffy eyes in your wedding photos.'

'That's what photoshop is for, dear,' Mum says with a shrug. 'If we cry, we cry.'

Rox sticks me a little harder than necessary with eyeliner while I try to control the spike of adrenaline coursing through me as I envision myself snatching the pencil from her fingers and snapping it in half. 'Ow!' I say as she gouges me once more.

'Soz.' Her eyes glitter with triumph as if she's enjoying this.

Why didn't Miles and I elope? That's more my speed. We could have married atop a mountain in Peru. Exchanged wedding rings underwater while snorkelling in Tahiti. Shared our vows in a helicopter above Maui. Oh, that's right, he said no to all of those ideas.

After a close-up inspection, Rox declares me ready. 'Wait!' she screeches. 'Setting spray.' She unleashes what looks (and burns) like a can of hairspray onto my face. I cough and splutter, worrying about aerosols and the ozone layer. You never hear about damage to the ozone layer any more. Why is that? It's a problem for another day because right now I'm trying hard to pull oxygen back into my lungs amid the toxic cloud I'm engulfed in.

'Was that really necessary?' I eventually choke out.

She arches a perfectly manicured brow. 'Probably not.'

'For the record, you are the worst make-up artist I've ever met.'

Rox gasps. Mum sighs. My maid of honour Freya shakes her head.

'Now now, girls,' Mum says. 'Don't argue. Aubrey, it's nice of your sister to do your make-up on your wedding day, even if she's a little overzealous with her products…'

'A little?'

Rox shakes her head. 'May I remind you I'm doing your make-up gratis and if we're dropping truth bombs left and right, you're not exactly the easiest subject to work with.'

I roll my eyes. This is how it always is with us, but the bickering is a good distraction.

Rox suffers from younger sibling syndrome. You know the

type: spoiled, petulant, attention seeking. I try to make allowances for her, but it's not easy.

'I can hear you, Aubrey. Mum, she's doing that weird under-breath life narration thing again. Please tell her I do not suffer from younger sibling syndrome. I'm sure she made that up to get back at me because she's jealous.'

I scoff. 'Jealous! Of what?'

'Of not being the cutest since I came along.'

'Oh please.'

'Girls.' Mum gives us a warning glare. Really, I'm too old for this kind of carry on.

'Sorry, Mum,' we mutter, but only one of us is contrite and – spoiler alert – it's not Rox.

Mum thanks her own make-up artist and comes to check out Rox's handiwork. I don't like to admit how talented my sister is, but she's managed to transform me from the clichéd plain Jane I am into a princess. 'Wow. You're beautiful, Aubrey, just beautiful.'

Rox beams. 'You have Charlotte Tilbury to thank for that.'

Mum frowns as if trying to place the name. 'I don't know who this Charlotte person is. I'm more inclined to think it's good genes, complemented by your wonderful cosmetic artistry, Rox.'

'No, Charlotte is the...' Rox's voice peters off as she figures there's no point educating Mum about make-up brands.

'Mum's right,' I begrudgingly admit. 'You've done a great job, Rox. I'm sure with that amount of "setting spray" the make-up won't budge for the next millennia or so.'

Freya wanders over, glancing at the time. 'Let's get you into the dress!'

They gather around as Freya pulls my dressing gown from my shoulders and I'm left standing exposed in my barely there wedding lingerie, chosen for its claims of no VPL. Mum helps me slip into the ivory satin gown that's been cut on the bias and features a low draped back. It falls around my curves like liquid. There's a fur stole to complete the look and stop me from freezing to death in the draughty church.

Mum's eyes glisten with tears. Before I can console her, Rox shoots her a cease-and-desist glare, vehemently shaking her head as if tears are contagious and will somehow jump from Mum's body to mine and ruin the cosmetics she's just spent the best part of an hour applying. 'Don't do it,' Rox warns.

Mum fans her face with a hand. Why do people fan their face like that when they cry? It's a mystery for later because Mum gulps back tears and sputters, 'Ma-maybe Rox is right. If I start crying, you'll soon join in. Ignore me!' A fresh sob escapes her, but there is no time for hugs as Freya motions for me to sit on the loveseat, so she can help me slip on my heels.

Heels that now seem perilously high. 'Why didn't I choose a more practical shoe?' I have visions of tumbling down the aisle with all those eyeballs on me as I awkwardly somersault towards my groom.

I'm more of a ballet flat than heels sort of girl, but really I have no one to blame except myself for getting swept away in the romance of wedding planning and choosing shoes normally found on a runway, not real life. Don't we all want to be the princess for just one day, even if I do resemble a newborn foal trying to walk in them. Weddings, eh?

'Just walk slowly,' Freya advises. 'Or pretend it's the aisle of a plane; you can walk down those just fine!'

Mum laughs. 'I'm happy you'll have a lifelong travel buddy for all those adventures around the world. It puts my mind at ease.' Mum always frets about me travelling solo. Now I'll have Miles along for the ride. Even if we settle here in the village for good, that doesn't mean we can't zip off when adventure calls.

'That's if Aubrey lets him tag along,' Freya jokes as she

absently rubs her bump, which is a bit of a misnomer as she's eight and bit months along. 'You'll be too busy, moving in together and making babies...?' She lifts a questioning brow.

'My nomadic days might be on pause but I'm not so sure about the baby part just yet.' When I picture my future, I don't see gurgling toddlers with spaghetti-sauce-stained faces. That clock has never ticked for me. And Miles is happy to wait and see.

Mum's fussing with my veil. Freya's fluffing my hair. When they finally step back, the room falls silent.

I turn to face the mirror and gasp in surprise. In the dress, the transformation is complete, despite my slight wobbling in the heels. Mum bites down on her lip as tears slide down her cheeks.

'Don't mind me,' Mum says. 'You're just so... so...'

Freya hands Mum a tissue and throws a comforting arm around her. 'Breathtaking,' Freya finishes while my poor mum blinks back tears. 'Today, you're the main character, Aubrey. You're stunning, like a golden age of Hollywood movie star.'

Rox gives Mum's shoulder a squeeze. 'Get it together, Mother. We don't want panda eyes.' At that she abruptly turns away and dips her head.

'Are you welling up too, Rox?' Freya teases.

Rox spins back to face us, her eyes glassy as she snatches a tissue from Freya. 'So what if the ice queen melts every now and then. Blame global warming. It's not every day your big sister gets married, is it?'

'Let's cheers to that. A glass of champagne is in order; well, I'll have sparkling apple juice...' Freya goes to the ice bucket and returns with a bottle of bubbles and three glasses. Mum goes to the kitchen to find Freya a drink.

Once we all have a glass in hand, Mum gives a speech about

finding true love, which makes us all well up, make-up be damned. 'Here's to Aubrey!'

'Cheers!' We clink glasses. 'Here's to the honeymoon of my dreams!' Oops, it just slipped out. I forget that most people hold the whole wedding part in much higher regard, whereas for me, it's the stepping stone to the fun part, the romantic holiday, with my brand-new husband.

Mum frowns. 'You'll enjoy the wedding first though, won't you, darling?'

I guzzle champagne too fast, my mouth parched as if I've run a marathon and not simply sat there all morning being pampered. 'Yes, yes. But the honeymoon is what I'm most looking forward to. Just me and Miles…'

I run an online travel agency curating exotic itineraries for loved-up couples. Now it's my turn to experience romantic travel with my soon-to-be husband. Having been a solo shoestring nomad for so long, our bougie honeymoon seems so wildly glamorous, I'm practically vibrating with excitement.

Tonight, we're staying in a swanky hotel in London with a view of Tower Bridge. And tomorrow we'll catch the Eurostar to Calais to board the famous sleeper train, the Winter Wonderland Express. While the train has been offering five-star holidays for decades, this is the first time they've curated a Christmas-themed tour, highlighting all the festive markets along the European Arctic Circle route. We disembark in Lapland and enjoy an igloo stay in the hopes of catching the spectacular Northern Lights. Luckily, I got our tickets for a song. One of the perks of being a travel agent is generous discounts, so even Miles had to agree it was a once-in-a-lifetime opportunity that we had to grab with both hands.

'The cars are here!' Freya calls just as my dad knocks and enters. My dad is the taciturn type, so I don't expect any blubbering from him. I envelop him in a hug and hold tight, like I have so many times in my life when I needed reassurance, needed comfort. He shores me up and reminds me that today is special, but marriage doesn't mean I lose my identity simply by taking on a different surname.

'I love you, Dad.'

'Love you too, Poppet.'

'Are you ready to get married?' Mum asks.

'I'm ready.' All my worries evaporate as I consider marriage for what it really is, once you push the pomp and ceremony to one side.

A promise to each other.

And what more can I ask for, except a promise from the man I adore that he's committed, that he wants to do life with me as his sidekick?

2

16 DECEMBER, KENT, ENGLAND

Wedding Day

Mum and the bridal party go ahead in a vintage Rolls Royce. Dad and I take the second car, trailing a few minutes behind them.

'Are you OK?' He gives me one of those paternal stare-downs that he's used my entire life to get me to fess up on my small crimes, like pulling my sister's hair or hiding her Barbie dolls.

'I'm OK. I just wish we were marrying in front of our nearest and dearest, not the entire village, in case I fall over on these ridiculous heels and knock out my two front teeth, or mess up my vows. Like, what if I say I don't, instead of I do? There's a lot to worry about.'

My toxic trait is to blurt out the most ridiculous things when I'm under pressure. It's like my mouth speaks before my brain engages, so there's a very real chance I might let slip an oddity that will raise eyebrows.

Dad gives me a sage nod. He's circumspect, like those inscrutable detectives on TV who remain stubbornly silent; a silence you can't help but fill, blurting all your secrets as you go.

He's doing that now, as if he knows I'm not quite being honest with him and he's prepared to wait me out.

I wring my hands. 'What if my wedding ring doesn't fit? What if it slips off? What if the dog Miles doesn't have ate it! I guess I wish I'd held my ground and kept our nuptials small, but this is important to Miles, so...'

Miles proposed early on, very early on, so this has all moved rather fast, but he, *we*, felt certain it was time to get serious, grow up. Marriage, house, responsibilities.

'None of that matters in the scheme of what today really means – a celebration of your love and the commitment you're making to one another.'

'Why can't you tell me I'm being dramatic? I'm making mountains out of molehills. Why do you have to be so wise?' I laugh. He's right though; if anything goes awry, we'll deal with it.

'You're not being dramatic, love. It's natural to feel a gamut of emotions on your wedding day. Miles has invited hundreds of people, while he gets to wait safely at the other end of aisle, wearing flat shoes that grip to the earth. Blame the patriarchy,' Dad jokes.

'The bloody patriarchy strikes again.'

He laughs. 'To combat your nerves, I suggest that you think of the guests naked.'

'Dad!'

'What? It's a real strategy, I read about it on the internet. It's meant to help nervous public speakers and the like.'

'Then it must be true. Can you imagine picturing straitlaced Uncle Harold naked?' The mood is suddenly jubilant as we laugh. The pretty village church comes into view, stunning under a blanket of light snow. Under grey skies the Christmas tree out the front sparkles with twinkling fairy lights, lending a festive air to the day.

'Here we go.' Now the moment has arrived, a burst of excitement races through me. It's not so bad, this wedding lark.

'Ready, darling?' Dad gives my hand a comforting squeeze.

'As ready as I'll ever be.' Don't think of all those eyeballs. Don't think of naked guests. Think of Miles, my handsome groom, waiting patiently for me. For our shiny new unwritten future where anything is possible.

Dad frowns. 'Where's the bridal party? Your mum said they'd be waiting to help you out of the car.'

Their car is here, but no sign of them. 'They're probably inside on account of the early snow, and it's not like I'm wearing a meringue-type dress that I need help with.'

The driver opens Dad's door and a blast of cold air fills the space. No wonder the bridal party chose to wait inside the church walls. They'll freeze to death outside in their bridesmaid dresses. 'Let's get you into the church, then.' Dad holds out a hand to me as soft snowflakes cascade down like something out of a fairytale.

Before I take his proffered hand, Freya rushes from the church doors. Her high heels slip on the icy ground. 'Freya!' I screech. My heart leaps to my throat as I watch my very pregnant friend sliding like a roller-skater looking for purchase. She manages to avoid slipping over and gives me an apologetic smile.

Dad jogs to her, much surer on his feet being a six-foot tall beanpole with no baby bump upsetting his balance. He takes Freya's arm and guides her across the slick ground and safely back towards the car. The wind whips their words away before I can catch what they're saying. Whatever it is, it has stolen their smiles. Miles forgot the rings, I bet.

With her free hand, Freya holds up the hem of her ruched gown as she approaches the car door. Instead of helping me out, she slides in beside me in the space my dad vacated.

'Aubrey...' Her voice cracks. Worry flashes over her features, then something else. Pity, maybe?

'What? What is it?' My eyes drop to her belly. 'Are you...? Do we need to go to the hosp— Is the baby coming?' That would explain her urgency in trying to run in heels in the inclement weather.

Freya shakes her head. Grips my hand and squeezes hard like she needs to cling on tight for whatever she's about to tell me, as if I might float away. 'No, no, it's not the baby. It's Miles. He's not here.'

'What? Where is he?' My mind goes to wardrobe malfunctions. A car accident on the icy roads. Perhaps he left his vows at home? That would be a very plausible Miles thing to do. But deep down I sense the truth, and it's not good.

In fact, it's very, very bad.

Freya swallows hard. 'Apparently, he was here, but he left about ten minutes ago, in a bit of a state. He told his parents that he's changed his mind and doesn't want to... get married. He thinks maybe he's rushed into the relationship and it's all moved too fast.'

My head is going to explode. 'I did tell him he was rushing things but he insisted on marriage – he did! What the actual hell.' Mortification colours me scarlet. 'And he's waited until now to share this?' My blood pressure spikes. Rage and shame fight for supremacy but shame wins the race. How utterly humiliating. 'Is he really not coming back?' My voice comes out strangled.

Freya gives me a slight nod as if not trusting herself to speak either. This whole situation almost feels like a practical joke – albeit a distasteful one.

Aren't jilted brides just fodder for romcom movies? Films starring Julia Roberts and Adam Sandler?

It's all so familiar, like I've heard this song before. None of my relationships ever go the distance and I'm clueless to what I do wrong, but it must be me; after all, I'm the common denominator. Gah! I'm not a fan of the whole blame game, but this betrayal... well, it gives a girl the urge to hold up a magnifying glass to herself to look for clues. A jilted bride! You can't get much worse than that.

'I'm so sorry, Aubrey.'

I give her a useless nod. I mean, what else can I do or say here? The man decided to run instead of commit to me.

Stupid me thought that I'd finally found the one. As if Cupid, that cherubic little fallacy, had finally shot his arrow especially for me. How could I have been so gullible? I have always been unlucky in love, and this proves it.

No, this can't be right. There must be another explanation. I find my phone and call Miles. He's switched his off! I call his best man Leo, who awkwardly confirms Miles has had a change of heart and isn't up to speaking to me right now. Leo is so apologetic, so concerned, that suddenly this nightmare becomes very real indeed.

A sob escapes Freya. This all feels so strange, like I'm floating outside of my body. Is it the shock? It must be. I'm grappling with what to do next. There's no guide for this. No one gives you a list of appropriate reactions for when your fiancé abruptly leaves you at the altar. Is this why he's been so withdrawn recently? He was having doubts. Why didn't he voice those concerns?

Even my dad, who usually has all the answers, stays glued to the spot like he's unsure of how to proceed.

'There's one other... problem.' Freya gulps. 'Rox saw red and has stolen one of the guest's e-scooters. She's on her way to Miles's cottage.'

'Oh, God,' Dad says, clutching his head. 'It's very likely that she will kill him.' Suddenly galvanised, Dad sprints into the church, perhaps to pray that Rox doesn't catch up to the runaway groom, or possibly that she does. Jury is still out on how Dad's feeling at the minute.

While my sister and I bicker like children, we stick together through thick and thin. Yes, we might torment each other – but that doesn't mean anyone else is allowed the privilege. Rox is fiercely protective of her family, but I do worry there's a little too much homicidal maniac languishing just under the surface, and any excuse will do to act on those urges.

Right now, I've got bigger things to worry about, like being on display as guests wander from the church and swing their confused gazes squarely at me. Great, now I have an audience to witness my humiliation.

I can imagine the whispers around the village: *Poor boy left that travel-obsessed Aubrey at the altar, so her crazy sister ran him over with a stolen e-scooter and now he's missing a leg! Those girls need taking into line. No wonder he changed his mind, family like that!*

Wait, no! Miles doesn't get to be dismembered to avoid the blame! I fumble for my phone and call my sister, who answers on the first ring. 'I'm almost at his place. I'm going to take great pleasure in hurting him, like he hurt you, Aubrey!' Her words come out breathless, choppy, as if she's riding a wave of adrenaline.

Oh God, she is going to kill him! Let's just say she's never taken to Miles; well, except that one time she literally took to him with a hammer after a slight misunderstanding between the pair, and ever since then, Rox has been leery of the guy. Was she right about him all along?

'Please don't, Rox.' My little sister strikes me as the type who'd enjoy a bit of bloodshed now there's a reason to warrant it. The very last thing I need is this to blow up into a grievous bodily harm charge. Part of me hopes this is just a kneejerk reaction and Miles will be right back, red-faced, full of apologies. But isn't his desertion unforgivable? 'Let him run away like the fool he is!' I cry.

'What!' she screeches. 'Where's the fun in that? No, he needs to pay for his crimes. I want to manslaughter him.'

I gasp. 'This isn't manslaughter, Rox. This is premeditated—'

'Slaughter all the toxic men who dare hurt women. Manslaughter the man-splainer!'

'Oh right. I see the difference.'

While I wouldn't mind him suffering a spot of pain right now, any retaliation will paint him as the victim and I need answers first. What if there is a valid reason? But then why isn't he talking? Nothing makes sense! 'And he will pay, Rox, but if you hurt him, which you're very capable of, he then becomes the wronged man, and everyone will be sympathetic towards him. Let's be clear, he doesn't deserve that!'

How am I thinking so straight? Why aren't I curled up in the foetal position? I suppose all that's still to come. Unless I escape.

Is there a town in this big wide world that has zero men in it? If not, I'll make one. A community of jilted brides. We'll burn effigies of cowardly men and—

'How would anyone in their right mind be sympathetic towards him? I'm not planning on killing the snake, just maiming him a bit, for crying out loud!'

Maiming him! How to convince her, and fast? 'Mum and Dad live here too. They don't want to face any blowback, Rox. They'd never live it down. Wouldn't it be better to hurt him in, say, a year or so when no one will connect those dots back to you?' Buying time is the best I can do for the damn man in the hopes her anger will wane.

Rox is quiet while she contemplates it. 'You're right. He is the type who'll press charges. A future stealth attack is much smarter. Fine, this calls for plan B then.' With that she abruptly hangs up.

'What's she doing?' Freya asks, peeking out through her hands as if she doesn't really want the details. Probably wise.

I shrug helplessly. 'Plan B.'

When the stragglers by the church doors become a crowd and a few break off and make their way towards the wedding car, I'm spurred into action. There's no way I'm having a conversation with these people before I've talked to Miles. Mum and Dad are still inside, probably with Miles's parents, so I leave them to it.

I call to the driver, who doubles as the local postman, and now has a front-row seat to this disaster show. 'Can you take me home please?'

'Sure.'

3

16 DECEMBER, KENT, ENGLAND

Wedding Day (that wasn't)

We arrive back at the cottage I share with Rox. Miles and I haven't officially moved in together yet – he still shares a bachelor pad with Leo – but I usually sleep there most evenings, even though I rent a room in Rox's cottage. The plan is (was?) to find our own house after the honeymoon. Now I'm thankful I have this private space in which to fall apart.

Freya wrings her hands while I question every little thing before collapsing on the sofa in a messy, sobbing heap. Were my own doubts earlier a sign that things weren't right between us, or were they simply the doubts of a nervous bride?

Truth be told, settling in one place always felt like a huge sacrifice, but I'd been prepared to do it because of my love for Miles. What changed for him? What made him baulk at the idea of matrimony?

Our phones simultaneously beep with a text. Freya swipes her screen. 'Your parents have told everyone at the venue,' she says. 'They want to know if they should invite guests to enjoy the reception, or not?'

The reception. All that catering going to waste, a decadent Christmas feast with all the trimmings. And all those staff hired for the day. Not to mention the effort our guests have made to be here, a few even coming from abroad. 'Yes, yes, they should have lunch. We've paid for it. I'm sure there's no refunds on the day of.' I clench my jaw as I call Miles again. Nothing.

The front door opens with a blustery bang, making me jump in fright. Rox appears as the wind whips her black locks around her face. With her mussed hair and wild eyes, she looks like something out of a horror movie.

'Ah... is everything OK, Rox?' I ask. 'You didn't catch up with Miles, did you?'

I surreptitiously survey her for blood spatter and am relieved when I find none.

Rox gives me an evil grin that can only mean a form of retribution has been meted out.

'What have you done?' Freya whispers, holding a protective hand over her belly. Let's hope her unborn baby isn't about to hear its first murder confession.

Rox shuts the door and throws herself next to me on the sofa. 'Nothing drastic. But let's just say, Miles won't be enjoying his wedding night safely tucked up in bed.'

My stomach flips as I debate whether to pry any further. If I don't know, I can't tell, right? But dammit, I care about the man. 'Erm, where will he be enjoying it?'

The bottom of the river? Six-foot underground? In a vat of chemicals that will dissolve...

'He'll be praying to the porcelain gods.'

I exhale a thankful breath. He's still alive. While I'm mad at him too, I don't want the guy dead and I especially don't want to spend my aborted wedding day at the police station protesting Rox's innocence, an innocence, I might add, that precisely no police officer around here will believe.

'Praying to the porcelain gods – what on earth does that mean?' Freya carefully asks, her face pinched, probably because even hearing these admissions makes her an accessory. And no eight-month pregnant woman wants to be pulled into a drama like this, not when she's already battling swollen ankles and the constant need to pee. But this is Rox's love language, balancing the scales. And she only does these acts of love for the ones she holds dear, so really, I should be grateful. It's just I'm not really the revenge type, but that's subject to change.

'It means I snuck in and filled up his beloved protein drinks with horse laxatives. It's the least he deserves. More fool him for leaving his back door unlocked – he was asking for trouble. He didn't commit to the "'til death do you part" bit, so this will help excise the demons from his system.' She flashes me a triumphant smile.

I'm no pharmacist but a quick mental calculation about potential outcomes equals trouble. Big trouble. 'Rox, wouldn't horse laxatives be way too strong for a human? His – his insides might become his outsides!' I pale as I imagine him suffering a violent digestive upset with medication meant for an animal that weighs four times what he does.

'One can only hope!'

I'm struck by a sudden onset of giggles. Could this day get any crazier? When I compose myself, I ask, 'Where did you get such a thing?'

'I took a slight detour on the way to his place and got them from... actually, never you mind. The less you know, the better, Aubrey. That goes for you too, Freya.'

There's no question that he won't ingest the drinks. Miles is obsessed with his protein intake and consuming exactly 130 grams per day. He does this by mainlining pre-mixed protein drinks 365 days of the year, no exceptions, and records it all on an app. His body is his temple, and why oh why didn't I see that as problematic?

I need to warn Miles, but then I run the risk of getting Rox in trouble. This will have to be handled delicately...

Freya turns to me, rubbing my arm, trying to mask the alarm on her features. 'Shall I make those calls and tell the guests to make their way to the reception?'

'Can you call my parents? Ask them to sort all of it?' I send her a pleading look that I hope translates to: Tell them to fix this! Today, the disaster of all days, a bit of delegation is acceptable.

Freya picks up her handbag, suddenly all business. I'm so glad she's here to help with the practicalities and Rox's revenge plot. My mind is scattered, like all my hopes and dreams. 'I'll go back to the church and chat with them,' she says, giving me a look that implies she understands the assignment. 'Oh, and the London hotel? The honeymoon? Is there any chance you can defer? I know how excited you are about the Winter Wonderland Express but I can call them, explain the situation?'

We were supposed to stay in a ritzy hotel in London this evening and catch the Eurostar tomorrow to Calais for our... Scratch that – *my* dream honeymoon.

'Can you please cancel the hotel for this evening? I'm not keen to stay in London alone on what would have been my wedding night.'

'Of course.'

'But... the honeymoon.' I hold in another sob. 'They won't accept a last-minute cancellation and the tickets were so expensive, a splurge, even with my travel agent discount.' A Christmas train ride to remember, full of festive activities at every stop. My lip quivers at the thought of missing out. It's the first time they've offered this particular festive-themed journey. Usually they run shorter snow trips, without all the Christmas activities on and off board.

'You'll go and you'll enjoy every damn minute,' Rox pipes up, eyes blazing.

'I could go with you?' Freya says, then glances at her belly.

'At eight months pregnant? And who'll look after the brood you already have?' Rox scoffs. 'And I can't go, because I've got brides galore marrying in Christmas wedd— Sorry. Half of those marriages will end in divorce, so don't feel bad, Aubs. Really, you've dodged a bullet. There's a lot to be said for being free. Untethered. Single. Alone. Unmoored.'

I hold up a hand. 'I get it, Rox. Thanks.'

Whatever chemical – adrenaline maybe – that was keeping me present evaporates and fatigue hits me like a brick. It doesn't matter that it's just after lunchtime, all I want to do is crawl into bed and sleep, forget today ever happened.

Their voices drone on as they try to bolster me and come up with a plan, but I tune out, closing my eyes and flopping back on the sofa. Honeymoon for one? For a travel agent who specialises in romantic holidays for couples, it's upsetting but it could also be the perfect solution. A faraway place to cool my heels and avoid the worst of the gossip. Avoid the truth. I am alone again. At Christmas, my favourite time of year, no less.

Sod it. I'll find my Christmas spirit, even if that spirit is at the bottom of a bottle of spiced rum. 'I'll go on my honeymoon for one and I will be merry and bright even if it kills me.'

'That's the way.' Rox fist-bumps me. 'Do you want me to sort another train ticket so you can go direct from Kent to Calais now that you're not staying in London this evening? Save the extra running around?'

I consider it. 'No, I'll head into London tomorrow and then catch the Eurostar to Calais like I planned. No point throwing good money away.'

'Good plan,' Rox says with a nod.

The satin of my dress strangles me the more I sink down the sofa. 'Thank you both for everything, but if you don't mind, I'm going to throw myself in the shower and pretend today was all a bad dream. Freya, if you could help my parents and—'

'Leave it to me,' Freya says. 'If you need me, just phone anytime. I'm sure there's a perfect explanation for all of this. Miles loves you and he's a good guy.'

Rox boos. 'Hardly, even my cat can't stand him.'

'To be fair, your cat hates everyone.' Freya gives Rox a long look.

'You've got me there,' Rox concedes. 'But she hisses at Miles like he's the devil incarnate. A very clear sign he's no good.'

To defuse any argument for or against Miles I jump in and say, 'Thank you for your help today, Freya.' I pull myself up from the sofa and give her a hug.

'Should I come back?'

I'm mindful of her pregnancy and go to reassure her I'm OK when Rox says, 'I'll stay here. I swiped a bottle of champagne from Miles's place, so it's only fitting I toast to the misfortune coming his way.'

'Thanks, Rox.' Knowing she's not out committing further crimes does ease my mind.

After a lengthy shower trying to remove make-up that has formed its own dermal layer, I fall into bed and swipe open my phone. There are a lot of texts and social media notifications, but nothing from Miles. No apology, no explanation. I call him again; his phone is still switched off.

I send him one single word:

> Why?

Clearly Miles is not Mr Right. As of today, he's won the honour of being Mr So Very Wrong. What excuse can he give me that will make sense? None. But is it for the best? I wilt when I stay in one place; the urge to explore this earth runs deep. It also makes me a better travel agent having first-hand experience of the places I recommend. Only love made me pause, stop to catch my breath. But that love must've been one sided.

My honeymoon for one can't come quick enough. The desire to get out of town is strong. I'll buy a festive mug at every Christmas market and drink mulled wine until the world around me softens. I have a thing with finding festive mugs that I usually send home to Rox for her ugly mugs collection. I'll visit Paris, Bruges, Amsterdam, Hamburg, Copenhagen, Stockholm and Lapland, and finish at the swanky igloo stay to catch the Northern Lights. I'm used to travelling solo, and even though this trip is marketed as a romantic journey for couples, I'm sure I won't be the only singleton…

4

17 DECEMBER, CALAIS, FRANCE

Boarding the Winter Wonderland Express

The next day I catch the early train out of Kent and arrive in London, then board the Eurostar to Calais. In Calais, I spend a couple of hours exploring but find the port city rather lacking. It's more of an industrial wasteland in parts and uninspiring. Being a transit point, it's filled with impatient tourists hurrying to make their next connection – if my toes are run over one more time by suitcase wheels I'll scream. Under different circumstances I'd find the silver lining, but today I don't have it in me.

Mid-afternoon I ditch the idea of sightseeing further and find the platform for the Winter Wonderland Express, in the hopes they're offering early check-in.

Damn, I'm not the only one who had that idea. The long queue snakes down the platform. The train sleeps up to one hundred people plus staff and by the looks of it, a good chunk of those have arrived already. According to my research, the train is divided into two identical sections, with fifty passengers a side.

This duplication is so that guests can enjoy the amenities without too much crowding.

There's nothing else to do but join the end of the queue and wait. I plan on keeping a low profile and my heartbreak to myself. I peek at people ahead of me. Gah – I'm smacked in the face by the sight of loved-up couples as far as the eye can see. They're kissing. They're canoodling. They're speaking baby language to each other. And wearing matching Christmas outfits. It's sickening. Probably my jealously talking, but still. I'm so obviously alone in a sea of sweethearts. At Christmas.

'Tis the season for resting Grinch face.

The line moves relatively quickly as couples board the train. I'm so busy tuning out the many lovebirds and their saccharine sweet nothings that I don't notice the life-size gingerbread man until he taps me on the shoulder.

'Ho, ho, ho, welcome to the Winter Wonderland Express!'

'Thank you,' I say. 'I've never seen a life-size gingerbread man before.' Not only is there a group of giant gingerbread men waiting to greet guests, but there's also a band of merry elves singing jaunty Christmas carols. I can't help but be swept along in song, and my mood lifts. How can anyone be gloomy listening to 'Jingle Bell Rock'? Maybe this won't be so bad.

'I'm actually a gingerbread woman, but it's hard to tell under all this fur. Between us, it's horrifically uncomfortable but I'm not supposed to say that so forget you heard,' she says in a conspiratorial tone. 'I'm your official welcomer, Sabrina.'

The gingerbread outfit does look rather cumbersome, but Sabrina is doing a good job navigating it.

Sabrina lifts a clipboard to her chest. 'Can I get your name? I'll check you in and you can go and find your cabin.' I'm impressed she can read through thick plastic gingerbread eyes.

'Aubrey Evans.' Thankfully, I hadn't even looked at changing any ID to my married name; figured I'd do all that much later.

'Evans. Evans...' Sabrina runs a pen down the list of names. 'Ah – here we are! Evans and Walker. Oooh, our "Just Married" lovebirds! You've certainly picked the most romantic holiday for a honeymoon!'

Her gingerbread costume doesn't hide the volume of her voice that rings along the platform, drawing the eyes of many of my fellow passengers. All those damn canoodlers. With some effort, Sabrina lifts her sizeable gingerbread head from the clipboard and searches over my shoulder. 'Where is Mr Walker then?'

I suffer a moment of sheer and utter panic with so many loveheart-for-eyes twosomes within earshot. Who wants to be known as the jilted bride among these kissy-wissy pairs packing on the PDA? Not me.

'Ah, he, umm...' I didn't factor in that I'd have to explain my missing spouse, a huge oversight on my part. I can't tell the truth and risk ten days of pitying stares, whispers behind hands. What if they think I'm defective or something? No, I need a solid excuse, one they won't question. It feels oddly quiet on the platform, like they're all waiting for an answer. I creep close to Sabrina and say as quietly as I can, 'He died. Tragically. In London.' I want to slap my own face. He died! In London! I suppose it works in the scheme of things. They won't question a widow, will they? 'Not long after our wedding.' Why I feel the need to blurt further details is beyond me.

There are gasps from the couple behind me, and I feel so very seen and uncomfortable in my own skin.

Sabrina's gingerbread hand flies to her gingerbread mouth. It's quite comical under the circumstances but I do my best not to laugh, or else she'll assume I'm a sociopath. 'He died not long after you said I do? Oh, it's too sad to even fathom.' Why does she need to broadcast it like that when I have so clearly spoken in a whisper? 'What happened?' I'm not sure Sabrina is cut out for this role. Shouldn't she be a little more circumspect?

'There was an... accident.' Oh, keep going, Aubrey, sheesh!

'What kind of accident?'

Should she be questioning a widow like this? Still, I need my story to work, so I roll with it.

How do people routinely die in London? I have no clue. I recall my morning in transit and all the ways in which I might have come to harm. Ah! 'Miles didn't... He didn't mind the gap.' I use my pointer finger, showing his rapid descent from here to down there.

'What! He died falling down the gap?' She's obviously realised I don't want all of Calais to hear and has lowered her voice accordingly.

'A little bit,' I mumble. Surely I've done enough to stave off any further queries?

'Oh my God, this is terrible. Was he... tiny?' Sabrina says, choking up.

'In a lot of ways, yes.' I'm not going to shame the man about the size of any of his appendages, and it's strange of her to even ask. 'I'd prefer not to discuss it.'

'Of course. Of course. I'm so sorry for your loss.'

'He's in a better place.' A place where it's acceptable to wear your insides on the outside without judgement.

A big, buff, broody guy appears just to my side, gorgeous with striking bluey-green eyes framed by thick dark brows. He's got an enigmatic smile and a quiet intensity about him. He's earth-shatteringly hot and quite knocks rational thought from—

Oh no.

I can't think. Of words. Of reasons. Or why I'm still staring at him, mouth agape. It's not like I'm married, is it? I'm resolutely single, aren't I? Or should I say widowed when I'm among this crowd? It's not illegal for me to appreciate this very fine specimen of a man. It, that, him, would be a bad idea. A complication. Holiday flings are fun, sure, but I'm rather vulnerable right now and men are dead to me. D.E.A.D.

He does that hot-guy head lift, eyebrow-raise thing that sends a shiver down the length of me. Oh, this is not good.

But that's not all that catches my attention. It's the sceptical tilt of his lips that makes me slightly uneasy, as if he doesn't believe my extremely plausible tale of woe. Will he call me out? Surely not!

He must sense my appraisal – not hard given I'm openly staring at him dumbstruck – because he holds out a hand and says, 'I'm Jasper. I'm travelling solo too.'

I take his outstretched palm and feel a zap. An actual zap. As if a current of electricity runs between us. What on earth? This is some weird off-the-charts chemistry. That or I'm hallucinating, which would be more my luck.

'I'm Aubrey.'

I'm transfixed by him, and how can that be? He's said exactly six words and all I manage to pick up is his rather sultry American accent. I slip off to fantasyland. I bet he lives in some cosy cabin in Vermont where there's a fire roaring, shelves overflowing with well-thumbed books, a charming space where we could cuddle on a wrinkled leather sofa— WHAT. Clearly, some broken part of me is running the engine – I cannot trust myself to be rational. And I'm not transfixed, like the heroine in some kind of insta-love wintry romance movie. I'm simply overwrought. Aren't I madly in love with Miles? Yes, he might have massively let me down, but love doesn't switch off overnight. Does it? Or does it? Right now, I'm having a hard time remembering what Miles even looks like.

Wait. Did Jasper mention he was travelling solo too?

'Last year my wife left me for her personal trainer. That didn't feel too good at the time,' Jasper says matter-of-factly. 'They're spending this Christmas in Aspen and asked me to pet-sit their schnauzer for them, which I declined.'

'Declined because of this trip?' Their split must've been amicable if they're still in touch and she's asking him to pet-sit her schnauzer.

'Yeah, that and the fact that we're now officially divorced, so a clean break is for the best.'

What woman would trade this love god in? She must be mad. Or…

It's more likely that Jasper is faulty. Yes, that's it. He's got some huge flaw. Probably a gaslighter. And so what if he's good with schnauzers. Is that really enough in the scheme of things?

'Perhaps she's still in love with you?' I mean, I'm not one to pry but the signs are all there. Who asks their ex-husband to look after their schnauzer? Is that actually a breed of dog or some kind of euphemism?

Jasper shakes his head. 'No, she's in love with her personal trainer, and I'm happy for them.' Really? If this were me, I'd be visualising all the ways in which karma might bite her for leaving out of the blue.

I find myself feeling sympathetic towards Jasper. Divorce is heavy. And being alone over the silly season while taking a romantic holiday for one amid a sea of couples isn't easy either. 'Leaving you for her personal trainer, sorry, but that's just' – I make a face – 'such a massive cliché.'

'Yeah.' Jasper grins, which makes his dark eyebrows dance, his expressive eyes twinkle. Who knew eyes actually twinkled? He looks like one of those all-American Abercrombie model types with a rugged edge that saves him from being too perfect. Really, he's quite disarming. With a loose shrug he says, 'You never know, he might break a leg skiing.'

I return his grin. That's more like it. 'There might be an avalanche.' I sound like Rox with the whole 'vengeance is mine' mindset. The difference is Jasper and I are using gallows humour for a morale boost. At least, I hope we are. 'The world is an unpredictable place.'

He flashes his pearly whites. 'It sure is.'

Sabrina coughs to get my attention. My cheeks pinken at the thought I've held up the line for so long and they've all been too polite to hurry me along.

Am I flirting with Jasper? The day after I was supposed to be a Mrs. Trauma will do strange things to a gal. No, it's not flirtation! I'm simply comforting a fellow singleton because I empathise with his pain. There will be no flirting for the rest of my natural-born life. Men are not just paused, they're cancelled. I'll get my fix with book boyfriends who, so far, have never let me down.

'Follow me, Aubrey.' Sabrina breaks the spell. 'And I'll show you to your cabin.'

'Sure,' I say. 'See you around, Jasper.' *Don't make goo-goo eyes at the damn man.* God, maybe Rox put some kind of love drug in my coffee. I wouldn't put it past her. He's probably a regular guy, regular height with regular-sized muscles, and she's put a potion in my cup of Joe that morphs Mr Average into a buff, brawny mountain man. That girl is always concocting evil.

'Bound to.' He gives me a look I can only call sizzling. Maybe he's not aware of his off-the-chain super-stud energy. I don't hold it against him. When I travel, I always make friends. It's one of the best parts of any trip, connecting with strangers and hearing their stories. Jasper and I have our singledom in common, so if I can get my overworked brain to stop misfiring and behave normally, then he just might make this couples holiday a little easier to stomach.

5

17 DECEMBER, CALAIS, FRANCE

I follow gingerbread Sabrina through the well-appointed interior of the train carriage. The design is luxe with an air of timeless grandeur, with decadent velvet upholstered seating, rich navy and gold carpets with matching drapes. Brass lamps are dotted along the carriage, giving the space a warm glow. If that wasn't enough, it's elevated by the addition of elegant Christmas decorations, delicate festive garlands made of Swarovski crystals.

We exit the lounge area and enter the dining carriage, which is just as elaborate and features the same navy and gold colour scheme. Cut-crystal wine glasses sparkle under the lights, waiting to be filled. Sabrina manages to swish her gingerbread body just enough to swipe leatherbound menus and gold cutlery from tabletops, but she's walking too fast for me to point this out.

Making our way past the dining carriage, we enter a small hallway with windows to one side and cabins on the other with sliding wood-panelled doors with ornate brass handles.

It's like being on the Orient Express, transported back in time to another era. The more I get swept away in the beauty, the better I feel. This five-star treat holiday can be a reset, a rejuvenation. New motto of the trip: 'Miles who?' How hard can it be to wipe it all from memory?

Close to the end of the hallway we come to a stop.

'Here we have number twelve, your cabin, Aubrey.' Sabrina slides the door open, revealing a double bed decorated with Christmas baubles that spell out: JUST MARRIED! Above the bed, glittery Mr & Mrs bunting drapes prettily across. Two fluffy dressing gowns hang on a hook, and I make out a patch of embroidery that says *Newlyweds*. I gulp. Wow. OK, slight setback in the 'Miles who?' thing.

Sabrina rushes in and tries to scoop up the baubles from the bed, but her little gingerbread arms just aren't long enough. 'I'm so sorry! I'll get this fixed right away. Can I bring you a glass of champagne in the meantime?'

I nod as pesky tears start again of their own accord. Poor Sabrina thinks I'm crying over a dead guy. If only it were that simple! The hurt is amplified because Miles hasn't even bothered to reply to any of my calls or texts. Am I that unimportant that I don't even deserve a response?

Sabrina dashes off, tripping over her awkward gingerbread feet while I try to push all thought of Miles deep down into a lock box in my mind and instead focus on the beauty of the cabin. It's travel agent crack, if I'm honest.

The suite is compact, as you'd expect on a train, but elegant, and it'd be oh-so-romantic if you were cosying up with the love of your life. There's a pulldown writing desk with a chair. A tiny bookshelf is tucked into the corner. I run a finger along the spines, delighted to find they're all travel memoirs and holiday romances, the type of novel to awaken your wanderlust and your regular lust, as the train chugs from one exotic clime to the next.

I've always found escapism in two concrete forms – travel and books. For me, they go hand in hand. There's a lot of downtime in travel, and being in transit is when I like to lose myself in the pages. I read a wide variety of genres, but travel memoirs or destination romances are my favourite. I love learning about new places through the eyes of another explorer or by a fictional couple holidaying in a patch of paradise.

I peek into the en suite. It's stunning with gorgeous emerald fish-scale-shaped tiles and bronze taps; very regal despite its efficient size.

Sabrina returns with a glass of bubbles. 'The Christmas activities are about to start so why don't you go ahead and join them in the lounge carriage and I'll get your suitcase unpacked and all of this' – she points to the 'just married' decor – 'taken away and set on fire.'

I stifle a laugh. 'Thank you. But I can unpack my own suitcase.'

She holds a hand up against my protests. 'Absolutely not. It's all part of the five-star service.'

I give her a warm smile. 'I'm not really a five-star person, Sabrina.' I'm sure it's obvious by my clothing, which is anything but designer label. Airs and graces will never be my thing. 'I'm a travel agent who got a hefty discount on this trip in the hopes that I'll offer this itinerary to my clients...'

'Ooh, a travel agent, nice! Don't worry about a thing, seriously. I've got new recruit George assisting me today. He's sweet, like one of those cinnamon roll cutie pies, so eager to help, although between us' – she darts a glance over her shoulder – 'the guy is a little clumsy.'

Sabrina removes her gingerbread head to reveal long blonde locks that are pasted to her forehead.

I gasp. 'You're... human?'

She flashes a grin. 'Don't think less of me, will you?'

I laugh. 'Ha. We're going to get along just fine.'

The pretty blonde is around late-twenties with wide doe eyes and cute dimpled cheeks. I feel ancient in comparison at almost forty. There's no dewy complexion and well-slept glow about me; just the opposite, in fact. For a moment I ache for my own twenties, when life was simpler. Still, I feel an affinity with Sabrina. She's a breath of fresh air and we seem to have clicked.

'There are a few hoity-toity passengers on board, but you're not the only one here in the tourism biz. As this Christmas itinerary is new, tickets were offered at a discount to travel agents, to media and marketing types to help with discoverability later.' Perhaps she means some kind of influencers? Social media stars who'll take stunning pictures and share them to the masses. It does make me feel a little more comfortable, knowing among the wealthy aboard there's some regular folk too. Where does Jasper fit in? I didn't see him snapping pics. Could he be a travel agent like me, or in the industry at least?

Sabrina hoists my suitcase on the luggage rack. 'There is one person aboard,' she says with a hint of mischievousness in her voice, 'who has more money than the Kardashians combined but lacks the sky-high ego to match. Even so, do you think she's offering to unpack her own suitcase? Hell no. Enjoy being spoiled, because you deserve it, especially after what you've been through.'

Guilt blooms inside of me. I shouldn't have made up such an elaborate lie about the death of my beloved, especially to someone as genuine as Sabrina, who is being supportive and lovely, while also giving me the inside scoop on my fellow passengers. But honestly, I'm so mad at Miles, I did enjoy a dopamine boost at sharing his tragic demise. It's not as if he's really dead, and I'm proud I managed to persuade my sister not to manslaughter the man-splainer. Still, I should be honest with Sabrina.

'Miles isn't really dead, you know.' There, secret shared, problem solved. We can move on and I'll tell her the awful truth that I've been rejected by the man who used all his wiles to convince me to put a ring on it.

Her face crumples and she moves to take me in her arms. She croons, 'Ooh, hon, I know, I know. He'll always be with you in spirit. In your heart forevermore. Never forgotten.' She chokes up a bit and rocks me in her arms like my mum would do. Oh God, I've made it ten times worse.

'No, it's not that. It's—'

She stands back, holding my shoulders like a pep talk is imminent. 'Look, let's make your time on board fun! It's the only way to wade through grief. There are a lot of interesting passengers for you to befriend, and if I may, I suggest you seek out Miss Moneybags, not her real name of course. She's a hoot and will be the perfect distraction for you.'

'Ah – OK. Who is she?'

She arches a brow. 'You'll know her when you see her, trust me. She's hard to miss.'

I'm not sure the cloak and dagger is necessary if she wants me to befriend this woman, but I don't press. 'OK, I'll keep my eyes peeled. And aside from Jasper, are there many singles on board?' I don't mention how the overt displays of romance are like a stab to the heart or how Jasper electrified me back to life for one sad moment.

'A few. But I wouldn't worry about all of that. At the end of the journey, I'm sure there'll be a few more.'

I frown. 'What do you mean?'

Sabrina motions around the small cabin. 'Spending time

together in a tight space can test the mettle of even the strongest relationship. Trust me, I've seen it all. I used to steward on cruise ships and yachts, and the only difference here is the view. Holidays can just so easily swing the pendulum of love ever so quickly back to hate when you're living in such close confines.'

I'm a little morose that a much-anticipated romantic holiday can potentially end in a break-up. Have any of my clients ended their relationship after a meticulously planned trip? Now I consider it, of course statistically, it's possible. Spending time with anyone 24/7 on a boat, or a train, even a hotel room, peels back all those layers and gives you nowhere to hide literally and figuratively.

Would Miles have got on my nerves here? Unequivocally yes. He would smile at Sabrina and when the door shut behind her, he'd let out a litany of complaints; minor infractions that peeved him. And stupid me in love bubble land would've put his micro annoyances down to him being a nervous traveller, but would that be the truth or would I be giving his bad manners a pass? Either way, close travel companions are an important consideration on any trip, especially if you're sharing your space with them.

Without Miles, I'll enjoy the sanctuary of my cabin. All those books. I don't have to pander to him with his travel quirks. There are certain types when it comes to travel: the meticulous planner, the nervous Nellie, the spontaneous explorer, the high-octane thrill-seeker, and so many more. Miles fit into the nervous Nellie category. So if you put the whole jilted bride thing to one side, this is the perfect scenario – travelling alone, enjoying all the five-star perks the Winter Wonderland Express has to offer without having to worry about anyone but myself.

A phone trills and Sabrina blushes. 'Oops, don't tell anyone you heard that.' She pulls a mobile from her gingerbread outfit.

'I'm not allowed to carry this around but I'm waiting on confirmation that my boyfriend can join me in Lapland for Christmas. I booked a few days off, but it won't be quite as magical if he doesn't make it there.' She flicks through her messages, her face giving away her disappointment. 'Ah – he hasn't had time to broach it but he's going to ask his boss tonight. We haven't seen each other for months!'

Long-distance love, ah, it's such a hard road. 'Is that him?' I point to her screensaver picture of a twentysomething lad with one of those mushroom haircuts that always remind me of Lego figurines for some reason. Why are they all the rage? Still, I'm not the demographic so I don't quiz her about his choice of hairstyle.

'Yes!' she trills. 'He's so fit. But it's not just his looks, he's also got a sensitive side to him. Look at this pic.' Sabrina shows me a picture of them on a beach under the shade of a palm tree.

'He's still in the Caribbean. We met when I did a stint over there but then I was offered this role and I couldn't turn it down. It's almost impossible to get a job on the Winter Wonderland Express, and it can lead to so many other opportunities within the company. But I miss the lovable goofball.' She lets out a sigh. 'Also, the long-distance won't be forever. I'm hoping I can get him a job here too so we're not apart for too much longer. While the workdays are long, the stops along the way are worth it, especially on this new Christmas themed route. And guests are always fascinating and tip generously. Oops, shouldn't have said that! Scratch that from the record.'

I laugh. 'I bet you've got some tales to tell.'

Sabrina waggles her brow. 'I'm going to write a book one day, *Confessions of a Travel Insider*. But don't tell anyone or I'll get blacklisted. I'm joking! Sort of. I mean, I'll change their names and details. But aren't travel escapades of the rich and famous oh so juicy?'

I sense Sabrina is only being so open because she feels sorry for me. A voice down the hallway calls for her. 'Wait!' I hold out a hand. 'I need to know more about these juicy escapades!'

Sabrina creeps forward and drops her voice. 'Well, between us, that's Mrs Delacroix yelling out for me. She's one of the wealthiest women in France and is well known for her scandalous affairs.'

'Why are they scandalous?'

Sabrina picks up her gingerbread head and holds it under her arm. 'Firstly, she's married, and her travel companion is not Mr Delacroix. The man she's bunking with just so happens to be thirty years her junior. Apparently, she's in an open marriage and anything goes. More power to her, I say! Lover boy is not bad either, if you're into that whole Timothee Chalamet look.'

My eyebrows shoot up. 'That is juicy! So I take it she's the person with more money than all the Kardashians combined.'

'Nope.' She laughs. 'But don't tell a soul. I really shouldn't be speaking so freely, it's just with you being in the industry, you've probably seen it all too.'

'The few wealthy clients I've had requested NDAs so I can't even tell you their names or where they've travelled to without risking a lawsuit. I've had a few celebrity doozies over the years, some sweet, some utterly dreadful with their demands. All part of the job.'

Her face falls. 'And you can't tell me who, not even a hint?'

I laugh at her expression, but so far Sabrina hasn't exactly been tight-lipped and I take my job seriously in that respect, even though their names would blow her hair back. 'Not even one! Truthfully, those kinds of clients are few and far between. I mostly deal with...' A lump forms in my throat. God, when will my body stop betraying me? '...honeymooners.' And just how will I cope with that once I get back to work after Christmas?

Maybe I can pivot to post-divorce holidays? Is there a market for that?

'I'll get some gossip out of you eventually.' She flashes a grin. 'Why don't you go and join the Christmas activities? Have some festive fun. If all else fails, drink your body weight in gingerbread martinis. I'll have your cabin sorted when you get back.'

6

17 DECEMBER, CALAIS, FRANCE

I leave Sabrina to unpack my suitcase, feeling slightly uneasy about what she might find, like the range of feminist serial-killer thrillers I tossed in at stupid o'clock this morning after ditching all the romances I'd previously packed. Titles like: *How to Slay on Your Wedding Day* and *Homicidally Ever After*, a couple of tomes I bought tongue-in-cheek to make Miles laugh in the lead up to our big day. I hope Sabrina doesn't get the wrong idea what with him plunging to his death down the gap and all…

I head towards the noise, passing through the dining carriage, where gingerbread people hold trays of colourful Christmas cocktails aloft.

'Can I offer you a Mistletoe Margarita or perhaps a Jingle Juice?' says a staff member dressed as the reindeer Rudolph, complete with bulbous red nose.

'Thanks,' I say, with a laugh at the festive drink names and the wild staff costumes. They really have gone all out in making the atmosphere Christmassy and fun, if a little kitschy. 'A Jingle Juice please.' I take the proffered glass and sip. It tastes like fruity punch mixed with Moscato, cranberry juice and fresh mint.

The dining carriage is packed with guests enjoying a range of Christmas canapés. 'Can I tempt you with a smoked salmon blini or madeleines with lemon curd?' I take a salmon blini, popping the bite-size morsel into my mouth, enjoying the rich crème fraiche layered with the saltiness of the salmon.

A woman wearing a ballgown, an actual ballgown, is parading up and down the small area, as if she's a catwalk model. Is this a fashion show for guests? It seems unlikely. I try to edge past her, but she spins and flicks her hair, which manages to catch me straight in the eye. My vision blurs, then doubles as I rub at the sting.

A few steps away, a man in a suit lays prone on the plush carpet, camera in hand, encouraging her. 'Katya, darling, tilt your chin... Smize, the way the model Tyra Banks does, smile with your eyes.' Smize?! What fresh hell is this? Are they simply passengers taking up almost all the thoroughfare to get pics for the 'gram? Ah, these must be the influencers Sabrina alluded to. By the hostile glares directed their way from other guests, they've been taking up the walkway for quite some time.

'Excuse me,' I say, failing to get around the woman's elbow as she drops her hip and poses once more.

She totally ignores me. I tap her on the shoulder and motion for her to move so I can get past.

With a frustrated sigh, she says, 'Wait until Igor gets the shot.'

Being nomadic by nature, I run across people like this all the time. The trick is not to give an inch, or next minute they'll act like they own the place. The rules are, there are no rules when it comes to travel photos.

Once at the Colosseum in Rome, I waited patiently for my turn at a photo platform to capture the arena backdrop. When I finally got to the front of the line, a horde of people pushed past until I was smack bang at the back of the queue again. A little war cry was needed that day, one that defies all rules of language. It's a dog-eat-dog world in tourist-land.

'No. Igor is the one who should wait, for me and all the other passengers to pass,' I say haughtily, 'then you can continue your photoshoot.' I give her a stiff smile, even though I'm not exactly in a people-pleasing mood.

I nudge her to the left and step over Igor's large frame. Honestly, they couldn't have picked a tighter space for their photos. Also, they could have done this in their cabin. Igor is determined not to move a muscle or give up his position on the ground, so it's not surprising that I manage to catch his leg with the heel of my boot.

'Ow!' he cries out.

'You're a tripping hazard, mate,' a sixty-something man with an Australian accent says. 'Move out the way before someone gets hurt, please.'

Igor's face is like thunder as the rest of the passengers make their feelings known.

Could either Katya or Igor be the person with the extreme wealth? Somehow, I don't think so. They're too showy, too theatrical, as if they want all eyes on them, and aren't stealth-wealth types more discreet, less flashy? I'm sure these are influencers who'll be posting up a storm. I make a mental note to check out #TheWinterWonderlandExpress online later.

I keep moving to the lounge carriage, which is far less crowded with only a handful of guests partaking in an activity making Christmas cards. There's a cute little post box to send their creations. Miles would have scoffed at such a twee activity, whereas it appeals to me. But right now I want to investigate what else is on offer along each carriage.

Another gingerbread person pops up and asks if I'd like to

join in. I politely decline. 'Where's the bar?' I'd read up on the recreations area, which sounds like a lot of fun if you're a game nerd like me. There are board games and cards tables, chess and other pursuits to pass the time. I love games, cards and quizzes. But chess for one? Gah.

A roving staff photographer jumps out of nowhere and chirps, 'Here for your happy snaps!' It's a little disconcerting, like she's been lying in wait for her first victim. 'Would you like to pose for a photo in front of the Christmas tree? It'll be a great memento to take home.'

A great memento of my honeymoon for one – I think not. Before I can politely decline, the influencer couple are hot on my heels, jostling me out of the way.

'We'd like professional photos.' Katya snaps her fingers and Igor jumps into action, switching on the spotlight on his phone. He barks an order to me, of all people. 'Hold this over us, would you? Not too close. And not too far away.'

Is he for real? Like I'm some kind of groupie of theirs. Of course, I don't want any photographic reminders of my honeymoon for one, but now that these two are shoving their way in, fight mode is activated and I might just be petty enough to pose just to make them wait.

I'm about to blurt some choice words when Jasper makes his way over, and my knees almost buckle at the sight of him. It's the intensity of his eyes framed by thick brows, and when he locks his gaze onto mine, I swear the earth stops spinning. How did I not notice his full, kissable lips? Golly, this is not good. Not good at all. You cannot lust after someone when you're one day post break-up. The day after your aborted wedding, even. It's obscene!

It's probably not even lust. Just desperation at the thought of being alone in my honeymoon happy snaps.

'Shove over, Igor,' Jasper says in a jocular tone. It doesn't surprise me he's made Igor's acquaintance already. I bet most of the passengers have bumped into Igor and Katya, because they're not exactly good with spatial awareness. 'I'd love a photo with you by the Christmas tree, Aubrey, if you don't mind?' Jasper winks and it sends a shiver down the length of me. I must be so desperate for affection I'm losing control of my capacity to function as a regular human.

'Umm,' I say, trying to think of an excuse but coming up blank. 'Sure.'

'Then Igor and Katya can have their turn, eh?'

Igor playfully slaps Jasper on the back as if they're the best of friends. 'Sure, sure, comrade.'

Comrade?

It's interesting how Jasper's sudden appearance has changed the dynamic with Igor and Katya. Is it his off-the-charts charisma that appeals to people? It's grossly unfair that hot people have it so much easier in life.

Jasper slips his hand into mine and positions me in front of a Christmas tree decorated with Swarovski crystal snowflake ornaments that bathe us in prisms of rainbow light. Katya pushes Igor in the back and next minute he's holding an iPhone spotlight above us. It's all too much. My head feels like it's going to explode.

'Lift your chin,' Katya directs me. I fight a grimace. Poser I am not. In fact, I'd say I'm a failure to my entire generation when it comes to posturing. I'm not all that comfortable when a camera is trained on me; my facial muscles seize up, I blink at the wrong time, or I'm caught with my mouth open at some weird angle when they yell 'Say cheese!'

'You are such a gorgeous couple!' the photographer gushes, her lovestruck gaze trained directly on Jasper. I'm no expert on photography, but how is she going to take any photos if she doesn't lift the camera to her eye and press a button or two? So in light of her ogling the poor man and so blatantly, I don't educate her about the fact we are absolutely not a couple.

Jasper pulls me closer, probably so I'm actually in the shot, as the camera is now trained more his way than mine. Typical. The photographer is going to cut my head off.

'I'm a sucker for travel mementoes. You should see my magnet collection.'

I replay the words to look for the joke, the euphemism, but find nothing. Is he legit talking about a magnet collection or am I missing something?

Jasper does not look like a guy who collects magnets. Collects a bevy of women vying for his attention, maybe. I struggle to think of a response. 'Magnets are cool, but have you ever seen a souvenir spoon collection?' Ooh, good one, Aubrey! Kill me.

He groans good-naturedly. 'Oh God, my mum was an avid collector of souvenir spoons back in the eighties. They still hang in a wooden cabinet in pride of place in her dining room.'

I laugh. 'My mum was the same. It was the go-to back then if anyone went on holiday, to bring a precious spoon back as a gift. It makes you wonder who thought, "Ah, souvenir spoons, that'll take off!" And it actually did.'

Jasper pauses like he's really considering it. 'Isn't that so strange. Why souvenir spoons? Then some genius thought of a way to display them, thus compounding that need to continually fill the cabinet with one more after every holiday. Marketing mastermind.' He gives me a wide smile. 'Do you travel often then?' he asks as the photographer snaps away, the flash making me blink, so these photos should come out about as well as normal, my face contorted like I'm stuck in a silent scream.

Jasper will have the most attractive travel memento to look back on and regard me fondly. Good-oh.

'Yes, as much as I can. Up until a year and a half ago, I worked as a digital nomad. Loved that lifestyle.'

He does a double-take. I'm not sure why. 'Nice. So what put an end to living that dream?'

'I came home to visit my family and reconnected with an old crush from high school. And I fell in love.' It's unusual for me to speak so openly but Jasper has got that way about him that makes me feel like he's invested in what I have to say. It's the way he's hanging on every word. 'It felt like time to settle down, like everyone else was doing.' Which didn't go according to plan, but hey ho.

He considers it for a moment. 'It's one of those great mysteries, isn't it?'

It's very hard to remain on topic when my mind has other ideas and goes off into some strange fantasy realm about Jasper. It's jarring to say the least. I'm not usually that fantasy realm kind of person. Quite possibly after all the upset I've faced, my brains have left the building and the system is running entirely on muscle memory. 'What's that?'

'That whole debate about following the crowd. Is it settling down, or is it settling?' He goes far away for a moment, as if the question is not really meant for me. When he snaps back, the dreamy-eyed gaze drops and he says, 'Sorry. I just wonder why we can't have the fairytale and still travel. Why do we have to give up the one part of us that gives us life? But it always ends up being a choice of this job or that relationship, never both.'

Jasper must be a bit of a hodophile too. By the sounds of it, his divorce had a lot to do with his career choices. And I relate. More than anyone probably.

When I consider his words, my chest tightens at the stone-cold truth of the matter. Did I settle because of pressure from every camp? To put roots down. To follow the crowd, like Freya, pregnant with baby number three. Even Rox, with her wild untameable nature, has a mortgage and recently adopted a rescue cat which shows a level of responsibility. Did I truly want that life too? Or did I feel compelled when Miles and my family and friends urged me to stay put? I can't blame anyone, I've got my own mind, but did the power of suggestion weaken my resolve? Hard to tell.

Was I in love with the idea of love and not the reality? The thought gives me pause.

'Sorry,' he quickly adds. 'I shouldn't speak like that when you've just lost your husband.' He gives that same sceptical moue, as if testing me. Does he know I'm lying about Miles plummeting into the next life, or is it something else? I'm convinced Sabrina believed me; either that or she's very good at hiding behind her bubbly smile because she's being paid to be kind.

All of this ruminating reminds me to be wary. Men in general have always let me down and so it's best if I don't get too friendly with Jasper. Or next minute he'll be getting under my defences, being sweet, caring, interested. This is exactly how it started with Miles, and then boom – he yanked the rug out from under me. I absolutely cannot let anyone in until I'm on stronger footing.

'And what about you?' I train the spotlight back on Jasper, metaphorically at least, while Igor still has the camera light haloing above me like the Christmas angel I am not. 'Do you travel often?'

He nods. 'I'm a travel writer, so I'm always on the go. Makes it hard on relationships. According to my ex-wife Olivia, it's the main reason we divorced. She says it's impossible to love a man who's never there. And I get that, I do, but trust goes a long way in relationships. Still, I wasn't home enough and that is the crux of it.'

Ah – trust issues. Olivia started her relationship with the personal trainer while they were still married. It's nice that Jasper doesn't lay the blame squarely at her feet for cheating, but understands it was part of a bigger tapestry. Must've hurt though. 'Has it been a theme with your relationships then? Your constant travelling for work is a problem?'

He smiles, gives me the full constellation of pearly whites. 'Yeah, it's been mentioned a fair bit in the past. I love my job, writing stories about far-flung places, but it takes a toll. As my forties creep closer, I want to find my person without giving up what I do. But it seems that's a deal breaker in the end. Each and every time.' There's a hint of frustration in his voice. 'How do I fix that without giving up a job that I'm passionate about? I'm beginning to think it's just not possible and so here I am, writing a story about the Christmas itinerary for the Winter Wonderland Express.' Ah, he's been invited aboard to write about the adventure!

Just when I'm ready to keep him at arm's length and am suspicious of his motives, he drops a truth bomb, showing his vulnerable side. Jasper and I have more in common than I'd first thought. And while he's mostly upbeat, I sense his sadness at the crumbling of his marriage and the idea that he can't have both a career and a long-term relationship. I'm sure his partner thinks he's having a wild old time every time he does a story on location, but I presume it's similar to my life, where it's actually just a hard slog like any job with the added bonus of a new vista and place to explore. It's not the same as travelling purely for fun with no work pressures.

'You don't ever give up the thing that gets you out of bed every day.' My voice comes out more heated than I intended, but it can't be helped. I don't share with him that if my recent experiences are anything to go by, changing who you are to fit the mould is a huge step backwards and will only end in tears. 'My family and friends treat my travels almost as a frivolous pursuit. As if I'm getting something out of my system. And when you hear something enough, you start to believe you're the oddity, the one who is doing life wrong. People don't understand the need to roam, do they? It's one of the biggest issues for me – they question what I'm running from, as if there's a solid reason, some secret that propels me to be on the move. As if it's unnatural not to want the house, the car, the two point four kids.'

He turns to me with something like wonder in his eyes. 'That's exactly it, Aubrey. I feel like I'm the anomaly when really it's not that unusual these days, the way technology has opened up the world for those who can work remotely as long as there's an internet connection.'

'Yeah. It really has.' The rise in numbers of digital nomads is huge, especially in countries with a low cost of living. It might not be for everyone, but it's an option for those who want to see a bit of the world instead of the inside of a commercial or corporate building.

'Do you think your marriage would have survived if you'd wanted to up sticks and live abroad again?'

When I put this question to Miles, he always dodged it, swept it away, and to be fair, I didn't press either. Perhaps neither of us wanted to face facts that there's no way Miles would live abroad and give up the stability of home. Would that have eventually soured our marriage?

One of us would be sacrificing their dream. But who would that have been?

'I guess I'll never know.'

Jasper and I lapse into an awkward silence.

A minute or two later the photographer says, 'You're all done. It's so much easier to take nice photos when you're not talking.'

Wow. If I didn't know better, I'd say the photographer is suffering a pang of jealousy. If only she knew the truth – that I barely know Jasper and in reality I'm dealing with a lot more than a bad photo or two.

'Yikes, passive aggressive or what,' Katya mutters under her breath.

'I better—' I say.

'I'm going to—' Jasper blushes. Huh. I didn't peg him for the blushing type.

The silence hangs, yet we stand frozen, staring into the abyss of each other's eyes. My pulse is thrumming, as if my body is trying to alert me. But alert me to what? That I've never felt this kind of attraction to a guy before? The fleeting thought feels like such a disservice to MIA Miles, somehow. Besides, attraction is only superficial. I need to put some space between me and this man mountain, because he's not good for my health.

This must be some weird rebound urge and my poor distressed mind hasn't got the memo that weird rebound urges are always best avoided. Even thinking lusty thoughts is a betrayal to what I believed I had with Miles, and so soon in the piece! Yeah sure, Miles doesn't deserve my consideration, but the sanctity of what we had should mean I cannot move on this quickly. Isn't that so? And there I have my answer. This isn't real – this is simply the broken part of me, the abandoned bride, looking for some kind of validation that I'm still worthy of love, and Jasper happened along vibrating with rebound-candidate energy. It's best if I avoid him at all costs.

I go to pivot just as there's a shove in my back that propels me directly into Jasper's arms. I turn my head to catch the culprit, but there's no one there. Gah, will he think I'm a stage-four clinger, catapulting towards him like some kind of desperado?

'God, sorry. I'm sure someone pushed me...' My hands find their way to his chest, I can feel the thrum of his heart through the fabric of his jumper. It beats staccato like mine. Probably because out of nowhere I flew at him like some lovestruck idiot.

Katya gives me a cat-that-got-the-cream smile. So here we have our culprit. I glare at her for good measure and step out from the warmth of his arms. He really does give good hugs – is there anything the man lacks? Even his ego seems to be within the normal range, and shouldn't it be bigger? Next minute he's going to tell me he donates to dog rescue centres and helps little old ladies cross the road.

'Sorry!' I trill. 'I have to go now. Arrivederci.' Arrivederci. Far out.

In front of the Christmas tree, Katya strikes a pose as Igor ogles her like she's all his dreams come true, while I rush away. My poor bruised heart is clearly searching for a distraction. For a safe harbour. It's only natural that my subconscious has scanned the crowd and landed on hot guy Jasper. That makes sense. I just need to switch off the old brain for a bit. Pretend I am a happy-go-lucky holidaymaker with no emotional baggage.

Wine, I need wine.

The bloody Christmas tree is not the only thing getting lit this year – where is that bar? I find it in the next carriage along. And hallelujah, there are plenty of empty seats. I'm not a big drinker but a little numbing is exactly what the doctor ordered.

Gingerbread Sabrina is here, showing a passenger the same photos of her boyfriend on the beach that she showed me. I guess the no phone rule for staff is a just a suggestion, as Sabrina doesn't seem too bothered.

She catches sight of me. 'Oh, Aubrey, this is George!' She

points to a tall twentysomething dressed up as the Grinch, and yet somehow, he pulls it off. 'If you can't find me to assist, George is the next point of call.'

'Hi, Aubrey,' George says with a nervous chuckle. 'Can I get you anything?'

I'm still rather flustered about the whole flying into Jasper's arms thing and the way my body is reacting to the damn man. I have half a mind to call Rox and ask her if she orchestrated this Jasper meet-cute disaster. I wouldn't put it past my shifty sister to find the passenger manifest, do a deep dive on socials and then intimidate the hottest guy on board into being nice to me. She's wily like that, especially when I've been hurt. Would my sister really go that far? What am I even saying?! I scrape my fingers through my hair. I'm in a bit of a right old state here.

So this is what it feels like to lose your marbles.

'Thanks, Sabrina, nice to meet you, George. I'll, uh – just head to the bar. A drink is in order.' They give me a wave, yet I catch the fleeting look of confusion in their eyes, as if I'm acting strangely – I do feel rather... scattered. To be expected; I'm running on fumes as it were. It's been a helluva time and really, I should be commended for not having a monumental breakdown of epic proportions.

Wine will take the edge off. Give me some much-needed clarity. It can't hurt, can it?

Propping up one end of the bar is a fashionably dressed mid-fifties woman with an immaculately made-up face, who slugs back a candy cane shooter in a way that contradicts my first impression of her that she's almost regal by the way she holds herself.

She glances my way and surveys me before saying, 'Hello, stranger. Tell me – what's got your tinsel in a tangle?' She pulls a silly face that is contrary to her impeccable style and poise. Ah, is she the Miss Moneybags who Sabrina told me about?

'My – my tinsel is fine. And you? Looks like that candy cane shooter went down well.' I flash a grin and order a glass of white wine from the bartender, who is dressed like Buddy the Elf. Really, I wish I were in more a Christmassy mood to enjoy all this festive schtick.

'It was worth a shot.' She guffaws at her own joke. 'I'm Princess. It's not just a name, it's a way of life.' She lets out a witch-like cackle, and the volume is startling coming from such a diminutive woman. I like her already and sense that Princess – who suits her name, dressed in her finery like she truly is royalty – is going to bring the fun on this trip.

'I'm Aubrey. Nice to meet you.'

The smile falls away and her expression becomes stoic. 'Ah, *the* Aubrey. Your name precedes, you, dear. Now it makes sense, you know, the tangled tinsel thing. I heard about husband numero uno and the way in which he left this mortal coil. Wild mushrooms, eh? Not suspicious in the slightest.'

She's already heard about Miles's unfortunate faux death? 'Sorry, wild mushrooms?'

Princess waves me away, her fingers swathed in rings with gemstones that catch the light and sparkle. Are they real diamonds and rubies? Yes, this chic woman is definitely a contender for the role of Miss Moneybags. 'No need to apologise.' She flashes me a smile. 'No judgement here. Death caps, skullcaps, easily misidentified. You're not to blame.'

I double-blink as I piece the puzzle together. 'Those are poisonous mushrooms.'

The regal Princess frowns as she glances over a shoulder, as if to make certain we're alone. 'I'm sure you weren't to know, right? It's not like you prepared the wedding feast, is it?'

Ooh! Is she implying that I poisoned Miles with death cap mushrooms at my very own wedding? The idea is so preposterous that I burst out laughing. I suppose he was poisoned, but not by wild mushrooms. Has word spread that my husband died and, like school kids playing the whispering game, it's taken on a life of its own up and down the train carriage?

'Princess, I didn't poison him with mushrooms, wild or otherwise.' The bartender deposits my glass of wine in front of me and narrows his eyes suspiciously as if he's weighing up whether I'm capable of poisoning the dearly departed, like I'm some kind of matricidal maniac. I do my best to assuage his fears by flashing him a toothy grin – the smile of an innocent – but am confounded when he blanches and promptly dashes away. What on earth?

'Don't worry about him. I believe you.' Princess winks. 'Take your drink and let's go.'

'Go?' I'm only half listening while I sit in the knowledge of my bad choices – admitting I'm a jilted bride might have been the better option when compared to being cast as a murdery murderer.

'To the library carriage.'

'There's a library carriage?' How did I not see that on the website? I'm slipping as a travel guru!

Princess clucks her tongue, as if disappointed in me. 'You're not going to be one of those types who repeats everything I say, are you?'

I quickly shake my head.

'Good. We're going to decorate Christmas baubles. And between us, it's about as close to any balls as I'm going to get. All three of my husbands died too, so I happen to know a thing or two about how you're feeling.'

Yikes, I can't let her think we're both suffering when I'm not really a widow and she truly is. 'I'm so sorry for your loss, Princess. That's tragic, losing three husbands.' How old is the glamorous woman? Her complexion is smooth, as if she's had a little surgical help, but done sparingly to appear natural so it's hard to pinpoint an age. But to be married thrice, perhaps she's older than she looks.

Truth bomb time. I suck in a breath for courage. 'Miles, you see, he didn't really die.'

'Yes, yes, darling, save the whimsy, I've heard it all before. He's transitioned. He's gone to a better place. You don't have to use all those platitudes with me. Some husbands live and some die. It's the luck of the draw. I've been cursed, so I can't love another man without fear he'll meet his maker just like the others.'

Cursed, as in someone put a spell on her? I itch to repeat her words back and ask for clarification, but she's already outlawed that. 'Can you tell me a little bit more about... that?' I say, almost laughing at how robotic I sound.

She lets out a sigh, as if it's a long story but pushes on nonetheless. 'All three of my beloveds died. Can you believe that? I plucked up the courage to open my heart and take the leap into love, time and again, only to have them ripped away from me. I must be cursed; what other explanation is there? When you're filthy rich like I am, self-made by the way, before you go thinking this is some inheritance plot, or that I rely on a man to keep me in the style I'm accustomed to. You have to be aware there's an extreme amount of envy out there. Whoever is behind this took away what I value most – love.'

I'm not sure about the science behind this. 'If you don't mind me asking, how did they die?'

We amble from the bar and go through another carriage.

'Natural causes, all three. Please tell me how such a thing is remotely possible, unless I've been cursed by a jealous rival?'

I slip behind Princess as we dodge couples. 'Yes, ah – a jealous rival cursing you makes sense. Or—' Dare I try and help this poor woman? 'Could it also be that they had underlying health conditions that led to their deaths?' I'm no forensic pathologist but surely a cause of death was determined at the time, and the findings weren't death by jealous rival!

She holds out her arm to me, and I link mine through as she practically drags me forward to the library carriage. 'Isn't that a bit farfetched? Underlying health conditions! No, Ricky, my first husband, died in hospital the day after he had major surgery for an unrelated matter, after years of refusing to take medications. Arturo, my second husband, died on his way back from a visit to the convenience store to buy cigarettes. Smoked like a chimney, that man. I was always at him to cut back, to quit. And my third husband, Miguel, drifted off peacefully in his sleep the day before his eightieth birthday. Four years ago, to the day.'

'I'm sorry for your loss, Princess, but may I also ask, do you think it's possible that Ricky's avoidance of medication for years coupled with a major surgery, Arturo's chain smoking, and Miguel's advanced age might have been a precursor for their deaths?'

She gives me a look that implies I'm totally off my rocker. 'No, definitely not! They were all fit and healthy men, despite their vices, of which they had many. I've been cursed, plain and simple. I don't dare give my heart to another man, lest he also dies of "natural" causes. It's safer that way. I'll die alone and I've made my peace with that. Until that day comes, I've dedicated my life to enjoying decadent pursuits, like travelling on opulent carriages such as this.'

Princess is the five-star type of traveller, one who only travels in luxury, probably the most coveted kind of tourist, who enjoys all those perks that come with lavish holidays, like flying first class or by private jet, butler services, personal shoppers – the list is endless.

'Who is your rival, do you know? Do you have a suspect list or…?' I can't believe I'm asking such a thing but here we are.

She lets out a world-weary sigh. 'It could be anyone. Over the years many people have been jealous of my success, and so they aim for my heart in an effort to take me down. Haven't you heard the saying "jealousy is a curse"? Well, I'm the living definition of it.'

'Right. I… see.'

If you believe Princess, her success and wealth is the root cause of her solo existence because a jealous rival has cursed her and made a future relationship impossible. The mind boggles that such a thing is possible but it's obvious she truly deems it so.

When Princess talks about her husbands, real love shines in her eyes. I'm not sure what I can say to make her trust in love again, it's not my place, but I sense that the woman yearns to have a committed travel buddy, someone to enjoy these exotic five-star adventures with.

I'm not quite sure what to say and wrack my brain for a positive spin to lift her spirits. I eventually muster, 'The love of travel is almost an affair of the heart itself.' We come to the library carriage, and Princess pauses before the door to face me.

'That's a nice way to look at it. If I didn't have these holiday escapades, I'd be a very morose woman indeed. Travel is the best part of my life, and I've still got so much of the world to see, so many places to leave a part of my heart in.'

Perhaps Princess and I have that in common – falling for a place, an adventure, a city with bright lights and dazzling faces can be a heady thing. It's a different sort of love story but a love story all the same. Is it enough to sustain a person though? In order to sustain that high, you have to keep moving, keep searching, and those connections made along the way fizzle out, are forgotten. Friendships tail off as time moves on. I wonder if this has an impact on Princess. While travel can light up your soul, it can also be intensely lonely at times after all those goodbyes.

'It's such a big place,' I muse, 'this world of ours.'

Princess flashes a smile. 'Made smaller when you meet like-minded people along the way.'

That's the thing about travel – it strips back those protective layers, and you become a person who lives in the moment, who says yes, and once you jump out of your comfort zone in such a fashion, the way you view the world changes. Is that the mistake I made – hoping that I could be the Aubrey that Miles wanted when in reality that version of me isn't quite real?

I let the thought slide and focus on Princess. 'And not one travel fling?' I tease.

She gasps, as if scandalised. 'And risk his life? No! My heart is closed to men and hidden out of sight high on a shelf. Instead, I flirt with everyone who comes my way, because flirting doesn't kill anyone. I'm almost certain of that. And I can get away with it now that I'm seventy-five.'

My eyebrows shoot up. 'You're seventy-five?'

'Didn't we agree you wouldn't do that terribly annoying repeat-after-me thing?'

I grin. 'Sorry, I forgot. It's a surprise, is all. I'd have guessed you were mid-fifties.'

'Want to know my secret?'

'Sure.'

'Eight glasses of water a day and always protect your skin from the sun.'

'Ooh.' I'm a little underwhelmed, expecting some solid

secrets to her youthful glow, not that I'm the type to follow a ten-step skincare routine. I'd rather buy books than beauty products.

Princess cackles again. 'Joking, darling, although I'm sure that's great advice. I have the best plastic surgeon money can buy.'

'Amazing.'

'That I am, darling. Tomorrow, we'll explore Paris together. I've lined up a driver.' Her tone brooks no argument, and her decisive nature is a godsend after my plans for the trip were thrown in such disarray. 'Now, let's go play with those balls.'

7

18 DECEMBER, PARIS, FRANCE

At breakfast the next day, I inadvertently catch Jasper's eye and quickly avert my gaze. He's sitting at the next table over with Igor and Katya, who are taking photos of their food and each other. The next time I sneak a peek his way, he pulls a face and gestures towards the influencer couple, who are now tangled in a steamy embrace, as if all the world is a stage and they're in the middle of a pivotal performance.

It's beautiful to witness two people who are so infatuated with each other that the rest of the world blurs, but it's not as beautiful when it's almost everyone on board and you're a discarded bride who suddenly feels rather unlovable. I smile at Jasper in solidarity as I ball up my napkin and ready myself to leave the dining carriage when Sabrina approaches.

There's a sort of giddiness to her movements, like she's had some good news.

Ah! 'Did you hear from your boyfriend then?'

Sabrina nods, her face breaking into a wide smile. 'I did!' She takes her phone out and shows me a message from him that reads:

> Boss man gave his approval. Can't wait to see you!

'He's checking flight prices as we speak. Unfortunately, we'll be paying a premium since it's Christmas time and so last minute but none of that matters, as long as we get to see each other.' Sabrina closes the message and flicks through screenshots of their video call. 'Look at his adorable face! I hope to convince him while he's here to give up his sous chef position in the Caribbean and apply for a kitchen role on the Winter Wonderland Express. Staff changeover is high and even if he has to start a bit lower than sous chef, he can work his way up.'

'It sounds like a good plan to me.' It's romantic, the way they've found each other but still live nomadic lives with Sabrina crisscrossing Europe by train while he's cheffing on a luxury yacht on the Caribbean Sea.

I'm itching to explore Paris. The city of lights, of love, is one of my favourite places in the world. No matter what you're suffering – a dead husband, heartbreak, humiliation, ennui – it's the cure. At least I hope so.

Princess arrives in a cloud of headache-inducing perfume and instructs me in her usual bossy way to grab my handbag and meet her outside on the platform to go through the checkpoint together. Sabrina launches into an account of her Christmas plans with her boyfriend, which includes showing Princess a range of photos of him. 'He's very cute, but why does he wear sunglasses inside? I will never understand your generation.'

Sabrina laughs. 'I'm sure it's so he can sneak naps and no one is any the wiser.'

'So he's clever too. I like him already. I'm thrilled for you, darling, love really does make the world go around. I hope we'll get to meet him in Lapland.'

'I hope so too. We'll be staying in a hostel close by so we can definitely meet up.'

I say my goodbyes and return to my cabin. I packed a cute little beret to wear, Parisian clichés be damned. After slipping the hat on, I wrap myself in a fluffy woolly striped scarf and slide on my gloves. As an afterthought, I shove a pocket travel guide into my handbag. I've been to Paris many times due to its proximity to Britain, but there's always more to discover.

Outside, Princess and I get through the customs checkpoint into the fresh Parisian air. I inhale like it's a tincture for my soul. If you're going to be sad and jilted, you may as well be sad and jilted in Paris.

I gaze towards the street, searching for the driver Princess has arranged, as she's distracted rummaging in her oversized handbag for her phone. 'Where on earth did I put it?' A car pulls up to the curb and a man lifts his hand to wave. It's an old beat-up runabout; surely that's not to Princess's standard. Part of me thinks it would be funny if she turned out to be the sort of person who has oodles of money because she's frugal to the extreme and only splurges on fashion. Somehow, I don't think that's the case.

'Darling, wait.' She places her hand on my arm to halt me. 'Jasper's not here yet.'

'Jasper's coming with us?' Why does my voice betray me so and come out high pitched, almost gargled?

'Yes.' Princess does the duck-lips pout as if pleased with herself. 'The more the merrier, wouldn't you agree?'

I pause, debating the idea. Jasper is sweet, isn't he? So why then does my mind scream no? It's not a crime I'm attracted to the guy. Really, that's all surface level anyway, not a big deal in the scheme of things. It's not as if I need to shout about that from the rooftops. Still, I feel a prickly sensation at the idea of being stuck with him all day. As if I'm not quite in control of the motherboard as I usually am. 'Ah – yes, of course. More the merrier!'

'There he is!' Princess waves at Jasper, who jogs over. Great, he's athletic too like some striking buff Norse God. If you're into gods like that. Which I'm not.

'*Bonjour, bonjour,*' he says, his breath coming out in puffs of foggy air. 'Are we ready to explore the best of Paris?'

'*Oui, mon amour!*' Princess says, letting out a fluttery little laugh and lightly touching his shoulder. As Princess warned, she's an incorrigible flirt and no one is off limits.

I give Jasper a curt nod. I mean, how curt can a nod be? But in the slight tilt of my head, I hope to convey that I'm averse to his charms. His charismatic nature affects me not.

'Here's the car.' Princess points to a black limo with windows tinted so darkly that it's impossible to see in. She must sense my thoughts because she says, 'Tinted, bullet-proof glass.'

'Are we in danger?' Maybe Princess is some kind of mafiosa boss. I narrow my eyes and take in her bling. Today she's dripping in diamonds and swathed in gold chains. She never did tell me what line of work she was in, only that she's self-made.

'No, darling, but imagine if we were! What a story we'd have to tell.'

I have to find out. I can't just willingly, obliviously, step into a fancy stretched limo with the head of a powerful mafia family, can I? 'What did you say you did for a living again, Princess?' I make my voice light.

'Assassin. But don't worry, I'm retired. Come now, darlings.'

Walked into that one. Damn it.

The stretched limo is the kind of car that celebrities travel in, and so out of the norm for me I can barely wait to tour Paris in such luxury.

The driver opens the door for us. We barrel in, delighted to find chilled bottles of Taittinger. 'First stop. Le Tour Eiffel!' Princess takes charge and pours the champagne, and the bubbles revolt, scaling the side of the glass.

'Not wanting to be the fun police or anything but isn't it a little too early for this?' I ask. 'All I've done since we boarded is drink to excess. I'm worried my blood stream now operates purely as an alcohol stream.'

Jasper laughs, as if I'm truly funny, and the sound is melodic, beautiful. It's quite captivating, I force myself to look away from him. The thing is, I wasn't actually making a joke. Usually, I am the fun police, the boring one, who counts her drinks and makes sure there's no hangover on the horizon. Here, I've been knocking back festively named drinks like they're going out of style – probably a numbing device; I have just lost my husband after all…

'Maybe you're right.' Princess nods. 'We'll have mimosas, we've got a long day ahead of us.' She presses a button on the door panel. A hidden compartment opens outwards to reveal a mini fridge full of soft drinks, sparkling water and juice.

She dollops a whisper of orange juice into our champagne glasses. Mimosas duly mixed, we clink glasses and relax back into the plush seats, falling quiet as we admire the view of Paris as we get closer to the city centre itself. The city is dressed in its finery for the festive season. There are Christmas trees dotted here and there, and each shopfront is luxuriously decorated.

While our driver battles early morning traffic, I press my face against the glass until my breath fogs up the incredible view – chic cafés on every corner with striped rattan chairs that face the street. Historic buildings and beautiful architecture. A lithe woman wears a long caramel-coloured coat and knee-high boots, looking like a fashion icon as she walks her tiny dog. Could I live in Paris? It's a dream worth contemplating. Perhaps I'll crunch the numbers and do some research into the cost of living in a metropolis like this.

My chest tightens. Am I really moving on already, making future plans, just like that? The fairytale Christmas winter wonderland wedding, the man of my dreams, gone like a puff of smoke. The pain catches me unawares, as if it's been lurking, waiting for me to remember.

'How are you, Aubrey?' Jasper asks as Princess flirts up a storm with the driver through the partition. 'We didn't get to speak at breakfast.'

'I'm good.' There's such sincerity in Jasper's eyes I wish that I'd been honest from the get-go about the Miles fiasco, not that anyone actually listens to my protestations. 'I'm considering where I'll go after this trip. I haven't lived in Paris before, only ever had flying visits. Could this be my new home for a while?'

He lifts a shoulder. 'Why not. Paris has it all. Where else have you called home?'

'Southeast Asia mainly. There's a huge digital nomad contingent there and the cost of living is so affordable. My favourite country is Indonesia. There are so many islands to explore and who doesn't want to live in a tropical paradise?'

'Funny you should say that. I was in Bali a year ago, doing a story on the digital nomad life in Canggu. Interviewing expats who'd made the island home and how much bang they got for their buck.'

'Really? I lived in Canggu for about six months.' How strange that all the places on the planet Jasper could visit for a story and he picks Canggu?

'I'm sorry I missed you. How did you wrench yourself away from there? I stayed for three weeks and I didn't want to leave. I found Indonesians to be the happiest people on the planet, always laughing, teasing, ready with a joke.'

'Yes! The locals are a lot of fun. I miss it, actually. The chaos of the island, the smiley-faced Balinese, four family members squished on a scooter.'

'Would you go back then?'

Would I? Even though it's only been eighteen months since I left Canggu, it seems like a lifetime ago. So much has happened since then, and it's like the Aubrey who lived there then – so free and unencumbered – is gone. While I loved my time on the island, there's no point going backwards. My relationship with Miles proves that.

'I'll visit again one day,' I say. 'But for now, I'd like to live somewhere new. Just me, a new horizon, a different vista.'

Jasper glances away for a moment. 'Then Paris seems about as good a place as any to hunker down for a while.' Again, I get the feeling he's reflecting about himself at times. Is he missing his ex?

'It could be. Or maybe one of our other stops along the way.' I haven't explored as much of Europe as I'd like, aside from some family holidays and many, many destination weddings as my friendship group hit their thirties. The invites are now mostly for baby showers and children's birthday parties.

'You're lucky to live the way you do,' Jasper muses, running a finger over his lips. I double-blink and quickly look away. The gesture is subconscious but it draws my attention to the fact he's got the most kissable lips I've ever seen. In fact, I don't recall noticing another man's lips before – kissable or not.

I forget to answer again so he continues. 'I travel, but have a home base in Connecticut.' He's from Connecticut? My earlier guess of Vermont wasn't far off then. 'When I'm working, I only just scratch the surface of each city. To know the heartbeat, you have to live there long term, at least that's how it feels when I have to leave so soon.'

'Why do you bother with a home base? Why not stay?'

He gives me a rueful smile. 'Well, Olivia expected me home at some point.' He stops short, a frown marring his features. 'Or... maybe she didn't. Either way, now things are different. I could live a more itinerant life, but would I yearn for home? I'm not sure. As much as I enjoy my work trips, I also like my own bed, my own space. Did you ever miss having a home base? A place to land, family around to love on you? I guess you must have, to have decided to settle down?'

I smile as my family and close friendship group spring to mind. 'Well, I always visited home a lot. There were family functions I couldn't miss, or a friend's wedding, so those visits shored me up, and they reminded me that it would always be there and so I didn't need to be. Does that even make sense?'

'Perfect sense. You could dip in and out when you like and still get the benefit of living on some island paradise.'

I grin. He gets it. It's unusual. There's always pushback when I talk about how I live, like people want to pick holes in my story, as if I can't possibly enjoy not having a home to go to. A mortgage. Or at least the dream of one.

Sure, I suffer bouts of homesickness, but they don't last long and a quick call home usually eases it. It's not like I'm pining for bricks and mortar; I'm pining for my family, or for a deep and meaningful conversation with Freya.

Princess throws herself back between us.

'Am I interrupting?' Her witchy cackle rings out.

I shake my head at her theatrics. 'Not at all. We were talking about our travels and where we call home, or would like to.'

'Ah, you're both nomadic by nature! I suppose the three of us are. Isn't that something? To find others so similar?'

It is, but it doesn't surprise me, since according to Sabrina this trip has been offered at a discount to many travel industry insiders. If not for that, then I'm sure Jasper and I would not be sitting here right now, as the cost for a ticket on the Winter Wonderland Express is somewhat prohibitive for the average Christmas holidaymaker.

Just what type of tourist is Jasper when he's not working? Spontaneous, I bet. The sort of person you'd call when you're suddenly inspired for a last-minute road trip to visit some crumbling ruins, or when you spot sale airfares and know they'll say yes without hesitation. I sense he'd be up for any adventure, and take it all in his stride.

'Yeah, it is,' Jasper agrees. 'What about you, Princess? Where do you call home?'

'I'm from the Philippines originally. Now that I've retired, I'm a rolling stone, but when the urge for my own bed calls, I visit my castello in Tuscany with its verdant rolling hills and vineyards as far as the eye can see. Or if I'm feeling energetic, I have a loft in Tribeca – I enjoy the New York nightlife, jazz clubs, nightclubs. My villa in St Lucia is perfect when I'm in the mood for sunshine and cocktails. My condo in Manila is fun when I'm craving Filipino food like sisig or adobo.' She waves her hand as if it's nothing. 'I have a few other abodes here and there, but I don't want to come across as pretentious.'

At that, we burst out laughing.

'Are you ready for a whistlestop tour of Paris?' Princess asks.

'Ready,' Jasper confirms. 'I'd love to find a gift for my mum for Christmas if we have time.'

Loves his mum – check. Actually, no, I'm not checking boxes for Jasper!

'Would you mind switching with me?' Princess gives Jasper a coy smile. Switching means Jasper will be seated next to me, instead of opposite.

'Sure thing.' Jasper switches and Princess's eyes sparkle with amusement. I give her an almost imperceptible shake of the head, so she knows I'm not interested. I'm sure she takes absolutely no notice.

As we zoom around Paris, Princess has us in fits of laughter, sharing stories of hijinks she got up to around the city on previous visits, most happening in underground clubs – she's got the energy of a teenager and it doesn't ever seem to ebb.

Princess has paid some kind of premium for tickets as we're whisked in an elevator to the top of the Eiffel Tower, which is not for the faint of heart but the stunning view of Paris below is worth it. We're back in the car and taken to the next stop.

Once again we skip the queue at the Louvre with a private guided tour to visit the Mona Lisa. I only wish we had more time at each sight, but it's enough to whet my appetite for an extended return trip. 'She's so tiny!' I whisper to Jasper, who is shoved in close beside me due to the crowd pushing us forward.

'Tiny but powerful,' he agrees, cocking his head to survey the small painting as the crowd push forward, a sea of arms holding phone cameras aloft.

'I see power too,' Princess agrees.

Jasper puts a protective arm around me when a burly man gets too close. 'The hint of a smile shows her quiet determination. She's a woman who has faced many challenges but persists and ultimately prevails.'

When I gaze back at Mona Lisa with that in mind, the painting changes; a different history takes shape. Was she a mother, a wife, a woman who suffered heartrending loss but persevered? Questions that will never be answered but that make the artwork sing its own sweet melody; it becomes not just an object but a story.

This is why I love touring with people. Jasper's comments have changed the way I view the painting. Art is subjective and up for interpretation and now I'm lost imagining a world this woman once walked.

Sainte-Chapelle is next. Sunlight pools through the stained-glass windows, colouring us in soft rainbow prisms. It's like being in the belly of a kaleidoscope. Jasper's mouth is agape, as if he can't quite believe this is real, and the sight of it makes me stifle a laugh.

'What?'

'You look like you're in love.'

He considers it. 'I am, I think.' He flashes me that same winning grin of his, but it's laced with something else – wonderment, anticipation? Well, who wouldn't be feeling those same emotions being bathed in vivid light like this?

'It's not just the beauty or majesty of these cathedrals that tug on the heart strings, it's a bigger feeling than that. I struggle to put it into words...' I say, unable to express the complexity of what I mean.

Jasper and Princess wear the same rapt faces so perhaps they feel it too.

Jasper nods. 'There's a word that might fit: numinous, which describes a strong religious and spiritual feeling signifying the presence of divinity. I take it to mean it's that bolt you feel deep in your soul when you walk into a place like this.'

How can this man be so perfect? A wordsmith who understands big feelings, big thoughts. The philosophy of things. 'That's exactly it, Jasper. Numinous.' I roll the word on my tongue; it feels right. While I don't follow any one religion, you can't help but feel the presence of the divine inside these walls. It adds a buoyancy to my spirit. This is why people truly believe. It's hard not to when it touches you like this, like it's an almost physical thing.

We leave Sainte-Chapelle and are driven to the 1st

arrondissement and stop at Place Vendôme to share a bottle of champagne and canapes at the Ritz, which Princess insists on. I'm not going to argue. It's all very fancy. The limo door is opened by a doorman and we're ushered inside to the sumptuous hotel famous for so many reasons, including being the home of Coco Chanel for over thirty years.

'Let's sit in Bar Vendôme,' Princess says. It's as lavish as you imagine, and I pretend for a moment that I eat canapes in swanky places all the time. The bite-size morsels are exceptional, the company more so, Jasper surprising me with his intellect and his big heart. Just as I suspected, the guy is the type to shovel snow off his neighbour's drive and carry shopping to the car for a frazzled mum. One of the good ones that you only see in romcoms. But there must be a flaw under all that, right? There always is. Maybe I can ask Rox to do a deep dive on his background... Until I remember I'm not interested so there's no point.

After Bar Vendôme, we're driven to Montmartre. Princess buys gifts at A la Mère de Famille, an artisanal chocolate shop, and I buy a book about the history of the shop, which is so utterly Parisian it's hard to leave.

Princess points out Café des Deux Moulins, where the French movie *Amélie* was filmed. We drive past the Vignes di Clos Montmartre, the last operational vineyard in all of Paris. I'm grateful we've had the car in which to zoom all over Paris as we covered some distance and managed to fit so much in.

As the day escapes and night falls, my energy ebbs. Princess is still lively chatting away with Jasper and the driver, while I soak up the view of Paris at night, a sepia-hued river Seine, the Eiffel Tower sparkling against the inky night.

'This is the last stop,' our driver informs us through the speakers. 'Marché de Noël de Notre-Dame.'

The facade of the Notre Dame cathedral looks different as

evening falls. The gothic structure fills with brooding shadows, the gargoyles perched above like sentinels guarding the city.

Square Rene-Viviani in front is alive with Swiss chalet-like stalls, selling an array of delights such as mulled wine, roasted chestnuts, Christmas ornaments and artisanal crafts. With the medieval towers of Notre Dame as a backdrop, and the lapping of the Seine close by, it's the perfect place to stretch our legs and do some Christmas shopping.

'There's a Ferris wheel! Who's keen?' Jasper asks. 'I bet the view will be even more stunning from that vantage.' He points high into the sky. It's sweet to see his childlike spirit come alive when faced with a carnival ride. If Miles were here, he'd insist that was for kids and no way would he be seen dead on it. Why am I comparing the two of them?

'I'm keen!' I say. 'What about you, Princess?'

Excitement shines on her face. 'I've got my eye firmly on my prize. Those big, thick, fat sausages. Look at the girth on those things.' Before we can respond, she's marching towards a choucroute stall. I have to practically bite my lips off to stop laughter spilling out.

'I'm noticing that Princess sees many objects as phallic,' Jasper muses, trying to rein in his own grin.

I don't dare tell him about our bauble-decorating experience. For a widow, she sure knew a lot of inappropriate jokes about balls. But who am I to judge?

Is the bawdy humour just a bit of schtick, a persona that Princess puts out to the world in an effort to hide her real heart, a heart that is hurting? Don't we all do that to some degree? Show the world what we think they want to see? Act a certain way to protect the vulnerable parts, the scars, the damage that we hide from the light?

'Should we get one too and then ride the Ferris wheel?' Jasper asks.

I'm not sure I can now eat a sausage without thinking of penises and not choke to death on it, and with Jasper in such close proximity. I swallow back a giggle.

'You're thinking of penis sausages, aren't you?'

I bite my bottom lip and fumble with an appropriate answer. 'Yes.' We knock into each other, laughing.

8

18 DECEMBER, PARIS, FRANCE

Later that evening, Princess bursts into my cabin while I'm meant to be freshening up for dinner but am really checking my phone for any contact from Miles. Nada. The longer I don't hear from him, the more I worry that he's truly suffering some sort of strange malady that prevents him from getting in touch. Or knowing Miles it's more likely he doesn't want to get the earful he deserves when I officially end things with him.

'Don't mind me, darling.' It seems that the normal rules like knocking and waiting for a response don't apply to Princess, and that makes sense in the scheme of how the confident woman walks this world.

I clip on cutesy Santa earrings that I picked up earlier at the Notre Dame Christmas market.

'You're really getting into the Christmas spirit, darling. That jumper.' Her eyebrows shoot up so high I worry that she'll fall over backwards. She adds to the dramatics by clutching her chest, tottering around and feigning a heart attack. Talk about hamming it up for effect.

'Tell me how you really feel,' I joke.

I survey her outfit. She's wearing a figure-hugging designer two-piece pantsuit that even my decidedly unfashion-conscious eyes can see is expensively made. In comparison, I look exactly like someone who got a cheap polyester jumper off the rack at the kind of department store that Princess would never step foot into.

'Sorry, darling, it's just you're so pretty and then you wear... that.'

I do appreciate that Princess doesn't mince words. 'This might be on the cheap and gaudy side, but it's the designated "ugly Christmas jumper" evening. Didn't you get the invite? There's even a prize for the ugliest. I hope I win.'

She blinks and blinks as if clearing a blockage that's not in her eyes but possibly in her mind. 'Yes, of course I did but that doesn't mean we have to surrender our standards. Darling, I don't know how to say this any other way, but it looks like you've taken that reindeer... hostage.'

'What? Hostage!' I check my reflection in the small mirror on the wardrobe. 'Ah, because of the bridle?'

'Because of the... the everything. I could lend you one of my dresses?'

'And risk spilling wine on actual couture? No thanks. Besides, this is fun! Who doesn't love dressing up in ugly Christmas jumpers? The uglier the better. Aside from you, who has impossibly high sartorial standards.'

Usually I'm only found in athleisure. Because I work online, I can get away without a corporate uniform and after so many years living out of a backpack, I'm used to a capsule wardrobe. But I did splurge on some outfits for my honeymoon, mostly because I didn't have anything remotely suitable in terms of formal or festive wear, and that included this ugly Christmas jumper.

'I suppose you'll win the contest, that's for sure, and I will happily celebrate with you, but I'm also worried about you wearing all that polyester and sitting so close to candles. You're a walking fire hazard and liable to go up in flames at any moment.'

'I've always wanted to light up a room,' I say mock dreamily.

'Very funny.'

'Don't sit too close to me, just in case I become a tinderbox.'

'Good idea. Let's go. If you keep adding more plastic jewellery like those earrings, you'll only make things worse.'

We find our name cards on a table in the dining carriage. 'Here we are! Hello, hello to one and all.' Princess sweeps in, as always announcing her arrival as if the table of strangers have been waiting for us. It's our first formal dinner and we've been assigned seats this evening.

Princess takes her place, exaggeratedly motions to the man who has the seat beside my place setting – Jasper, of course. I bet Princess had a hand in this. Wouldn't have taken much for her to find his name card and do the old switcheroo.

It's fine. While he might be fun to look at, that doesn't matter one jot. I steal a glance at the man in question and, oh my God, even dressed in an ugly Christmas jumper, he takes my pulse from regular programming into adrenaline rush. Why does he have such a visceral effect on me? With his mussed hair and intense unfathomable eyes, he's all masculine energy, even in a silly jumper that somehow makes me dream of snuggling sessions on the couch in front of a fire, slow kisses…

I flop into my seat as my legs struggle to hold me. Probably from the long day. What else could it be? I practically inhale a glass of water; I have a thirst I can't seem to quench.

'Thirsty?' Jasper asks with a lift of his brow.

Can he read my mind? He is a thirst trap, that's for sure. He wiggles the water jug.

'Yes. Please.'

I'm confused when he laughs. Confused and woozy.

Oh no.

Lovesick, is that what this is?

I've read about this phenomenon in the books. But this cannot happen. Because a) I'm in mourning and b) I have a steadfast rule about no rebounds and 3) It's so hot in here, is the heating stuck on high?

Ah. It's a glitch in the matrix. That's all it is. My subconscious wreaking havoc again.

Besides, I hardly know the guy, so all of this is just some surface-level lust.

But maybe Princess is onto something with the polyester-being-flammable thing because I feel like I'm on FIRE.

I focus intently on Princess so I don't self-combust. 'Who here is single?' Princess moves her gaze from person to person and is met with eyes downcast or slow nods. 'Ah. All of us, then. That's why they've grouped us together. A better outcome, if you ask me. I don't know about you, but I for one am a little tired of the obnoxious displays of affection from the couples aboard, aren't you?' Her voice carries, and we're met with a lot of smug side-eye from all the lovebirds on other tables in the vicinity.

I'm sure Princess is just trying to bond and not make our table of singles feel so alone, because she's been very friendly with the loved-up couples, but I agree their canoodling has been next level. Or maybe that's the bitterness talking; who can tell?

'Why are they so overt? Like there's a prize for most smooching? Is there a prize for that too?' Princess trains her gaze on me. She's barely taken a breath but her soliloquy seems to put everyone at ease. They're smiling and relaxed now that Princess has broken the ice.

I laugh. 'No prize that I'm aware of. But you're right, they do seem rather fond of kissing like their life depends on it.' I let out a little trill of a laugh to show that I am not jealous – no siree, I'm just observant. 'I'm Aubrey by the way.' I give everyone a little wave.

'And as most of you know, I'm Princess. It's not just a name, it's a way of life.'

I grin at her customary introduction. She's a social butterfly, and a very nosy one at that. I'm relieved to be with other lonely hearts but do feel a little sad at the thought we're all effectively spending Christmas alone. Not a loved one in sight. Why are my fellow singles solitary at this time of year? Even if they're not in relationships, usually the festive season would be spent with family. Or are they like me and thought this trip – despite the circumstances leading up to it – was too good to pass up?

Princess continues. 'We're footloose and fancy free! We've been thrown together amid those in love-bubble land, so let's introduce ourselves and explain why we're alone this Christmas. I'll start. I've been cursed by a jealous rival, culminating in the loss of three husbands who left this mortal coil under suspicious circumstances. Even though they deemed those deaths "natural causes", it makes not an iota of sense to me. Hence I have decided to close my heart to love so that no further men are carried off by the Grim Reaper. And you?' Princess asks the woman seated beside her, who is about mid-fifties with fiery red hair and dark dramatic winged eyeliner and scarlet-red lipstick. Her eyes hold a certain sadness, as if she's got a lot on her mind. Around the table are shellshocked faces, probably at hearing such a frank admission from Princess. There are lots of reasons people choose to remain single – being cursed by a jealous rival is rather unique, so it's no wonder they're all stunned silent.

The woman coughs, gathering herself. 'I'm Karen, it's nice to meet you all.' Karen's made one concession to the theme and wears a jumper that says *Too Intelligent to Wear Ugly Christmas Jumpers*. 'I'm alone for the holidays because I chose to be. After fifty first dates, where they all gave me the ick, there was no need for a second. I've concluded that I'm simply unlucky in love and it's time to live my life sans man, and so here I am.' I admire her directness and sense Karen is a what-you-see-is-what-you-get type of person. 'I travel once a year, always during the festive season because it's my favourite holiday and I enjoy experiencing different foodie traditions around the world.' Karen gestures to a grey-haired man in his sixties wearing a uniquely Australian Christmas jumper featuring festive jars of Vegemite.

'I'm Barry. Hail from Australia, as you can probably tell.' He points to his green and gold jumper. 'I'm alone for the holidays. Again. Can't seem to make a relationship stick – and I'm not sure why. I send flowers, voice notes, texts, love letters, call every hour on hour and it's still not enough.'

Yikes. Not enough, or far too much? Barry is dangerously close to stage four clinger territory. I debate whether to mention it but decide it's far too early to gently probe if he's aware that kind of behaviour might be seen as smothering. And really, what would I know? I'm not exactly an expert on relationships myself.

'I'm open to love though.' He lets out a booming laugh and stares hard at Princess, who reels back as if slapped. It's the first time I've seen her lose her composure and I bite down on a smile. 'A mate of mine suggested that I needed to broaden my horizons. I'm a late bloomer when it comes to travel.' He lets out an embarrassed chuckle. 'This is the first time I've ventured from Australia, to see a bit of the world. Who knows, love might find me that way. Any takers?' He guffaws. Really, he's quite sweet in that typical jokester Australian way where they don't take life too seriously.

I jab Princess in the ribs and she gives me the stink eye. Sure,

Barry doesn't have her style or grace, but he seems like a man who'd make life fun and be up for anything just like she is. If anyone can handle a man who is a little overzealous, it's Princess. So what if Princess has sworn off men? So have I for the minute and yet she's still nudging Jasper towards me at every interval she can. Two can play at that game.

'And what about you?' Barry motions to a woman wearing a festive tracksuit adorned with candy canes. She sits to his left and smiles broadly when the attention is directed her way. She tucks a lock of mousy brown hair behind her ear.

'I'm CJ from Canada. I'm a divorced single mother and likely to remain as such because the dating pool in my town is more of a pond. I don't hold high hopes I'll meet my Prince Charming there, where everyone knows everyone. I want a partner who enjoys outdoors pursuits, but he must also love K-Pop. Extra points if he adores K-Drama, or Korean zombie flicks. Unless he meets that criterion, I'm not interested.'

'K-Pop, K-Drama, and Korean zombie movies? That's very specific,' Karen says, giving CJ an approving nod.

Karen's not prepared to commit to a second date if they don't pass muster and CJ's not willing to compromise on sharing similar hobbies – it's refreshing that these women are so aware of what they want in a partner.

'Yeah, and frankly, I'm at the point of giving up finding such a unicorn.' CJ laughs. 'But I figure, life is too short to settle for second best.'

CJ's sentiment hits home. 'I hope you find your perfect match,' I say, admiring her for sticking to a wish list. It makes me question my own standards for love. I've never really thought that deeply about it. I've been more caught up in the end of relationships, licking my wounds and piecing together what went wrong – should I be focusing instead on what attributes the perfect man needs to have?

'Thank you,' CJ says. 'It's my ex-husband's turn with the teens this Christmas, so I splurged on this trip. I'm up for anything, if the rest of you are? I'm mostly looking forward to our igloo stays in Lapland.'

'I am too,' I say with a smile. At the end of the line, when the train stops in Rovaniemi, we'll be driven deep into the snowy wilds of Lapland to finish out our trip in private igloos with domed glass ceilings, hoping to catch an unobstructed view of the Aurora Borealis if weather conditions are favourable. I sprang for an upgrade, an outdoor terrace with hot tub – which now seems like a huge waste of money. Hot tub for one? Damn you, Miles, for casting a pall over things. The Northern Lights have been on my bucket list for ages and to be able to experience them in the height of luxury must be magical.

'The igloo stays are fantastic,' Princess says. 'It's like being in a different universe under a galaxy of swirling green and pink sky. I've stayed there twice and am hoping to be lucky enough to catch the spectacle of colour for a third time.'

'Oh nice,' CJ says. 'Yeah, it's not so much about the Aurora Borealis as it is Lapland itself. I'm keen to try sauna bathing and Arctic-ice swimming! Going from the intense heat of the sauna to the extreme cold of the lake is great for your circulation. But I'm most excited about learning to command the husky sled.'

'Don't you just sit in the sled and enjoy being pulled along in the frozen forest?' Princess asks.

CJ's eyes sparkle with anticipation. 'There is that option but I found a company that teaches you how to command the huskies and drive the sled yourself. Apparently it's quite the skill learning how to navigate through such a dense forest of trees. The huskies can get up to speeds of twenty kilometres per hour.

Then there's snowshoeing! Oh, and I want to take a snowmobile out for a spin. What a rush!'

Ah, Canadian CJ is that rare breed of tourist, the thrill-seeker who enjoys high octane, adrenaline-fuelled pursuits. No doubt she's the kind of holidaymaker who bungees off cliffs and leaps from perfectly safe planes. I wish I had a little more daredevil inside me, but I like being alive too much to risk it.

'I'm stuck on the idea of ice swimming,' Barry says, anxiety flicking across his features. 'How on earth would you not freeze to death? Aren't temperatures forecast to be around minus sixteen degrees Celsius or so?' The big burly Australian shivers.

'Yes, those temps sound about right.' CJ grins. 'It will be a little chilly but that's exactly what the sauna is for, to warm the old bones up again afterwards.' Her face is lit up as she talks about the activities she's keen to partake in. 'It must sound extreme to you, Barry, coming from a country with all that sunshine, but the benefits outweigh the discomfort. Ice swimming reduces blood pressure and boosts your immune system and cognitive abilities. I need of all that, especially after raising teenage boys who zap me of my strength by their sheer rambunctiousness.'

'Aah,' Karen says with an understanding nod. 'Now it makes sense. This is your version of self-care – more extreme than, say, a spa day, but effective nonetheless.'

CJ gives her a knowing grin. 'Exactly. Shocks me back to life. Replenishes me for motherhood duties. And what about you?' CJ turns the conversation back my way.

Princess jumps in before I have a chance to respond. 'Aubrey's husband took his seat on the Afterlife Express. It's very recent, so the less said the better, and please, she can't stomach even the thought of mushrooms. It's too soon.'

Karen frowns and mouths 'mushrooms?' to Barry. He gives

her a blank look and a shrug. Oh God. Who started the bloody poisonous mushroom story anyway?

'Oooh. You're the... widow.' CJ's expression changes to one of sympathy. 'I'm so sorry. To lose the love of your life in such a way. Sinkholes are my worst nightmare.' She shudders. 'They seem to be on the rise too, don't they? Like, what is going on with that?'

Barry mouths 'sinkhole?' back to Karen. I will never live this down.

A sinkhole! Now I've heard it all. My backstory has grown legs, a head, and a life of its own so why fight it? Most people don't question me further once they hear Miles is pushing up daisies, and isn't that what I wanted? Not to be known as the abandoned bride?

But for the sake of being honest, I better give it a try because otherwise I fear there'll be detectives waiting at the next platform to interrogate me, what with all the deeply suspicious ways in which the other passengers seem to think my beloved departed the land of the living. 'Miles, he didn't really die, you know...'

CJ leans across and rubs the top of my hand. 'Of course not! His spirit lives on, while he rests in eternal peace, and one day' – she's moved to tears – 'you'll be reunited.'

I'm detecting a pattern. People are so alarmed by grief they stop listening and pivot to platitudes. Before I can assure CJ that he's not knocking on heaven's door, she's out of her chair and pulling me in for a hug that's so tight I struggle to breathe. I'm surprised at how strong she is as she squeezes the very breath from my body.

When I'm released from her vice-like grip, I inhale much-needed oxygen as Sabrina heads our way, bottle of wine in hand. This evening she's wearing her own ugly Christmas jumper that features Rudolph the Red Nosed Reindeer on the front, and has a tail sewed on to the back that bounces and swings with each step. As she fills guests' wine glasses, her tail swipes plates and glasses from tables, leaving a trail of devastation in her wake. Sabrina is blithely unaware, probably because she's also donned a pair of puffy reindeer earmuffs that serve no real purpose except maybe to prevent her hearing passenger complaints and cries for help. George trails behind, picking up debris and apologising to passengers.

'Aubrey!' she yells too loud when she spots me.

'Behind you!' I motion, but she's doesn't understand and just gives me a fluttery little wave while another table's cutlery clatters to the carpet.

She misinterprets what I'm gesturing to and says, 'Oh, you know George. He's always grovelling around the floor picking up bits and pieces.' She leans closer to us and lowers her voice. 'A bit of a klutz, but honestly, he's such a sweetheart.'

Poor George is a few steps back, dealing with the aftermath. Around the table we exchange hurried glances. Is anyone going to tell her that in actual fact she is the klutz? By the looks of it, no one wants to be the bearer of such news, so I let it go. I'm sure George will have a quiet word.

Sabrina goes around the table, topping up our wine glasses with a bottle of Burgundy. She doesn't seem to notice that some of us are drinking white wine, and she splashes the red in, oblivious. While she might be lacking in a certain attention to detail, she more than makes up for it with her bubbly personality, although tonight she does appear a little less sparkly. Staff work hours on board are intense, so I feel for her. In jobs like this, staff rely on generous tips from passengers at the end of the journey as thanks for their efforts. It's why this type of job is so popular, despite the toll the long hours take on staff.

'Did you hear the latest?' Sabrina bends to whisper loud enough for our table of six to hear.

'No?' I say. 'The latest about what?'

'There's trouble in paradise. A once-happy couple have hit splitsville!' Sabrina darts a glance around to make sure other tables aren't eavesdropping. 'Came out of nowhere too.'

'Really? Who?' I ask, surveying the dining room carriage for potential candidates.

Sabrina doesn't have a chance to respond as our group chatter excitedly about who it could be. 'Have you noticed some of them act like kissing is an Olympic event and their very own gold medal is on the line?' Karen puckers her mouth as if the idea is distasteful. 'Like, we get it, you're in love.'

'This train is nothing but sex on wheels... except for us.' Princess sadly shakes her head.

Sabrina acknowledges Princess with a nod and gives Karen a sympathetic pat on the shoulder. 'Tell me about it. I'm the one who has to turn down their beds every evening, and let's just say there are quite a few who need to learn that the "do not disturb" door hanger is as much for the benefit of staff as their own modesty, which seems to be grossly lacking.'

'Yikes.'

'Yikes exactly. I'm going to need years of therapy to wipe those visions from my mind.'

Sabrina's future Confessions Of tell-all book will be a gold mine of stories and most likely a bestseller because who doesn't want to hear the lowdown? 'So, who are they?' I ask, sneaking another peek at the tables close by. I feel a wave of sadness for whoever the couple is.

There's a pause as Sabrina bites down on her lip, as if wondering if she should confide in us or not. 'Think of this like... an Agatha Christie novel. You'll have to find the clues and solve the mystery.'

Jasper frowns. 'But someone always ends up dead in an

Agatha Christie novel, don't they? And there's one set on a train very similar to this.'

'Oh!' Sabrina chortles. 'I've never actually read any of her novels. Well, same principle – hunt for clues. I'll leave this little break-up mystery with you.' With that she moves to the next table as we scurry to save our overly full wine glasses and rescue our dinner plates as her tail shows no mercy.

'Well,' Karen says. 'This train ride just got a little more interesting!'

'It seems that we all have one thing in common.' Princess takes a sip of her mixed-up wine and grimaces. 'We're all consciously uncoupled, darlings, and at Christmas no less. Therefore I hereby dub us the "Unlucky in Love Travel Club".'

We clink glasses and celebrate our... misfortune.

'So,' Karen asks. 'Which couple is on the precipice of joining our ranks?'

I swear the dining carriage goes quiet to listen to our speculations. Our couple sailing stormy waters may well be one of them, but which one? Some pretend to be gazing at menus but peep over the top at us. Others kiss and croon while giving us the side-eye, which is a little strange. If you commit to a kiss in public, like, actually commit.

'Perhaps this is a conversation best kept for the library?' I give an almost imperceptible tilt of the head to our audience.

'Good idea,' agrees Princess. 'After dinner we'll move to the comfort of the library carriage where we can unpick this mystery without all these extra ears.' She lifts a regal brow.

9

18 DECEMBER, PARIS, FRANCE

In the library we sit at one of the bigger tables. The space has a dark academia aesthetic – the stuff dreams are made of. Having lived nomadically most of my adult life and even after staying put in Kent for a year and a half, my possessions are still rudimentary, basics that fit in a rucksack, but that doesn't stop me from wishing I had a library like this. Leatherbound books line dark shelves. All the classics are here, from Emily Brontë's *Wuthering Heights* to Jack London's *Call of the Wild*. Navy-blue wingback chairs sit awaiting guests to sink into. All it's missing is a fireplace and then I'd truly never leave.

'This gives "Professor Plum in the library with a wrench" vibes and I'm here for it,' CJ says with a grin. 'My kids love that game.'

'I love it too,' I say. 'It's a classic.'

Jasper arrives a few minutes later, having escaped to his cabin to take a work call in private. And there's one seat left, next to me, and I realise that's only because Princess has orchestrated it that way.

From his coat he takes a bottle of red wine. 'Sabrina insisted I smuggle this in – it's one of the fancier varieties apparently. She'll be along with fresh wine glasses very soon.'

I'm not sure why we need fresh glasses since Sabrina mixes the wine varieties anyway, but it's nice of her to think of us.

Jasper flashes me a grin, and boy oh boy, what a smile. Looking at this god of a man is like staring at the sun.

'I' – I momentarily lose my train of thought – 'enjoy drinking wine.' Kill me.

'Ah.' His brow furrows slightly as if he's confused. And I get that. 'Great to hear.'

Princess stands up and claps for attention. 'Welcome, one and all, to the very first meeting of the Unlucky in Love Travel Club destination: the Arctic Circle. Now, let's get down to business. First up, who do we suspect might just be about to become a member of our club? And secondly, should we stage an intervention and help them stay together?'

The group confers. Jasper leans so close I lose the ability to form rational thought. Why does he smell so good and why does it send my brain haywire? The decision is seemingly made, without any input from me, because I cannot compute words when Jasper's a mere whisper away.

Karen says, 'An intervention would be best, if we can do it subtly and try to help them on the sly. It's all dependant on who the couple is.'

'Agreed.' Princess nods.

'It's got to be that beautiful French lady – what's her name? Madame Delacroix, I think? The one who's married but is holidaying with another man who is thirty years her junior? Never fear, it's all above board, she's in an open marriage I believe,' Barry says. How does he know about that? 'I had a drink with the lad himself at the welcome party. A gentleman should never kiss and tell, but this lad was rather loose with the details, so much so that it all felt rather desperate.'

'Really?' I ask. 'Desperate how?'

Barry clears his throat as colour creeps up his neck. 'Well, he mentioned how long they'd been together – only a few months – and that he'd fallen hopelessly in love but that her attentions were slipping. He alluded to the fact that her petite affairs usually had a time limit and that meant he wouldn't be flavour of the month for much longer, despite his feelings for her.'

'Absolutely scandalous!' Princess says, eyes twinkling as if she's loving the inside scoop. 'Although I do love a woman who takes charge and knows what she wants from a lover, before ditching him for the next hero in her story.'

'But he's in love!' CJ cries. 'Maybe he'll be that special sort of someone who shows her what real commitment is all about and they'll live happily ever after... with her husband... Ah, maybe not. I don't profess to know much about open marriages.'

Barry presses his lips together and nods. 'He asked me what the best course of action is to woo the lovely lady. I suggested he shower her with affection, so she has no doubt about his feelings. You know, be there for her every minute of every day, write her love letters and leave them under her pillow, kiss her awake, read her poetry, open doors, close doors, the lot.'

I wrinkle my nose and face Barry. 'Wouldn't that be... a little suffocating?' While it might sound romantic on paper, that kind of constant attention would stifle me. 'A bit like love bombing, in a way?'

'Suffocating?' Barry reels as if I've slapped him. 'Love bombing? Why is that such an issue these days? My last girlfriend accused me of being overbearing, after I left her a number of voicemails over the course of a Friday. It was meant to be sweet –

I simply called her when she popped into my thoughts but apparently it was too much.'

'How many voicemails did you leave?' I ask, intrigued.

'Twenty-one... but we were newly in love, or so I thought.' Sadness flashes across his features as he dips his head.

'Barry's right,' Princess pipes up. 'That's romantic, a man showing up like that, being vulnerable, making his intentions and feelings clear – maybe it's an age thing, me being sixty and all and Barry a touch older perhaps.' Princess remains poker-faced, even though she's already admitted to me she's seventy-five. I let it slide, the crafty minx. 'I simply don't understand this love bombing nonsense. Or that a man can be judged so harshly for calling twenty-one times. It's sweet.'

Karen grimaces. 'Barry's intentions may be pure, but love bombers flip the switch from love to hate, so it's a bit different to Barry's scenario. Although, honestly, I'd still run a mile too if a man called me twenty-one times. Sorry, not sorry, Barry.' The Australian shrugs good-naturedly. 'In saying that, I can't get past the first date, so there's no chance of that happening to me, but I digress...'

I shake my head to clear it. How quickly our little mystery-solving turned the magnifying glass on our own shortcomings in love. Are they shortcomings though, or are we collectively making mistakes over and again in our quests for love?

So far, Princess won't risk dating due to being cursed by a jealous rival. Barry loves his partners almost too much. Karen's ick list stops her from getting past the first date. CJ won't settle for a man unless he's a K-Pop fan. Jasper's job keeps him away from home and causes issues. What about me?

Yeah, sure, Miles didn't turn up to our wedding, but do I have some fatal flaw that stops my relationships going the distance? What is my relationship kryptonite? I'm not clingy or needy. But maybe I'm too aloof, too self-sufficient? It's worth thinking about – as I can clearly see what behaviours or beliefs might be hurting my newfound friends as they navigate the search for a soulmate, so what are mine? My spontaneity has been an issue before, as has my indifference about starting a family. There are also the times I go quiet, craving solitude, which is occasionally seen as being cold, detached.

'So, the French lady is a possibility then?' Jasper asks the group, pulling me from my reverie. 'Perhaps she's tiring of the toy boy?'

'Yes,' Princess says, a gleam in her eye. 'The toy boy is on the chopping block and if this is her modus operandi and he's fully aware of that then I don't see an intervention will help but we can try for the sake of the poor lovesick man.'

Sabrina arrives with a tray full of wine glasses and another bottle of wine, white this time. 'It is it Madame Delacroix and her lover?' I ask as she opens the bottle of wine.

'Nope, not them. I have it on good authority that this couple split over a suspected cheating scandal. The guy went rogue, even though he professed his love for her morning, noon and night.' With that, Sabrina flounces off.

'Ooh no, then we can't stage an intervention if there's been a cheating scandal.' Princess frowns. 'I wouldn't want to encourage that type of behaviour.'

The group confers for a bit.

'Well, Sabrina did say "suspected" so I put it to the group that we find out who the couple is first and get the lowdown, and we can then decide if an intervention is warranted,' Barry offers.

Princess beams. 'Such a clever man. OK, so who do we suspect it could be?'

'Ooh.' Karen holds up a finger. 'Could it be the young couple from Hawaii? You can't miss them, they wear matching clothes and are so happy and bubbly, but almost too happy and bubbly, like it's a little forced.'

'Faking it, to get through a holiday?' Jasper gives her a sage nod. 'I'm sure we've all been there before.'

I'm not sure why that comment gets under my skin, but it does. Is the man mountain finally showing his true colours? 'So you've faked it before, have you, Jasper? That seems rather cruel. Do you have a thing against honesty in relationships?' My voice comes out taut, tense, possibly contaminated by my own heartbreak.

Jasper colours. 'No, God no, all I mean is...' He takes a moment to calibrate, or conjure a lie – who can tell. '...I've been there before with a partner on a holiday.'

Princess shoots me a warning glare, as if I should be giving Jasper the benefit of the doubt. 'And I'm sure the purpose of the trip was romance. Was it not, Jasper?' Princess asks.

He ruffles a hand through his hair. 'It was a last-ditch trip, booked on a whim in an attempt to save a relationship that was on the way to failing, but neither of us wanted to admit it and so there was this feeling of just going through the motions...'

He's rambling, just like a man trying to make excuses for his poor behaviour.

'Makes perfect sense to me,' Princess – ever Jasper's cheerleader – declares. 'You've got a good heart, Jasper.' I fight an eyeroll and lose, resulting in another glare from Princess.

'I'd prefer honesty rather than my partner "going through the motions" all because we were on holiday.' Is Jasper just like all the others? Probably. Why can't men be upfront? I give him a cool stare. Not that I'm very good with cool stares; that's more Rox's domain. I narrow my eyes to really emphasise the point.

He has the audacity to lay his hand atop mine, and it irks me no end that my body gets a buzz from his touch. I try to give myself a stern talking to, but apparently it's falling on deaf ears because when he looks deeply into my eyes, my body goes molten, like lava. This is the worst betrayal – myself against myself.

'Truly, it was just one of those situations where the love had fizzled out and like always when it comes to me and all of my relationships to date, I tried to save it far too late.'

'Aww,' Princess says, dropping her bottom lip. 'This is why you're part of the Unlucky in Love Travel Club, Jasper. We're all guilty of this, in one way or another. Making mistakes in love that we're not even aware of until too late.'

'Yes,' Barry says with a wide smile. 'I sure could use some help from Lady Love.'

Princess is on the same wavelength as me, but I don't want to encourage her where Jasper is concerned. He could say he's the love 'em and leave 'em type and she'd tell him how sweet he is for sharing his hot body with the masses.

'Maybe our club will be good for us! We can ascertain what we've done wrong in relationships and how to fix them. With the exception of me; my curse can't be fixed, but it's not too late for all of you.'

'I'm not sure I can be fixed either,' Jasper says. 'Unless I give up my job.'

'You just haven't met the right person yet,' Princess says. 'And by the stories I've heard around the table, none of you have, except maybe Aubrey, but her person now walks with Jesus.'

'Miles is not actually dead.'

Karen squeezes my shoulder. 'His journey earthside might have ended but his memory lives on.'

I let out a frustrated laugh, which makes them gather round, and the next minute I'm in the centre of a group hug, for crying out loud.

10

19 DECEMBER, BRUGES, BELGIUM

I'm languishing in bed, cocooned in sheets that undoubtedly cost more than I earn in a week. It's glorious. For someone who usually travels cattle class and stays in budget hotels and hostels, this level of bougie is a real indulgence.

My phone blares from under the bedding. Only one person would call me this early.

'Hey, Rox,' I say, making my voice bright when her face appears on screen.

'How is it going? Have you thrown yourself into bed with the nearest warm bod yet?'

Why does Jasper's face spring to mind? I blink the vision away. 'No, I haven't, but I am about to throw myself in the shower.'

'Urgh, boring. Anyway, an update: Miles is alive.' Her voice is laced with disappointment.

If Miles is alive (which I hope was always the plan) then someone has checked on him, which means he is able to communicate, and yet I still haven't heard from him. 'So that's a good thing, right? You didn't really want to kill him, did you?' I brace for her answer.

'Only half.'

'That's the issue with homicide though, Rox. It's an all or nothing kind of thing. And to be frank, you're terrifically unsuited for jail life. Sure, there's no doubt you could run a prison gang, but you're used to the finer things in life – hair, nails, beauty treatments. Imagine your skin care routine. There wouldn't be one.'

She gasps. 'The horror! I didn't think that far ahead. Anyway, according to my sources, he suffered a fair bit since so that's something.'

I fall back on the cloud-like pillows. 'Does he know it was you?'

'Apparently he suspects, but what's he's going to do? Get the police out to fingerprint the place? Not going to happen.'

'The perfect crime.'

'He might question his drink of choice in future. Anyway, enough about him, are you OK, Aubrey, really?'

I exhale all the lies that sit on the tip of my tongue. There is no point pretending with my sister – that inherent politeness that I use to make light of even the hardest situations won't wash with her. 'Not really, but I'm making the best of it.'

Rox grunts. 'It's OK to rant and rage and feel your feelings, Aubrey. All of them are valid. You don't always have to slip on that veneer, you know.'

My sister is many things, but she has a good heart. Sometimes I think she knows me better than I know myself. If only I had her chutzpah, her complete disregard for the opinions of others.

'Well, I have managed to find myself in a spot of bother.

When I was asked where my sparkly brand-new husband was, I blurted out that he died a tragic death. Plunging down the gap.'

Rox guffaws down the line. 'Oh my God, Aubrey – what made you do that? Wishful thinking, perhaps?'

I groan and hold a hand to my forehead. 'I got flustered and it came out. I tried to backtrack and explain that he's not really dead, but they take that the wrong way as well, like I'm talking about him in the afterlife, or as if he's still around me, in a spiritual sense. I've quite made a mess of it. And not only that, but the story has also changed from person to person. Princess thinks he died eating death cap mushrooms. I'm not sure where that nugget came from. Then there was a mention of a sinkhole. Who knows what else they've conjured.'

'Princess? These people sound fab! What a laugh.' Trust Rox to find it amusing when it's actually super awkward.

'Yes, she's a fabulous woman who introduces herself accordingly.'

'I wish I was with you.'

We lapse into silence before I ask, 'So I suppose it's all anyone is talking about in the village?'

Rox waits a beat before saying, 'Who cares what they're talking about? We live in a village full of busybodies. They'd have been gossiping about you, married or not.'

'True.' Small-town life is a hotbed for gossip, good or bad. 'I've met some lovely people on board already, there's—'

'Any potentials? And don't tell me it's too soon. Newsflash – you're thirty-nine years old. You're almost forty. It's time to make hay while the sun shines. Get all that sex in before you lose the urge. You're a strong independent woman, who can shag whoever she wants, whenever she wants.'

I gasp, faux shocked. 'Almost forty! I'm one step away from

spinsterhood. Quickly, call the cat rescue, tell them I'll take them all!'

'Very funny. If there's one thing I understand, it's my sister, and a break-up like this will have you closing the metaphorical doors to your heart, and other regions, I might add, for years to come. If you don't use it, you lose it. No, you simply don't have time for a sabbatical of the heart.'

I blithely ignore her terrible advice. 'I'm quite sure I do. In fact, I've already erected a sign that reads: Closed for maintenance. There's no man on this entire planet that… that…' I lose my train of thought as my turncoat mind pictures Jasper. The intensity of his bluey-green eyes, the way he holds my gaze, almost hypnotising me.

There's a sharp intake of breath from Rox. 'Oh my God, you have already met someone! Who is he?' Her beady eye is up to the camera, terrifyingly close. It's an intimidation tactic, but I'm well aware of it and it affects me not. 'Aubrey, who is he?'

I'm not having this conversation. 'There's no one.'

'Don't you lie to me or I'll be at the next platform waiting to board the Winter Wonderland Express.'

OK, that threat I take seriously, because she will act on it. 'Fine, you're impossible, you know that? There's this one guy, Jasper. He's hot, smouldering and it's all very superficial of me. There's nothing in it.'

'The perfect holiday fling with a side of rebound – hot and smouldering! It's like Cupid has set down the perfect snack for you.'

'Snack? He's definitely not fun sized.'

She makes a bawdy sound. 'Even better!'

'Rox!'

'There's hope yet.'

'Fine, can you let it go for now please?'

'I cannot. I'll need a pic of him. Today. Full name, stats. I'll do a deep dive for you. A quick rummage on the dark web. Make sure he's all good.'

'Sure, sure. I'll send you his details,' I lie. The dark web? My sister scares the life out of me at times.

'Now, just going back to the boring bit for a moment. Have you heard from Miles yet? Let me guess, that snivelling bottom feeder—'

I close my eyes and wish the bed would swallow me whole. 'No, not a call or a text. Nothing.'

'Give me ten minutes.'

'Wait!' Too late, she's already gone.

I should've seen that coming; instead, I got lulled into a false sense of security that my sister was offering her skills as a listening ear, not an avenger. And that's on me; I should know better by now. While I wait for the inevitable, I shower and dress for the day.

As I'm drying my hair, my phone bleats and I take a deep breath. Incoming video call from Rox. For a moment my vision blurs as I prepare for what I might be met with.

Rox with Miles in a headlock. Rox with...

I swipe the screen. 'Hello.'

Rox has her face so close to the camera all I see is her eyeball. 'He's gone.'

Dead? My stomach clenches. She's killed him for real this time. 'What! Ah, gone as in...?'

'Worst man Leo can answer that.' Another face comes into view. It's Miles's flat mate and best man Leo, wearing PJs and an abject look of pity with a hefty dose of fear in his eyes, probably due to Rox's impromptu visit.

'Hey, Aubrey.' His face contorts as if he's actually in pain. Poor guy. Out of all of Miles's friends, Leo is the only one I ever really liked. The others behave as if they stopped maturing back in high school.

I can't help but feel a pang of sympathy for the guy, being wrenched out of bed and forced to face us because Miles is in incognito mode. 'Hi, Leo. I'm sorry you're stuck in the middle of all of this.'

He hides a yawn behind his hand. 'You're not the one who needs to apologise. I'm really sorry to have to tell you, Aubrey. Miles is still in a right state. He... he...'

'It's not a bloody Michael Jackson song,' Rox rebukes Leo. 'He he... what? Where the hell is he and why doesn't he have the decency to apologise to my sister after what he did? I should have bloody well killed him.'

'Rox!' I'd hazard a guess there's a direct link to my sister's lack of people skills and my need to live elsewhere in the world. Captain Chaos means well, but it's a lot to manage at times. 'Let him speak.'

'Well, speak!'

I stifle a sigh.

Leo scrubs his face, and not for the first time I see the ripple effect this fallout is having on the people we love. It's not their circus, yet they've all been dragged into it like performing monkeys while Miles avoids me. 'I'm honestly fine.'

'She's not, you know!'

Rox! 'But it would be good to chat to Miles at some stage, put the whole sorry situation to bed once and for all.' I mean, I don't want to have to beg for common decency but here we are.

'Right. Yeah, hopefully he'll do that at some point.'

I clamp my lips closed so my anger at the situation doesn't spill out and I scare the poor man further.

Leo continues. 'The night before the wedding he didn't get a wink of sleep and he hasn't eaten much since, and you know what he's like if he doesn't have—'

'—a hundred and thirty grams of protein,' I finish for him and roll my eyes. God, how did I get swept away with a guy who cares more about his protein intake than me?

Leo's eyes fill with anguish. 'He does love you, Aubrey. I'm sure this is just a blip. But honestly, at the church he suffered a full-blown panic attack. He lost it in front of everyone. I don't want to make excuses, but it really knocked his confidence and I think he reacted in the moment.'

'Boo hoo!' Rox spits. 'He could have shared that with his bride-to-be. In sickness and health, isn't that part of it?'

A full-blown panic attack? Still, Rox is right. That doesn't excuse the radio silence.

'A few hours later, he finally calmed down and then suddenly he got violently ill.' Leo gives Rox the side-eye.

I take a second to process it. Miles is all about appearances, but he didn't care for me enough to worry about how I'd feel by forsaking me and leaving me to arrive at a church jam-packed with guests, a church that he'd absconded from. 'He could have called. Text. Sent a carrier pigeon. He still ought to. It's been three days now.'

'Yes, yes, he should have and I'd tell him that if I could.' Leo has dark circles under his eyes, as if he too hasn't slept. It's not fair on him, being bullied by Rox to field video calls from me. It's not his battle, and the fight goes out of me. 'That's the thing though, Aubrey. Miles is... missing.'

'Missing?'

'Missing. He left a note to say he needed time.'

My stomach turns. 'Time for what exactly?'

Leo gives a helpless shrug.

'I thought he was of the opinion he'd rushed into things and wanted to end it?' Which is it? Am I supposed to wait and see, like some dumbstruck idiot?

'He's just confused.'

'He's just a horrible troll with a bad haircut! Now he pulls a stunt like this,' Rox spits. 'Another attempt at garnering sympathy while my poor sister had to take her freaking honeymoon alone!' Her face appears on screen. 'I wanted to tell you so many times he was a dud. You can always tell when a guy ends his sentences with "Do you feel me?" Like, gross, but did you listen? No. Urgh.'

Now that she mentions it, that did always irk me. 'I'm not sure I have the capacity to worry about where he's gone missing to.' Am I supposed to worry about him? Does he deserve that?

Leo continues. 'Things got a little heated at the wedding reception, and word got back to Miles.'

'What do you mean?'

'Well, a few people were none too happy with his actions. I rather think he's missing to hide from the worst of the fallout.'

'Ah!' Rox yells in the background. 'He's not missing, he's hiding. That's Miles to a T.'

Leo's face is a mess of warring emotions, but he stays silent. Probably for the best. What else can he say? Miles has run away. Again.

'Thanks for everything, Leo,' I say. 'We'll leave it there for now and I promise you won't get any more visits from Rox.'

He nods, gives me a thankful smile. 'Chin up, eh?'

Rox snatches the phone from him and soon she's whizzing down the street, houses a blur in the background.

'Are you still using the stolen e-scooter?'

'It's not stolen. It's borrowed!'

'From whom?'

'How would I know? They didn't leave a forwarding address or anything.'

'You're going to get arrested for theft!'

She laughs high and loud. My sister is so wild, having the sort of self-possession that she does even when she's breaking the law or bending life to her will. 'They have to catch me first.'

I can only shake my head.

'Do you want me to track down Miles?' There's a gleeful shine to her eyes. 'Or leave him be?'

I stare her down. Although knowing Rox I have to make these boundaries abundantly clear. 'Do not under any circumstances track him down. No trailing, stalking, hunting, scheming, or plotting revenge.'

'Fiiiine,' she says like a petulant child. 'Take every ounce of fun away, why don't you?'

'Sorry, Rox. I'm just so confused by all of this. I'm going to try and forget about it all for a bit and enjoy exploring Bruges.'

'That's more like it.'

'Take the e-scooter back, please.'

'Yes, Mum.' She salutes and ends the video call.

11

19 DECEMBER, BRUGES, BELGIUM

After I hang up from Rox, there's a knock on the cabin door. Sabrina comes in, rolling a trolley offering a truly decadent breakfast in bed.

'Good morning, Aubrey. I trust you slept well.'

'I did, thank you. Didn't hear a peep, although that might be because of all the wine I drank. I want to blame Princess, but there are certain gaps to my memory.'

Sabrina laughs. 'Well, you're on holiday, so you can take your time and enjoy breakfast in bed.'

She lifts the cloche and presents me with a range of delicious morsels. Fresh fruit, crispy bacon, eggs, thick sourdough slices, petit fours, a beaker of yoghurt and gourmet chocolate truffles.

I snatch a truffle and take a bite. 'Ooh, you have to try these,' I say.

Sabrina takes a chocolate praline and sits on the edge of the bed.

I had the option of breakfasting in the dining carriage, but figured I'd try room service since it's all inclusive and a rare treat. And OK, I'm avoiding smouldering hot guy Jasper. Last night, under the influence of too much Jingle Juice, my interest in him only heightened most likely due to Princess picking up on the vibe between he and I and steering conversation to matters of the heart. And that's a not a road I want to travel down.

Actually... Don't I have to dwell on what went wrong with my 'wedding that wasn't' to make sure I don't make that same mistake again? And without hearing from Miles himself, it's impossible to move on. I'm stuck treading water, waiting for answers. Gah. I'm a mess.

'You look a little more comfortable this morning, Sabrina.' Today she's wearing a traditional uniform, a single-breasted navy-blue suit with gold buttons. The only nod to Christmas is a pair of candy cane earrings. 'No festive costume today?'

'Not this morning. Later I'll be wearing some hideous thing, I'm sure. Have you got much planned for today?' Sabrina asks, stifling a yawn. Her usual verve is missing, as if she hasn't slept well. I feel for her, having to always be 'on' around passengers at all hours of the day and night.

I motion to the generous breakfast, and Sabrina takes a bunch of grapes to nibble. 'Princess and I are going to do some sightseeing, not exactly sure what yet. I take it that she's Miss Moneybags?'

Sabrina claps. 'Yes, she is indeed! Isn't she hilarious? I've met her before when I worked in a five-star hotel in London. Princess can't help but bring the party atmosphere. Where she goes, fun follows.' The world of luxury travel is small, so it's not a surprise their paths have crossed.

'Yeah, she had everyone in stitches last night with her bawdy humour.'

There's another knock at the door. Princess peers in, her make-up expertly applied, her eyes bright, even though last night she sank enough champagne to fell an elephant. How does she do it?

'Speak of the devil,' I say with a smile.

'And she shall appear! How are you, my darlings?'

'Tired,' Sabrina says. 'I wish I could skip today, to be honest.'

'Why don't you make up my room?' Princess says. 'And instead of doing anything, take a nap? No one will ever find out!'

That brings the sparkle back to Sabrina's eyes. 'Don't tempt me, Princess. I'll be all right once I've mainlined some caffeine. Now, can I get you ladies anything before I head off to help at breakfast service?'

'Actually, darling, yes. Can we bring Aubrey's breakfast to the dining carriage, please? I'd never miss breakfast in the dining room unless my life was falling apart – too much gossip to eavesdrop on, and too many handsome men that need staring at. And I happen to know a thing or two about grief, and eating alone is a slippery slope into the depths of despair. Next she'll be wearing an ankle-length Victorian nightgown and roaming the halls at midnight. We can't have that, not with all those exit doors. We don't want her pancaked along the route now, do we? Her beloved will have to hold on and be patient for her join him in heaven.'

I shake my head. I've explicitly told them that Miles is not dead; in fact, I've tried several times now and they don't listen.

'I don't even own an ankle-length nightgown, Princess, Victorian or otherwise.'

'Not yet.'

There's nothing I can say to convince her that I'd rather eat alone because Princess has a way of sweeping everything up in her path, like a hurricane.

'Come on, darling! Get yourself ready and meet me in the dining carriage.'

12

19 DECEMBER, BRUGES, BELGIUM

After breakfast, I return to my cabin under strict instructions from Princess to 'not mess about' and meet on the platform for our day in Bruges. For someone who is a few decades older than me, she has a surprising amount of energy. Will I be able to keep up with her for another full day of sightseeing? Surely at some point she will slow down. Still, I'm delighted to have found a travel buddy so early on. It stops me ruminating about Miles and the fact he's still uncontactable. He's a ghost, which fits with his backstory of being dead and all.

I hurry to my cabin and don a few more layers for the frosty air outside and rush to meet Princess at the designated spot on the platform.

'Oh, darling, there you are! How are your ankles?'

'My ankles?'

'Must you repeat everything?'

I grin. 'Sorry, it's just a bit of an odd question. As far as I'm aware my ankles are... fine.'

'Great! If you're amenable I've sorted a plan for us, a horse-drawn carriage ride through the cobblestoned streets of Bruges, including a stop at Rozenhoedkaai, the picturesque quay on the Dijver Canal, with medieval architecture as a stunning backdrop.'

'Wow, that sounds great. I read up about the history of Bruges last night actually.' Rozenhoedkaai translates to the Quay of the Rosary, a place where rosaries were once sold but now is more famous because of its instagrammable allure. 'How does this relate to my ankles though?'

'Well.' She waggles a brow. 'After that we can check out the Grote markt, the Christmas market in the main square, and then... have a swish around the ice-skating rink! What do you say, are your ankles up to a bit of dancing on ice?'

'I'm not sure I can dance on ice but I'll give it a red-hot go.'

'I'd also like to visit the belfry in the town square. You can climb to the top for a panoramic view of the city.'

'Great. Although maybe we should leave the ice skating for last in case I do break an ankle.'

'Good plan.' She blows out her lips. 'Let's go.'

The horse-drawn carriage ride is a delight as our mare trots slowly around the charming cobblestoned streets and hidden laneways of Bruges while we sip on a glass of jenever, a juniper berry drink, the Dutch version of gin with a botanical fragrance. It warms me up on the inside as I take small sips under the cover of a fluffy blanket, all generously provided by our coachman.

We take photos at every remarkable stop. Princess hams it up for the coachman, who doubles as a photographer and has a lot of knowledge about camera angles and how to crop other tourists out of the shot.

Our coachman delivers us back to the market square and points out the belfry. Yikes, I have to crane my neck to view all eighty-three metres of it as it dominates the city skyline. And no doubt that means there's a lot of steps. He gives us directions to other Christmas events taking place as part of Bruges Winter Glow festival, including the pop-up floating ice skating rink situated by the Lake of Love.

We thank him and give the horse a pat on the nose. Princess tips the man profusely. All I see is a wad of euros, which makes my paltry addition seem rather stingy, but I'm not Miss Moneybags so it can't be helped.

'Wasn't he lovely?' Princess muses, linking her arm through mine as we wander Market Square, which is decorated to the hilt in festive flair. Wooden pop-up chalets circle the cobblestones and are doing a bustling trade, selling all sorts of festive fare like glühwein, spiced mulled wine, and roasted chestnuts. I turn in a circle to view the buildings that border the square. They're as pretty and colourful as a town from a storybook. There are chocolate shops everywhere we look.

'This city has oodles of charm, doesn't it?'

'Yes, somehow it's cute and quaint despite the size,' Princess says. 'Let's get in line for a ticket for the belfry.'

While we queue, I glance at all the festive foodie options on offer, from Belgian waffles layered with whipped cream and chocolate sauce to speculoos, a spiced shortbread, traditionally served at Christmas. And have you even been to Belgium if you haven't delighted in a cone of thick-cut doubled fried frites smothered in garlic mayonnaise? It's the stuff of dreams.

'Let's work up our appetite,' I say to Princess, wishing I was hungry.

Princess nods. 'I'm keen for a big stein of Belgian beer, it would be rude not to.'

'Beer, waffles, frites.'

'And Belgian chocolate.'

'Mulled wine.'

'Ha, we better do these steps twice over.'

The belfry stands before us, as if reaching for the heavens. 'I did a little reading about the history of it.'

Princess folds her arms against the cold wind that whips through the square. 'And?'

'It was built in the thirteenth century and is a UNESCO world heritage site. There are forty-seven carillon bells. I hope we get to hear them ring. Oh... and it's only three hundred and sixty-six steps to the top.'

'Three hundred and sixty-six! How can that be?' Her eyes flash with surprise which is swiftly replaced by a more cunning expression. 'If I run out of steam, I'll pretend to faint right into the arms of the first handsome stranger that comes our way and he can carry me to safety. Let him know that the only way to bring me back to life is with glühwein and chocolate. Kissing is verboten obviously, or he'll most likely die.'

My eyebrows shoot up.

'Because of the curse, darling.'

'Right. I'm sure if we take it slow, you'll be fine.' Princess doesn't do anything by half measures, so I sense her fainting performance will be of Oscar-winning proportions. She's got a one-track mind, that's for sure.

Princess tunes the rest of my fun facts out and is accessing the queue for handsome men. Under her breath she mumbles: 'No, definitely not. Maybe. Has potential. Yes, a big yes. No. No. Holy guacamole, yes.'

When she turns back to me, her eyes glitter with mischief but there's no time to figure out why as it's our turn at the ticket booth. Princess grabs my hand and pulls me ahead of people ambling upwards at a slower pace, you know, sensibly. She practically thunders up the stairs.

'What's the rush, Princess? At this rate you'll burn out your quads!' Or whatever muscle is needed to climb so many stairs.

'Save your breath, Aubrey, and pump those legs!'

What. A minute ago, she was lamenting there were three hundred and sixty-six steps; now she's trying to break the land-speed record for her ascent. And honestly, the woman can move. It must be her lithe frame that makes her so bloody fast and nimble. I'm regretting the big breakfast I ate, sure it's the culprit for my sluggish pace. It couldn't be my lack of fitness. So what if the only exercise I get is running for plane connections or reading romantasy novels – those epic tomes are heavy, I'll have you know, and are responsible for my biceps that have the tiniest amount of definition from so many late nights reading.

Princess blithely ignores protesters as she pushes past, like she's a thief running from police. Unfortunately, as I'm behind her, I cop the death stares and cries of 'You're pushing in!' Ah, travel etiquette; it seems Princess doesn't give a hoot about how long these people lined up before us. If they don't climb at her rate, they get pushed out of the way. Must be a rich person thing. Move or be moved. I blush and fumble and apologise in that usual British way.

'Don't apologise!' she cries. 'It's not your fault they move like slugs!'

How to win friends and influence people. 'Well, it's just that it's not polite…'

She comes to a sudden stop and I smack hard into the back of her, which duly sends her sprawling. Oh God. I'm going to have a real death on my hands this time!

'ARGH!' she screams with so much gusto it gives me pause. Wait. Is that…? The puzzle pieces click into place as Princess latches like a koala onto the back of Jasper. Honestly, the way she's clinched onto him is enough to make me burst out laughing, but we're supposed to be in the throes of a terrible stumble so I rein it in.

With Jasper's height and her tiny frame, it really does look like a koala latched onto a tree. Jasper turns and she turns with him. Both their faces are now directed at me. Princess winks over his shoulder but doesn't let go. 'Are you OK?' he asks, trying to turn again, but the mad woman does not give up her position.

Princess pops her head up. Really, she's impossible. 'I just need a minute.'

I shake my head. 'We might need a doctor to surgically remove her from you. She's locked in, claws and all.'

Princess glares at me.

Jasper laughs. 'I wasn't quite sure what hit me.'

'Aubrey was rushing me up the stairs as if my very life depended on it! My vision went blurry and for a moment I felt very lightheaded.'

'Is that so?' Jasper grins.

'Hmm, I remember it rather differently,' I say. 'Perhaps it's that hit on the head you suffered earlier.'

'But I didn't suffer a hit to the head earlier.'

'Well, the day is but young.'

Her eyes go wide.

'Would you like me to help you the rest of the way?' Jasper, ever the gentlemen, asks, as if she's a doddering old lady when she is anything but. I may just have found the only other human on earth that could give my sister Rox a run for her money.

'Actually, I need glühwein, as a matter of urgency. For my blood sugar. Perhaps you can accompany Aubrey the rest of the way as she's in need of a strong, capable man...' Wait, that wasn't the plan! She leaps from his back, like a sprite.

'I am n—'

'...to listen to her many facts about Bruges. Swallowed a guidebook, that one.' She jerks a thumb in my direction. Oh, she really is the limit!

'Sure, I'd love to,' Jasper says. 'As long as you can make it down OK?'

'I'll manage.' Princess spins on her heel and sprints away with footing as sure as a mountain goat.

'What just happened?' Jasper asks with a rueful smile.

'Hurricane Princess just happened.' I'm sure he knows as well as I do what she's up to since subtlety isn't exactly her strong suit.

'Shall we continue then?' Jasper asks. 'And you can tell me all the fun facts you know about the belfry.' He waggles his brow. 'I'm a bit of a guidebook nerd too.'

I raise a brow. 'Oh yeah?' I'm flirting, why am I flirting? It's not often you meet a fellow guidebook nerd, is it? 'Why don't you share your fun facts about the belfry first?'

His smile says: challenge accepted. 'Well, the belfry is known to be haunted...' Jasper goes on to tell me about the myths surrounding the history of the building, which I'm sure he exaggerates so it sounds spookier. 'And so there you have it. It's best to see these places in pairs, purely for your own safety.'

I smother a grin. 'I'm lucky you're here then.'

'Very lucky.'

We make it to the top. The view is a breathtaking panorama of the city and square below. The climb up now seems insignificant when rewarded with such a beautiful vista.

We spend the rest of the afternoon moseying around the Christmas markets and eating our body weight in waffles and chocolate. Princess plies us with beer; honestly, the woman can hold her alcohol, me not so much.

'Are we going ice skating?' Jasper asks.

'After all that beer?' I'm not all that coordinated at the best of times, less so after drinking Brugse Zot from a stein as big as my head.

Princess gives Jasper a solemn nod and says, 'Or we could do the Christmas light trail?'

It's still light out, but not for long. 'I've heard about that!' I say. 'It's three kilometres long and features ten different light installations.'

'With the theme of fire and ice.' Jasper grins. So we've both read the same Christmas guidebook it seems.

'Three kilometres long!' Princess whines. 'Count me out. I'll meet you two back on the Winter Wonderland Express. Toodle-oo!'

Before I form a response, Princess is gone and we've walked straight into another set-up of hers...

After a sit-down dinner back on the train that evening, I return to my cabin, face sore from laughing. Princess is a hoot, even if she's quite the stirrer of the pot. And Jasper is gorgeous and also open and sweet in that way that people who travel a lot often are. We fell down the rabbit hole discussing our favourite books and the evening just vanished. It's been fun to have new friends on board, even if Princess is hijacking things in her efforts to push us together. She means well, and they've both stopped me from succumbing to the doldrums about Miles and his lack of contact.

I shower and get into PJs and find my phone to check out the photos from the day in Bruges. Now I understand better why it's known as the chocolate-box city, not only for its colourful architecture but also because of the many chocolatiers who make high-quality Belgian chocolates.

I go to text my family some Bruges photos when my phone rings. It's Freya. 'Hello! Any baby news?'

She groans. 'No, not yet. The doctor says he's a very happy

little elf indeed and not in any rush. The little fella might make it until the due date this time, unlike his siblings.'

I smile, remembering their births. I'd been living in Thailand when her daughter Maisie was born ahead of her due date and flew home as soon as I heard. A couple of years after that her son Freddy arrived, almost a month early. I'd been on a retreat in India at the time, which I promptly pulled the pin on, and dashed home to snuggle with the baby while Freya caught up on sleep.

Which country will I be in when this little boy appears earthside?

'Ooh, he just wants a little more time in the oven.'

'Yeah, if only I wasn't swollen up like a Michelin man. You should see my ankles now, they're officially cankles. The joys of motherhood, eh. Enough about me, how are you?'

'Good, good.'

'OK, and now the truth?'

I laugh. 'Well, it's hard to explain. It's a bit like I'm on pause from my real life. I've managed to push down all the hurt and confusion into a lock box and I'm pretending that everything is fine. The Winter Wonderland Express is truly enchanting, and Bruges today was so much fun. I've made a few friends on board.'

'Nice! You always make friends wherever you go so I wasn't concerned about that, more concerned about the state of your heart. What about Miles? Have you heard from him?'

'No. Have you?' There's no point hiding the hurt, it's evident in my voice.

'No.' An awkward silence hangs for a moment before Freya says, 'Gosh. I'm sorry, Aubrey. I'm really surprised by that. It's not like him, is it?' Freya's been friends with Miles since high school. She married one of his good friends, James, so they've been in each other's lives for ages. When Miles asked me on a date, she encouraged me. Told me he was the real deal and while he might act the lad at times, he really was a good guy. And I found that to be true, right up until the wedding day when he let me down.

'No, it's not. I'm not sure what to think. Whether to be mad at him, or... worried.' Rox would berate me for allowing doubt to creep in like it has, but I can't help it. It's all so strange.

'Yeah, it is a bit of a worry. I'll go round and check on him, eh?'

'No need. According to Leo, he's gone AWOL. Needs some time apparently.'

'Time? For what?'

'Word is, he suffered a panic attack at the church.'

'Oh.'

'But I still don't understand why he hasn't been in contact.'

'Yes, he's obviously made a split-second decision with dire consequences.'

It's hard to reconcile such a thing. I'm not sure where the line is between being forgivable or being a pushover?

'I'm still hoping you and Miles can work this out. You know how much he loves you, right? Rox is ready to tear him limb from limb, but I just don't think he'd do this maliciously. Do you?'

Freya's heart's in the right place but I sense she's keen to have me home long term, for us both to have babies and book club and live the sort of life in close proximity that we dreamed about as teenagers. And for a minute there, with Miles, that very nearly happened. The settling. When I'm away from village life, like I am now, I understand on a deeper level that being of a fixed abode isn't for me. Could I just be telling myself that to feel better about being unceremoniously dumped on my wedding day? It's like I'm waiting for a fog to clear so I can see more plainly...

'No,' I finally admit. 'I don't think he's done this maliciously, but he's done it all the same. And by taking the coward's way out and ignoring me, it makes it so much worse. It makes the love I did feel vanish...' There, I said it. It doesn't feel good, but it's true.

Freya lets out a sad sigh. 'Yeah. It's all so out of character. Everyone presumes he got cold feet, but I think it's more than that...'

13

20 DECEMBER, AMSTERDAM, NETHERLANDS

We arrive in Amsterdam the next morning. There's something very relaxing about the way the train trundles slowly as we sleep to the next location and we wake to a new city – it's such an effortless way to travel, to unpack once and enjoy the ride. It's much like cruising where all the heavy lifting is done for travellers, leaving the day open for activities.

I glance at the clock and debate whether to ring for breakfast or go and find Princess and see what her plans are for the day when really all I want to do is stay put. Having spoken to Freya last night, that worry about Miles still lingers. I'm not sure I can be upbeat this morning, put on my happy face for the other passengers.

There's a knock at the door and I spring out of bed to throw on a dressing gown. Thankfully, Sabrina managed to switch the gowns so there's no embroidery announcing my newlywed status.

'Morning,' she says when I open the door. 'I hope I'm not intruding but you weren't in the dining carriage with the others, so I wanted to check-in and see if you'd prefer breakfast in bed?'

In the compact hallway the couple from the cabin next door are in the middle of a long noisy kiss. Seriously? They couldn't do that behind closed doors? I grab Sabrina's hand and pull her into my cabin. 'Those two, are... wow.'

'Noisy?'

'Last night, very. I'm guessing they're in the' – I swallow a lump in my throat – 'honeymoon stage of their relationship and can't keep their hands off each other.'

Sabrina rolls her eyes. 'Sickening, isn't it? The way everyone on board is so in love.' I'm sure she's only sympathising because she's under the impression that I'm a grieving widow, and right now, I'll take any sympathy I can get.

'Don't listen to me, I'm just a bitter, rejected, dejected, erm, sad sack who wants to wallow in misery when I'm on the world's most beautiful luxurious train.' Talk about wasting the opportunity of a lifetime! Hiding out in my cabin, waiting for the rest of the passengers to leave so I can ugly cry, possibly howl, and not have any witnesses. It's going to get messy. I can feel it bubbling away inside me, that gamut of emotions I've mostly been avoiding.

'Ah,' Sabrina says. 'This is to be expected after suffering a loss the way you have.'

'That's the thing, though. He's not dead! He's a horrible little man!'

Sabrina knits her fingers and her brow. I get the feeling she's about to impart some wisdom. 'You're in the anger stage of grief. And before you go to protest...' She holds up a hand as I go to do just that. 'Let me reassure you, this stage is necessary. It's OK to be angry at his sudden death. It's OK to hate him just a little bit – I mean, there are plenty of visual and audio warnings about minding the gap, so it's understandable you're peeved. Grief changes shape with time. One day you love the guy, the next you hate him. I'm not clinically trained of course, but I'd say these are all healthy responses to what you're going through.'

Oh God, here we are again. I'm too heartsore to argue further. 'Yeah. Today I just feel the heaviness of it all. As if it's only just caught up with me.' It's hard to nail down how I feel. I go from being sympathetic that he panicked to furious he can't communicate.

'That makes sense. You did seem rather chipper that first day – most likely wearing a mask, as we women so often do. The whole nothing-to-see-here thing.'

Well, she's right in a way. 'I don't feel like exploring today, and then I feel guilty about it, like I'm wasting the opportunity to visit Amsterdam.'

'You can always see it another time. Plenty of passengers miss stops along the way. It's the best time to soak up the activities onboard when there's fewer people about. I'd suggest a self-care day. Just say the word and I'll bring a tray of assorted cakes and treats for you. You could watch some Christmas movies? Have popcorn and hot cocoa. If you did feel like getting out in Amsterdam, there are certain cafés that offer certain substances, all perfectly legal here, that just might help you escape your head for a bit? A chocolate brownie with a twist, let's just say.' She waggles her brow.

I laugh at the thought of eating an Amsterdam brownie and wandering around in an even bigger daze. 'Thank you, Sabrina. I like the sound of watching Christmas movies and eating sugary treats.' If I turn up the volume on the TV that will help muffle my wailing. 'Wait, I don't have a TV in here.'

'You have everything in here, it's just hidden. Allow me to show you.' Sabrina is all brisk efficiency as she goes to the bed and crouches down. 'There's a latch here, you just pull it up and the bed moves to a sitting angle.'

There's a mechanical whirr as the bed transforms into a giant seat. 'That's amazing. I'll stay in this cabin for the rest of my natural-born life.'

'There's more.' She grins and presses a button that releases a white screen. 'It's top of the range, and there's mood lighting when you're ready to watch. With this remote you can scroll through a range of lighting options and also flick through all the movies on offer.'

'Wow.'

'Pretty cool, right? I'll be back with some tempting morsels.'

'That's my day sorted.' I flop on the bed lounge and pull the rug over my lap.

I decide that it's fine to have lazy day and if I spend the day crying along to Christmas movies it might just be the release I need. I need to fall apart so I can put myself back together again. Stronger, this time.

* * *

After an epic Christmas movie marathon watching all my favourites like *Love Actually* (Harry, what were you thinking!) and *The Holiday* (oh, how I love you, Kate Winslet) the tears fell unabashedly. I feel slightly better, if not a little puffy. I get to thinking about love and how we often make it hard for ourselves, when really, it should come much easier. It does for some, and then there are others, like me, who are decidedly unlucky.

Why? I mull it over, considering my new friends in the Unlucky in Love Travel Club, and deduce it can only mean we just haven't crossed paths with our soulmate yet – that's the only logical explanation. Jasper's ruggedly handsome face pops into my mind's eye, making me reflect on the guy. Yes, he's unequivocally handsome, but as I've got to know him better, he's so much more than just the sum of his looks. Still, I'm not here to walk into yet another mistake.

Speaking of mistakes, there's Princess, sabotaging her own love life when it's so obvious she yearns for a plus one. In the quiet of the afternoon, I do a little research on curses just out of morbid curiosity, nothing else. I stumble on a website of an albularyo and feel a bit like Rox must do when she does her dark web deep dives.

14

21 DECEMBER, HAMBURG, GERMANY

The next morning, I give myself a pat on the back for listening to Sabrina and enjoying a day in. I feel weirdly refreshed, as if I needed that time alone. The sob-fest and a metric ton of sugar helped flip my mindset. Sometimes you just need to wallow and wail and get it out of your system. And yes, I might look like I've suffered an allergic reaction from all that crying, but it needed to be done.

My phone beeps with a text from Freya.

> Miles still isn't back. Have been round twice now. Baby is keeping me up all night kicking, and cankles are now tankles. Miss you F x

I'm not keen to waste another day sobbing, and to be frank, my eyeballs probably need a rest from all that blubbering too so I push Miles from my mind as I text Freya back.

> Tankles? The size of tanks, I'm guessing? Don't worry about Miles. Put those feet up and rest please. Miss you too. Aubs x

Pregnancy is not for the faint of heart, that's for sure.

There are more messages from family and friends that I mindlessly flick through.

Mum and Dad have messaged on the family WhatsApp offering to meet me in Lapland for Christmas Day. A sweet idea, but one I'll decline, as I know they're hosting extended family over the holidays. Dad goes all out. Their house is so lit up you can see it from space, and Mum has dedicated festive décor, so it feels as if you're living in a real-life gingerbread house. Admittedly, their cooking skills leave a lot to be desired, but they try their best. I'm sure Rox only turned vegetarian after a debacle one year with some undercooked turkey. Lesson learned.

> No need to meet me in Lapland. I've made some wonderful friends on board already and I'm really enjoying myself. There are six of us singles who've connected, and a staff member extraordinaire has taken us under her wing. Honestly, I'm having a lot of fun, so please don't worry.

I attach a selection of pictures from each stop and one of the Unlucky in Love Travel Club that Sabrina took of us sitting around the table in the library. In the group photo I'm smiling, radiant like I haven't just had my heart broken, but more like I'm a happy-go-lucky holidaymaker. And isn't that strange? The more distance I have from Miles, coupled with the ongoing radio silence, makes me question if what we had, or what I thought we had, was even real. Were he and I simply two almost-forties in panic mode that we'd been left behind? I'm still so unsure. It felt real, at the time, that love, those dreams, but now, not so much and it's only been less than a week since it all went bust.

Before I can blink my phone rings with an incoming video call from Rox. Far too late I understand the mistake I've made.

Posting pictures of the Unlucky in Love Travel Club, when that club just so happens to have a member like Jasper, is an amateur move on my part. I really should know better, yet I never learn. There's no getting lax when you've got a sister like mine.

'Who the flip is that hot, spicy jalapeño? Even a lesbian can appreciate a man that hot. Please tell me he's the definitely-not-fun-sized snack of a man you're going to warm your body with on all these long, lonely wintry nights?' Her words come out thick and fast. How she's not blue from lack of oxygen I don't know. 'Jasper, was it? I hope that knockout in the photo is the same one you were alluding to before on our video call!'

'Have you finished? Take a breath, for goodness' sake.'

Rox sucks in the requisite air needed to stay alive. 'Don't you even think about deflecting any of the questions coming your way, Aubrey.'

I groan inwardly. Rookie mistake, how stupid of me not to guess Rox would zero in on the hot guy and declare us a perfect match. 'I'm not going to deflect but there's nothing to answer for.'

She furrows her brow. 'Liar! Who is that buff, bronzed hottie sitting next to you in the photo? Slightly mussed hair that gives him an edgy vibe. Husky-blue-green intense eyes that could almost make a girl like me swoon! The only thing that saves him from being too perfect is his ruggedness and that cute smile on his face, like he doesn't know the power he wields.'

'The power he wields, what?' I make fun of her, but she's bloody spot on. 'You got all that from a group photo?'

Rox stares me down in the way only my sister can. It means she's well aware I'm not being truthful. 'Don't start that crap with me. I can tell that man doesn't have a huge ego, not like some men who I won't name, Miles the no-good low-bellied bottom feeder. Yet you in your infinite wisdom are going to find a way to start hating on this hottie. Because it's "too soon". Or you'll pick apart something he says and call him untrustworthy. After all this stuff with Miles, you're on the man-hate train, and it's time to disembark, girl.'

Damn, she's got me there. It is too soon and I did pick apart a thing or two Jasper said, like when I took offence after he mentioned faking it on holidays to save any awkwardness. Am I really so transparent or is that my sister is so wily? 'I'm on the Winter Wonderland Express,' I state stiffly. 'Not the man-hate train.' And I'll try anything to change the subject, but no doubt always-one-step-ahead Rox won't be fooled.

'Stop trying to evade the question.' She presses her evil eye close to the camera. It's enough to make me shudder. 'Well?'

'Well, what?'

Rox lets out a frustrated groan. 'God, you're impossible! Look at the group photo, open it up right this second.'

I roll my eyes to let her know just how tedious I find her demands but I do it anyway otherwise I'll be here all day.

'Done, master.'

Her face disappears off screen, replaced by the photo in question.

'Look at the way he's leaning towards you! Look at his love-heart eyes, eyes that are not trained at the camera, but at you! That man is absolutely smitten. His lips are slightly parted like he wants to lean in and whisper sweet nothings before he scoops you into his arms and kisses you.'

'Have you swapped your fantasy books for romcoms or something, Rox?' I squint hard at the photo and, yes, Jasper's leaning close to me, but that's because we're all pressed together to fit in the photo. I'm not sure about the rest of her ramblings. 'We see what we want to see, Rox.' I try for diplomacy.

'Exactly!'

'What?'

'You're not seeing it, are you?'

'Because it's not there!'

I swipe the photo away and Rox's thunderous face returns. 'Do you like the guy?' Her voice is eerily low.

'As much as I like any of them, yes.'

'Aubrey.'

'Fine, there's a spark there, at least for me, and—' Her mouth drops open. 'Wait! And before you berate me for my post-break-up rules, there's not one part of me that thinks it's OK to lust after another man merely days after I was supposed to walk down the aisle. Besides, I love Miles. Or I did love Miles. I was going to marry him. Although… now I've found out he's not quite the person I thought I loved. God, I'm so confused. Not hearing from Miles, either, it's just – odd. Like, what if he's having some kind of internal crisis and I've gone and hooked up with some guy on a train? How would he feel? Awful. I'd be breaking the promises I made.'

'You're not really considering Miles's feelings on the matter, are you? He's done a runner to avoid the heat and now you're worrying he's having an internal crisis? Come on!'

I understand Rox's point of view, but still, what if there was a valid reason for Miles's abrupt exit from my life? 'After I spoke to best man Leo, I got to musing about the panic attack Miles apparently suffered, well it left me questioning everything. Shouldn't I give him the benefit of the doubt, in case there's more to it?' Imagine if we do make up and in the interim I've hooked up with a six-foot-two sex god.

Rox's mouth hangs open. It's not like her to be lost for words. I wait for the barrage to come, because when she gets hold of herself—

'ARE YOU CRAZY?'

And… there it is.

I purse my lips before saying, 'I know how it sounds and I'm not making excuses for him, but – and it's a very big but – what if there is a reason? I can't move on until I've heard from Miles, and even then, I'll need time to—'

'Time to process it all, yeah, yeah. And in the meantime, Norse God walks off into the sunset with some other lucky girl. The only excuse he'd have not to call is if I ripped every one of his fingers off. Actually that's not true because he could use voice activation to call even if he didn't have fingers! Point proven, there's no excuse for his silence.'

I shake my head at Rox's very violent and befuddling reasoning. 'It's not as simple as all that, Rox, and you know it.'

'Yet here we are, still waiting on missing groom Miles, and you giving him the benefit of the doubt here is mind boggling.'

We're not going to agree while Rox is still so mad at Miles. 'OK, Rox, so on that note...'

She lets out a sigh but her voice softens. 'Fine. On that note, have fun, be safe, and think about what I said, won't you?'

We say our goodbyes and I make a mental note to not send any more photos in such a willy nilly fashion, not if those photos contain Jasper, at any rate.

15

21 DECEMBER, HAMBURG, GERMANY

Over breakfast, there's much chatter about our plans for the day. Princess invites everyone in the Unlucky in Love Travel Club to share her limo to explore Hamburg. As they talk, I swing my gaze from table to table, trying to work out which pair of lovebirds are on the rocks. For some inexplicable reason, I'm invested, having this urge to find out what is going wrong, and feeling a strange sense of hope that they can fix their relationship. I realise that I want to love to win, even if it's not happening for me.

But at each table sit harmonious passengers, not a hint of discord among them. They're making kissy faces. Or intensely gazing at each other. There's much fondling of necks, backs, arms.

Our late-night chat in the library was fun but we didn't get far into our investigations as we got sidetracked, talking about our own love lives or lack thereof. Katya and Igor are my prime suspects. They're too polished. Too performative. It's got to be them.

I lean close to Jasper to tell him my suspicions but am

distracted by the scent of his cologne. It's a spicy floral blend that's somehow utterly masculine. I have a real thing with powerful colognes and what they evoke, which is somehow a little more X-rated when Jasper plays into the fantasy. Suddenly I have the strangest urge to sniff him. I'm sure that wouldn't be appropriate, no matter how much I explain it's not him I'm after, it's the smell of his skin. Probably a little too Silence of the Lambs'y for the general population to feel comfortable with.

I've frozen in place as Jasper turns his head to mine, and his eyes widen at the fact that my face is only millimetres from his. 'Hi.' Oh, smooth, Aubrey. I gulp at my awkwardness. Why can't I just behave normally? Instead when I'm flustered I become one of those close talkers, which is as sexy as hell. Not.

'Hi.'

I stretch a smile over my teeth to highlight how relaxed I am. My lips are stuck to my gums. Attractive.

'Ah, everything... OK?'

'Yes, yes, fine, good, great.' I press on and try to ignore how delectable he is. I mean, smells. When I'm in the vicinity of Jasper, the whole Miles fiasco pales in importance. Why is that? It doesn't make sense to me, but I don't have time to ponder it because Jasper is waiting for me to speak. 'Ah – with my detective hat firmly pressed on, I've come to a conclusion. Katya and Igor act a certain way; they're used to being camera ready at all times. Could it be all smoke and mirrors? I'm sure they're the couple who have split but continue to play their parts because what else can they do when they're stuck together like this?'

Just as the words leave my mouth, there's a commotion behind us.

I spin in my chair to see what all the fuss is about. To my utter shock, Igor is down on one knee, holding a box with a diamond that's so big it's got its own ecosystem. Katya's hand flies to her mouth when he asks if she'll marry him. It's a fast 'Yes, yes!' And then the couple embrace to many cheers on the train.

Joining in, I holler and clap for them, but inside I die a little death at the memory of Miles's proposal and how astonished I'd been and how quickly I changed the course of my life for him. It's bittersweet, more bitter if I'm honest. Jasper must sense my outward appearance doesn't match what I'm feeling inside; that or my usually foolproof rictus smile isn't convincing. I am happy for them, I truly am, it's more that I'm sorry for myself, and by the facial expressions around the Unlucky in Love Travel Club, I'm not the only one.

Sabrina wanders past and gives me a smile. George is trailing behind her, probably ready to jump into action if she knocks anything flying.

Jasper moves his chair close to mine and whispers, 'Are you OK?'

'Being surrounded by love's young dream?' I try to make light of the sudden heaviness but from the sympathy reflected in Jasper's eyes, I fail miserably.

The smile Jasper gives me is tinged with sadness too. For him? For me? For all of us on this table who have tried and failed to find our soulmates? It truly is beautiful seeing real love play out before us, but it still hurts the sensitive sides of my broken heart, and clearly my new friends feel the same.

'Do you want to get out of here?' Jasper is intuitive in a way most people aren't, or maybe it's not even intuition – since it's clear I am husbandless – but a deep sense of empathy.

'Yes.'

'We'll meet you on the platform at ten o'clock,' Jasper informs our group, who are now being directed to hold their phones with spotlight activated above Igor and Katya's heads in their quest for the perfect photo.

When Jasper takes my hand, it feels natural, as if he's just helping me dodge the crowd that has grown thick as staff and passengers gather to witness a proposal and an impromptu photoshoot.

This arouses my suspicions about the influencer couple once again, or maybe I'm as bitter as lemon pith, in my turmoil, that the pendulum swings between being happy for them to insanely envious.

My own proposal sits front and centre of my mind – Miles has surprised me getting down on one knee over a candlelight dinner at his cottage. Simple, sure, but more my style, without the crowds, and rather nice and intimate. Even so, I'd been hesitant to say yes – how could our different lives merge? And Miles didn't seem like the marrying kind. Turns out he's not.

Jasper leads me to the library and slides open the ornate gold door. We're met with the comforting vanilla scent of books.

'Do you think it's a sham?' I ask as I plonk on a plush royal-blue chaise, and I hate myself for voicing such a thing.

'Igor's proposal?' Jasper takes a seat next to me, but the cushion collapses and we sink and roll into each other, our faces almost colliding. He's so close I can smell the mint of his toothpaste.

'Sorry!' He attempts to scoot over but that seesaws me the other way – he quickly clutches my arm and brings me back to him. My heart stutters at his proximity. Am I so desperate that the touch of a guy I barely know sends shockwaves through me? Honestly, yes. Especially when that man is Jasper.

Even Rox, who usually has little regard for most men, can tell from a photo that Jasper is different. There is a certain aura, a charm about him. It could all be fake, but somehow, I don't think so. Jasper is sensitive in a way that's rare, not just in men, but all of humankind. Maybe it's the writer in him – he observes, stands back and reads the room so well.

'Right.' Jasper fixes his shirt. 'You were asking if Igor's proposal is real?'

I blow a lock of hair from my face. 'Yeah, mostly because it's become another performance, another photo opportunity. And who proposes at breakfast? Wouldn't an Eiffel Tower proposal have been more their style, or even under the Aurora Borealis in Lapland? At breakfast in the dining carriage just seems so... basic, especially for them.'

He rubs his chin as he contemplates it. 'There's a lot of natural light at breakfast.'

'Which makes for good photos. I'm being a bitter crone, aren't I?'

Jasper shakes his head. 'Not at all. And part of me wonders if this isn't some marketing ploy – wouldn't it be great promotional material for the Winter Wonderland Express? Not only the most romantic holiday, pitched to couples, but the perfect place to propose to your soulmate.'

I nod. 'Yes, exactly!'

Doubt flashes across Jasper's features. 'It makes sense from that perspective, but it's just... Igor's voice was trembling, his hands were shaking. It was as if he was really, truly nervous about her response. The man was sweating bullets – why would he fake that? If it was all a show, he wouldn't have the deer in headlights panic in his eyes, would he?'

I shake my head. 'No, he wouldn't. Now you say that, he really did seem worried about Katya's response.' Proposals must be so nerve-wracking, especially proposals done in public.

'So perhaps they're not the mystery break-up.'

I recall Katya's wide-eyed surprise, the hand on her heart, the way her usual haughty mask slipped into a real smile.

'It's not them, no.'

For the newly engaged couple I send a wish up to the universe that they find every happiness. And then I burst into messy tears.

16

21 DECEMBER, HAMBURG, GERMANY

At 10 a.m. we meet the others from the Unlucky in Love Travel Club on the platform. Jasper's trying his best to be subtle about it, but he keeps me in his direct line of sight as if I might suddenly dart away, never to be seen again. And truthfully, I might, if only to hide from him.

I cannot believe I let my emotions get the better of me like that, and in front of him, no less. My body is betraying me in the worst way and even now tears threaten to spill again. Being surrounded by people who have found their plus one is hard. I'm happy for them, and for Katya and Igor, but boy oh boy, it's not easy. That sadness stealthily crept up behind me and popped out when I least expected it.

When Jasper's concerned gaze lands on me again, I give him a small smile. I'm mortified – not only did I suffer a crying jag, but it was a bad one, a full ugly cry of epic proportions. The whole gasping, wheezing sob-fest. Jasper put his arms around me and told me death isn't final – I'll meet Miles again one day, and I had to blurt out I very much hope not after what he's bloody well done and so now Jasper claims that I'm dealing with my grief in a very healthy way and that anger is a natural part of the healing process. I assume that means Jasper isn't sceptical about Miles's faux death any more, and that is yet another complication.

When there's a tap on my shoulder, I turn and find Sabrina standing there. She's wearing casual clothes, athleisure; a girl after my own heart. 'Um... would you guys mind if I tag along with you today?'

'Sure, we'd love that. There's plenty of room in the limo, right, Princess?'

Princess grins and pulls Sabrina into a tight hug. 'Plenty, darling girl! We'd love to have you with us.'

Sabrina nods. 'Great. Usually I'd catch some Zs in the downtime but I haven't been rostered off in Hamburg before, so I've never been able to see it.' From what Sabrina's told me, staff work long hours morning and night but are on a rota system to get time off during the day when most passengers disembark.

'Great!' I loop my arm through hers, excited to spend the day with Sabrina where she gets to have fun for a change.

The car picks us up and drives around the centre of the historical maritime city of Hamburg. It's a snowy winter wonderland, decorated to the hilt for Christmas.

Hamburg is a blur as we spend the day zigzagging around trying to fit in as many sights as possible. We're taken on a boat tour along the Elbe River and learn about the festive traditions of Hamburg. Advent wreaths were invented here in the nineteenth century by Johann Hinrich Wichern, a local pastor.

Off the boat, we're dropped at the Rathausmarkt, the famous Christmas market in front of City Hall. The festive atmosphere is electric as we go from stall to stall. I buy some roasted almonds to munch on as we meander.

'I want one of everything,' Sabrina says, pointing out hand-made Christmas ornaments and keepsakes. There are wooden miniature sleighs and villages that are intricate and beautifully made. When Princess pulls Sabrina ahead to the gingerbread stall, I quickly make a purchase of a tiny snow globe keychain to surprise her with later. When I spot a little wooden library scene miniature, I buy it for Jasper, hoping being a writer he'll get a kick out of the tiny typewriter that sits on a table inside the small decoration. Like Sabrina, I'd love to buy them all; they're extraordinary and like nothing I've seen before being handcrafted as they are. Really, I wish I could find him a souvenir teaspoon, because I have a small suspicion when we spoke that day about it, it was really his collection and not his mum's, like he said. Which is kind of adorable.

Jasper sidles up next to me just as I'm stuffing my purchases in my handbag.

'For the lady,' he says with a grin and hands me a rather oddly shaped Christmas mug. 'Is it... a reindeer?' The mug handle looks like a tail gone wrong, and because of its ugliness I like it even more.

'It is indeed. It reminded me of your Christmas jumper. I can't believe you didn't win. Yours was the best.' The winner of the ugly Christmas jumper was a guy from table three named Silas who wore a festive knit that said *I do it for the ho's*. While we all had a laugh at his jumper, that laughter wore off quick when he did the old winky face at every woman with a heartbeat for the remainder of the night. Actually, I must bring that up with the Unlucky in Love Travel Club – could Silas be one half of the couple in trouble? And if so, I'm sure we'll be in agreement that an intervention is best avoided, since he is such a letch.

'Ha! Thank you, Jasper. I love it in all its clunky glory. Is it filled with mulled wine?'

'Glühwein, yes. And there's plenty more where that came from.'

I raise my brows. 'Are you trying to get me drunk?'

He blanches, puts up his hands. 'No, no, God that sounded creepy, didn't it? I just love these European Christmas markets where you buy a mug and then get it refilled at every pit stop. Usually I have hot chocolate because I've got a major sweet tooth.'

I grin. 'You're going to share this wine with me, because quite honestly, this is plenty big enough for two.' Is it too intimate sharing a mug of mulled wine like this? Jasper doesn't seem to care. He takes it from me and has a sip.

'Warms the cockles of my heart.'

When he hands it back to me, I follow suit. The warmth of the wine heats my blood, or maybe that's the Jasper effect. I take his gift from my bag. 'I got you a gift too.'

His face breaks into a wide smile. 'Ooh, look at that tiny typewriter! The little Hamburg library. Thank you, that's going straight on the shelf with my souvenir spoons.'

Aha! I mock frown. 'Weren't they your mum's spoons? You said you collected magnets!'

'Umm…'

Laughter burbles out. 'I knew it! I could see ten-year-old Jasper clutching his holiday teaspoon, marvelling at his new treasure.'

'Look, what can I say, I was a kid ahead of his time. And if you ever visit me for afternoon tea I might even let you use one.'

I gasp dramatically. 'You would?'

'Well, maybe not actually use it for its intended purpose, but I'd let you take it out of the display cabinet and look at it up close.'

I make a show of being amazed. 'Wow, I'm honoured. And

this reindeer mug will rival any that my sister has in her ugly mugs collection and she has many that are deserving of that title!' I say. 'I'm going to treasure this and let it be a reminder of all the ways in which making reindeers can go wrong.'

'And me, of course.'

'Nothing went wrong in the making of you, Jasper.' As soon as the words leave my mouth, I want to snatch them back, but it's too late. They float between us like a confession.

'The feeling is mutual,' he says, lips curving up at corner as if he's fighting the smile and losing.

My heart flutters at the compliment. Can a guy as perfect as this be real? He must have a flaw, a huge fault, or why is he still single? Yeah, sure, his job carries him away a lot, but so do lots of jobs. It's got to be more than that. Some horrible thing he's hiding, like maybe he uses all the hot water in the mornings, or drinks directly from the carton of milk and puts it back almost empty. Seriously, though, what if he's secretly a player? He could very well have flings when he's away, right? Maybe he cheated first?

'What are you thinking about?' He gives me a quizzical look. 'You have this intensity about you at times, like you're trying to solve a complicated maths problem or something.'

'Ha!' Is it so obvious when I disappear inside my mind? 'I'm... overthinking, actually.' It feels good to admit that. I'm an overthinker, and honestly, it holds me back. I'm aware of it but not sure about how to stop the behaviour. It stems from being independent and living around the world, a sort of survival mechanism, to figure out every possible scenario to make sure I'm safe, I'm making the right steps forward. I'm spontaneous but that comes at a cost of a lot of mental calisthenics.

He cocks his head and assesses me. 'What if you didn't think, you just acted on your feelings? Do you ever do that?' The question feels loaded, and it makes my heart bongo. The air between us practically sizzles and heat rushes up my face. I fight the urge to gulp because I am not some helpless heroine, I'm...

'I...' What did he ask? Something about kissing? Or did I join those dots? 'Is that mistletoe?' I point above me where a stem of mistletoe hangs, softly blowing in the wind, almost as if it's trying to get our attention.

'I believe it is.'

I'm not really doing this, am I? 'I'm a stickler for tradition.'

'It would be rude not to.'

'I agree.'

'So...?' He waits for definite consent.

I give him a decisive nod. The ground beneath me shifts, rumbles, or maybe that's my heart pounding inside my chest.

He lowers his head to mine as I stand on tiptoes to meet him, awkwardly holding the reindeer mug out to one side. We're a whisper away, a heartbeat. I close my eyes as he presses his lips to mine. A flash of longing steals my breath, and then too soon, it's over. Only a peck, a meeting of closed lips. Still one of the best kisses I've ever had, and why is that? The thundering of my pulse alarms me. In his eyes is the same wooziness I'm feeling reflected back.

I don't dare speak. I can't trust myself to utter mere words. It feels like someone shook me up and deposited me back upside down.

'Guys!' Sabrina shakes me. Shakes me hard. I come back to earth with a thud. 'Hello! You look like you've been struck by lightning.' She laughs, the sound tinny, high. 'Jasper, what's up with her? Jasper?' Sabrina ping-pongs her head from him to me. 'Ooh. Ooh.' A knowing smile plays at her lips. 'The thunderbolt. Now I get it. When you've, uh – composed yourselves – would you like to join the land of the living? We're going to Spezialitätengasse, which is a speciality street dedicated to food – take my money – and then Spielzeuggasse, toy street, so Karen can buy some presents for her nieces. Then there's a Christmas parade with floats full of dancing angels, elves and Santa we might be able to catch the end of.'

'Great!' There is no way I could eat right now, not when my belly is flipping the way it is. 'Let's go.' I avoid Jasper's eye and loop my arm through Sabrina's again and hold my Christmas mug in the other.

17

21 DECEMBER, HAMBURG, GERMANY

Back on board the train after a day full of festive fun, I hurry to my cabin. I'm eager for a moment alone to process the kiss. I fall on the plush bed and do a bit of doomscrolling. Nothing like not thinking when you're supposed to be thinking. An avoidance tactic.

My phone rings with an incoming video call. I swear to God Rox has some alert that tells her when I'm online and in an emotional bind. 'Hey, Rox. How are you?' I say smooth as anything.

Her face flickers on screen. Today she's gone for vampish make-up, which suits her edgy nature. 'Good, good. And you?'

I will myself not to blush or she'll see it and the interrogation will begin. 'Great. We spent the day in Hamburg, the most magical Christmas-filled city. I'd love to come back one day, there's so much that we just didn't have time to see.'

'Nice. Did you go to the St Pauli Christmas market?'

I try to place the name, but it doesn't sound familiar. 'No, we went to the one by the town hall. Why, is that one better?'

She nods. 'Yes, much better. It's situated in the red-light

district. An adults only, queer-friendly, X-rated affair with strip shows and live music, but still decidedly festive. Full of erotic gifts brimming with sensuality and spiciness. You still have time if you head there now.'

'Yikes.' I absolutely cannot handle any more sensuality for one day. I'm still reeling from the chaste-but-sizzling kiss with Jasper. 'That's more your speed, Rox. I'd be scandalised, I'm sure.'

My little sister gives me a wry smile. 'True. So, I have news.'

I sit up straight. 'Freya's had the baby?'

'No, no, she's still waddling around the village with ankles the size of arms. What's that about?'

'Poor Freya. She should be elevating her legs and resting.'

'Yeah, apparently... Wait.' Her eyes narrow. 'There's something different about you? What is it?'

I sigh. 'There's nothing.'

'Your cheeks are flushed.'

'What great powers of deduction you have, Poirot. It's bloody freezing here. I've spent most of the day outside in the snow. Therefore my cheeks are flushed, the tip of my nose is an ice block and my socks are wet through. In fact, I'm desperate to jump in the shower and warm up. So... the news?'

'No, it's not just that. There's a sparkle in your eyes. I can't quite put my finger on it, but you're different.'

'Rox. What's the news? You wave that carrot at me then go off on a tangent about the sparkle in my eyes, for crying out loud. It's not like you to speak so whimsically.'

Behind her, Catty Roan is attempting to swipe a glass from the counter. You get the cat you deserve, and Roan is Rox in feline form. 'I can spot it a mile away when you're withholding the truth from me.'

'You cannot.' OK, she can, but I'm not going to admit that, am I? I should inform Rox that she's about to have one almighty mess to clean up, but a smashed glass might get me out of this jam, so I stay silent about the hijinks happening behind her.

'Ah!' She clicks her fingers up at the screen, so I don't miss her theatrics. 'It's that guy, isn't it? Jasper. Did something happen? Bring your face closer to the camera. I want to inspect it for clues, you and your lying eyes!' Rox's voice rises in excitement, which catches Roan's attention, and her little paw retreats, dammit.

'I will do no such thing. A minute ago, I had a sparkle in my eyes – and now I have lying eyes? I've got whiplash from this chat, Rox. Can you tell me the news please so I can get in the shower, before the frostbite sets in?'

'No, I cannot, not until you tell me what happened to you.'

She's like a dog with a bone. I'll never get the so-called news until I give her some meaty bits.

'You are infuriating. If my toes die and fall off I'm never going to forgive you.'

'That's a risk I'm prepared to take.'

'Why, because they're not your toes?'

Rox drops her head, giving me a look that implies *duh*. 'Stop stalling. Did you kiss? Or dare I hope for more? If you did, how does he rate? Top ten, top three? Dare I hope he's taken up the number-one spot on the podium? After some of the duds you've dated, it wouldn't be hard for him to snag pole position, would it?'

I roll my eyes. 'I don't score men like they're Uber drivers, Rox, and it's also not very politically correct these days either.'

Catty Roan has grown bored of our conversation (that makes two of us) and is back to tapping at the glass, which now sits perilously close to the edge of the bench. 'Oh please, everyone does it.'

'I don't.'

'Well, maybe that's what's wrong with your love life. Yeah, sure, you want to find a sweet caring man, but unless he's dynamite in the sack, what's the point?' Rox's only saying all these inflammatory things to get me to fess up.

'Oh God, I'm not having this chat with you right now.'

'It's like talking to a bucket of rocks! Can I have some details or what?'

I make a show of huffing and puffing, mostly to keep her in suspense, the usual sibling microaggression. 'Fine. There was a brief moment of madness at the market.' A flush blooms, and my body warms at the memory. 'I don't even know what caused it. One minute we were sharing little gifts we'd got for one another, and the next minute there was this overwhelming sizzle of attraction, and we kissed under the mistletoe. Just a peck really. Nothing earth-shattering.' It was a little earth-shattering in all honesty, but I play it down.

'You kissed a guy! You kissed a guy without the requisite time of processing a break-up. And after being jilted! Well, I'd expected that processing time to last even longer. Far out, this is real progress! You'd normally go into spinster mode, shut the blinds, sign up: closed for business for the foreseeable. Padlock the chastity belt, throw away the key.'

'Wow, what a visual, thanks, Rox.' I silently will Roan to use a bit more force. The mischievous cat can usually swipe a glass, a mug, hell, even a full bottle of wine off the bench in a few swats. 'You speak as if I've had lots of breakups when I've only had a few serious relationships, and yes, after those I might have put some boundaries in place, and made time to recalibrate and figure out what went wrong...' And then it dawns on me that she's right. I would never usually move so fast after.

'Well, those breakups are memorable for how long you took yourself out of the dating pool, I guess. So, you had what sounds like a rather innocent peck under the mistletoe, then what happened?'

'Nothing. Sabrina – who works on the train – came along and we all went to another section of the market.'

'OK, this tracks. I suppose it would be too much to hope you dragged him back to your room and ripped all of his clothes off.' Her voice is laced with disappointment.

'You suppose right.'

'And what will you do now? Maybe you can progress to hand-holding later this evening!'

I roll my eyes with dramatic flair. 'Not funny.'

'I mean it, are you going to pursue this... whatever it is? Festive fling? Holiday hook-up?'

I laugh and manage to choke on thin air. 'No! The timing couldn't be worse. I'm obviously not in the best frame of mind for this to go any further.' But she makes a good point. If we did hook up, it would likely go the way of most holiday romances – burn hot like fire then fizzle out, and who needs that?

'But you kissed! Oh... was it bad?'

Lie or not, that is the question. With her bloodhound senses she'll sniff out an untruth. 'The kiss itself was glorious, as much as a peck can be glorious. I swear to God, the earth shook and that's exactly why I'll have to pretend it never happened. Not until I have closure and I've processed the Miles debacle. Now, the news?'

'Urgh! That's some peck! Fine, this might help. The news is that the snivelling snake in the grass Miles has resurfaced, but only to pack more of his things and leave again like the massive baby he is.'

'Leave to where?' What is he playing at?

Rox shrugs. 'Worst man Leo wouldn't elaborate, despite my many threats of violence. He's either growing immune to my charms or he really doesn't know; those two are as thick as thieves, so it's probably the former. Now he's gone AWOL too, unless he's just not answering the door. According to my source, his curtain twitcher of a neighbour Sandy – who is delighting a little too much in her mission of spying for me – Miles packed two big suitcases as if he plans on being away for a while.'

'But where would he go? He works in the village.' Miles is the sports teacher at the local high school. School is out for the Christmas break, but that's only a couple of weeks in total.

'Not sure, unless he's planning to live elsewhere until this dies down and commuting when school goes back? I wouldn't put it past him.'

'Hmm. Did she say how he looked? Like, was there any sign that he's suffered some sort of... medical problem?'

It's not that I don't get the most likely case is that Miles got cold feet and is now embarrassed, it's that I want to be sure it's not anything else seriously wrong that he's too upset to share with me. After everything, I'd still like to hear him out. Both of us deserve that. Tie that box up with a nice little bow and put it at the back of the cupboard where I'll never see it again.

Rox scoffs. 'Sandy said he looked the same as usual, fit and healthy and even shared a laugh or two with Leo as he helped him load his stuff into the car.'

I suppose any crisis of the mind may not be physically obvious, but I don't share that with Rox, because she'll shut that line of enquiry down before I get a full sentence out.

'Thanks for letting me know. I'll try calling him again.'

'Why bother?' Rox screws up her face.

Isn't it obvious? 'I want to know why. It's driving me mad wondering. You can't just ghost a person when you were set to marry them. Surely there's an unwritten rule about that, at the very least.'

'Yeah.' She lets out a long exhale. 'You don't see it, do you?'
'See what?'

'Miles realised he couldn't control you, not the way he wants to.'

Was he controlling? I think back on our relationship. There were times when Miles put his foot down and I acquiesced. But wasn't that just the give and take you'd expect from a couple, both willing to compromise every now and then, to be fair and keep the peace?

'I'm not so sure?' I'd been a little miffed when he didn't want any part of the wedding planning, but then he'd stepped in last minute and wanted the venue changed and the guest list expanded. Was that controlling, or just living out his idea of a dream wedding? It felt strange at the time, changing from an intimate wedding to an extravaganza, but I'd been so happy he'd finally taken an interest that I agreed, even though I didn't particularly want that. Is Rox right that it was some kind of power play to see if I'd cave to his demands?

There are other instances I flip through, but I'm not sure I'd label them as controlling. Not moving in together struck me as odd, but he'd wanted to wait until after the wedding, and I stayed at his place most nights anyway, so it didn't really matter.

It worried me a little that Miles acted more ambivalent, almost apathetic at the end – which I'd put down to wedding jitters, as I felt that nervousness too, especially once the guest list blew up.

And I admit, I tend to put my job first, because my work is all commission based, so if I don't put in the hard slog, I don't get paid. I'm used to hustling for every penny and I get a real thrill from helping my clients plan the perfect holiday – I live those holidays vicariously through them and I go the extra mile to make sure they have an unforgettable experience. I work in busy bursts, because I often take a month here and there for my own personal travel experiences.

'A few weeks before the wedding day, Miles asked me to pare back my work once we were married.' Why didn't that ring alarm bells?

Rox gasps. 'What did you say to that?'

'I said no, and that my schedule was unpredictable and that wouldn't change. It's the nature of the beast.'

Rox's eyes narrow in anger. 'And he was fine with that?'

I think back to the conversation. I'd only been half-listening as I was in the middle of an urgent quote for a regular client and told Miles that we'd chat properly once it was done, but he still stood there and said his piece. 'He suggested that I should find a job with regular work hours and a stable income at some point.' How did I not take offence to that? I'd been so focused on getting the quote right that I hadn't paid attention to what he said and had put it out of my mind until now.

'Red flags, red flags everywhere.'

'Maybe.' I'm a firm believer in learning a lesson when life gives you lemons, so what is the lesson here? Pay closer attention? Stop and listen to your partner, even if they're disturbing your workday? Don't let apathy become the norm for either of you? While I could easily lay the blame all at Miles's feet, that's not fair. Something between us clearly broke – but what? What was my part in it?

'Do you think Miles would have gradually pressured you to find a steadier job?'

I consider the question. 'There's absolutely zero chance I'd have caved in to a demand such as that.' Or would he have worn me down in the end? My job is what brings me joy and allows me the freedom to travel, so I don't see that ever changing... although I did agree to live in the village for a while. Would that have led to the next thing, and the next, until I become a Stepford Wives' version of myself?

'Honestly, Miles is just not good enough for you. He never was and he never will be. You're a free spirit, a wanderer, and he wanted to clip your wings. Thankfully, he realised that you can't – *won't* – be contained. Butterflies can't be caged.'

'Wow, Rox.'

'Yeah, I've got a soft side, don't you dare tell anyone or I'll rip those wings off myself.'

'And she's back.' Roan decides at that moment to take one last swipe at the glass. It careens to the floor with one almighty smash. Thank you, Catty Roan!

'Roan!'

After we say our goodbyes, I call Miles. The phone rings out. So it's at least switched on now and he's just choosing to ignore me. My chest tightens. Seriously! I'm done with him. Whatever we had is over.

I type a rage text, then delete and try again:

> It would be nice if you had the courtesy to call me. I deserve that much at least.

I freshen up and go to meet the members of the Unlucky in Love Travel Club in the library for another night of shenanigans.

18

21 DECEMBER, HAMBURG, GERMANY

We sit around the big table in the library, everyone claiming their usual spot, as people tend to do. Jasper saunters in and I look everywhere but at him. When he takes his place beside me, it's sort of hard not to say hello, since he directs his gaze right at me. 'Hi, Aubrey.'

'Hi.' Short, sweet, clipped. I can't believe I kissed this guy on a whim and am now stuck in the close confines of the train with him. A stupid move in retrospect, despite him setting my soul on fire. That's just his off-the-charts sex appeal and not something I should seriously consider. But if I did stop for one moment and ponder it, what power does the mere mortal wield to make a closed lip peck so earth shattering? The romance reader in me wants to say it's a soulmate thing – the practical side of me is more prudent: it's lust pure and simple, a lust that's exacerbated by the fact Jasper is drop-dead gorgeous.

He's wearing a different cologne today – a sweet candyfloss scent. I have to physically clamp my mouth closed so I don't lick my lips, like some sex-starved fool. Whoever invented perfumery has a lot to answer for.

After chatting to Rox earlier, I consider Jasper anew. Is he a controlling type? What type of man is he? Laid back, easy going – but doesn't everyone put on a performance when you first meet? Holidays aren't real life, either. People are generally happier on a trip, more likely to go with the flow.

As the others chat, I feel Jasper's gaze on me, like a laser beam. The kiss has to be addressed to avoid any more awkwardness between us.

'So...'

'So...'

'You go first,' I say, hating myself for the heat that pools inside me.

'I wanted to apologise. For earlier. I'm not sure what came over me.'

Oh God, he's regretting the kiss. Why didn't I speak up first? Now he's not going to believe that I also regret the kiss and he'll presume whatever I say is a knee-jerk reaction to his rejection of me, because that's essentially what he's doing, isn't it?

I will myself to smile. Do I go on the defence too? I run with the truth; it's less messy and Jasper can judge all he likes. 'I'm so glad you said that! I'm not sure what was in that mulled wine' – I let out a choked laugh – 'but I'm never hasty like that, and I'm sure you can agree it's not the right time. It was a moment of madness. Let's forget it ever happened.'

Jasper's eyes cloud. 'Oh. I mean... yeah, sure. Of course. I figured it wasn't the right time, is all, and I wanted to apologise if I acted hastily. But I...' His words peter off as confusion slides across his features. Why? Did he expect me to be upset at his rejection? He's probably used to breaking hearts left, right and centre. Well, not this heart. Clearly it's already under maintenance.

He falls silent.

When Sabrina walks in holding a tray of drinks I can't help but be relieved at the interruption. She's changed into an elf costume and from the looks of it, we should all be able to keep our drinks on the table this evening; there's no big tail or gingerbread fur to knock things flying.

I speak too soon, as she trips on her oversized elf boots. The tray goes flying as she takes a messy tumble. Jasper launches himself across the table and somehow manages to catch the tray and the bottle of wine. The glasses bounce to the carpet but don't break.

'Whoa,' CJ says. 'You're like a superhero, Jasper.'

I laugh. He did look rather god-like, flinging himself into the air like that.

'A superhero would have caught the glasses too.' Ever so humble, our own real-life hero.

I edge around the table and give Sabrina a hand up. 'Are you OK?' Her elf tights are laddered where she landed hard on her knees.

When she looks up at me, her eyes are glassy with tears, but she lets out a laugh as if she's fine, or is pretending to be at any rate.

'I'm such a klutz. Thanks for saving the day, Jasper. I've already had a run-in with my manager about my performance, which is "lacking" apparently.' She darts a glance over her shoulder. 'Actually, forget I said that. Me and my big mouth. I also got a warning about fraternising with the guests. Apparently that's forbidden too.'

I frown. 'You got in trouble for being out with us?'

She nods, expression miserable. 'Yeah, someone saw me and reported it.'

Princess pulls out a chair and helps Sabrina into it. On closer inspection, her knee is quite badly hurt; it's already swelling.

'Barry,' Princess says. 'Can you ask George for an icepack for Sabrina's knee?'

'Sure, hold tight.' Princess and Barry exchange a look and hold it for a fraction of a second too long.

What's going on there? Barry hurries away and Princess looks anywhere but at me. Is she thinking of chancing love? I'm dying to ask her but poor Sabrina's bottom lip is quivering as she tries to hold herself together, so I turn my attention back to my young friend.

'I'm so sorry you got in trouble,' I say. 'It's a ridiculous rule being told what you can do in your time off and, as for all the rest, I'm sure I speak for us all when I say you're the best staff member on board.' Yes, there have been a few accidents, but that's to be expected on a compact carriage, whilst wearing festive costumes that are more than a little extra.

Sabrina gives me watery smile. 'Thanks, Aubrey. It's fine, I have been rather preoccupied and not at my best. I probably deserve the telling off, it's just they're a little stricter here than I'm used to and my new manager does not mince her words.'

Barry returns with an icepack and some gauze.

'What about your knee with having to work this evening?' I ask. 'You may need to rest it?'

'Tell me who this manager person is!' Princess blurts out. 'No one threatens you, Sabrina. I mean it!' There's fire in her eyes, and I don't doubt Princess will march down the carriage to staff quarters and give Sabrina's manager a piece of her mind. 'WHO IS SHE!' There's a guttural edge to her voice that makes us all freeze.

We're wide-eyed when suddenly the tension breaks and we fall about laughing. 'Sorry.' Princess lets out an embarrassed giggle. 'Even though I don't have children, apparently I still have Tiger Mum DNA.'

That sets us off again. Once we're all composed, Sabrina says, 'Thank you, Princess. I'll be OK. Honestly, I did break the rules. But my manager was most upset by all the breakages on board, but like, what breakages? I'm sure I'm being blamed for someone else's fumbles. George probably, but I don't want to point the finger his way, do I? Not with him being new and all.'

Who's going to tell her? I move my gaze around the Unlucky in Love Travel Club and realise it's going to have to be me. No one wants to enlighten the poor girl when she's already feeling so low.

Gently as I can, I say, 'I'm sorry to say the breakages were all you, Sabrina.' She gasps, so I hurry on. 'But it was not your fault! Your reindeer tail was responsible, being the perfect height to knock glasses, plates, candles to the floor.'

'What! I'm sure I would have been aware if that was— Ooh.' She covers her face in her hands. 'The stupid reindeer earmuffs. I couldn't hear!'

I bite my lip and nod. 'And the furry gingerbread costume. Same thing.'

A burst of laughter escapes from her small frame. 'Why didn't anyone tell me?'

I pull my lips to the side. 'You make a very good point.'

Sabrina reties her ponytail. 'Well, at least there's an explanation for it. Every time I turned around, George was cleaning mess from the carpet and I just figured he had a bad case of butter fingers. And all that time he was fixing up my mistakes?'

I give her a solemn nod.

With a deep exhale she says, 'I'll be more aware tomorrow when I have to dress up as a flipping Christmas tree with gift box shoes, I'm not even joking. It's as wide as it is gaudy. Anyway, thanks for this.' She points to her knee. The swelling has reduced a fraction. 'I better get back to it and try to be a bit more spatially aware.'

'Are you sure?' Princess asks. 'I'm quite taken with the idea of having it out with your manager.'

Sabrina grins. 'I'm sure.'

'You could buy me a drink, how about that?' Barry says, throwing an arm around Princess.

'The drinks are all free, as you know.'

'We can pretend.'

'Very well. Can I offer you a glass of the finest' – she surveys the label on the wine – 'Beaujolais?'

'Yes, please. I'd love nothing more.'

Sabrina gives us a wave as she hobbles off. I can't help but feel sorry for her – even though she's made some blunders, she's a real asset to the Winter Wonderland Express. Often with travel it's not just the place, it's the people you meet, and Sabrina is proof of that. She's made this entire experience so much better.

Princess pours wine for the group.

'So,' Karen says. 'Did you see the kiss at the market?'

My belly flips. I'd been so sure they were all out of sight. Jasper stiffens beside me.

'What kiss?' Barry asks.

Karen throws her hands up in frustration. 'Don't tell me CJ and I were the only ones who witnessed the kiss? That British guy who wears the cravat, like he's Sherlock Holmes himself, kissed a woman right by the hot chocolate stand at the market, a woman who is not the one he boarded the train with.'

Princess cocks her head. 'Explain the kiss.'

'It was a European kiss, a peck on each cheek.' Karen holds up a hand as we all groan. Everyone kisses like that in Europe; it's the standard greeting. 'Wait, wait, I know what you're thinking, but ask CJ. He sort of stayed close, like he was whispering to her. It was all very clandestine. But here's where it gets interesting – we then bumped into his partner and she was having lunch with another man! What's that about? If they had friends here, and it was innocent, wouldn't they meet them together?'

'We're reaching,' I say with a laugh.

Karen shakes her head. 'I'm not sure we are, Aubrey. At lunch, the woman – you know, the one who always speaks at full volume as if she wants the entire train to hear her witty repartee – was speaking so quietly we couldn't hear a word. Isn't that strange?'

'Not really, I mean, it could also be innocent.'

Jasper must be on the same wavelength as me because he says, 'We might need an Agatha Christie-like murder to make things interesting, because clearly we're failing as investigators. A European kiss on the cheeks and using inside voices doesn't cry foul play to me.'

Karen deflates as if we've taken the wind out of her sails. 'Maybe you're right. Still, it's weird they didn't spend the day in Hamburg together. Don't you think?'

'Not really. Maybe the woman is conducting a bit of business, and so the husband wandered around the market while he waited and ran into an old acquaintance,' Barry says. 'If it were me, I'd like to think I'd give my significant other some space, but I'd message her to check in, or if I saw something at a stall I think she'd like…'

'They broke the mould when they made men like you, Barry,' Princess says with not an ounce of irony.

I stay schtum, but is there a development between these two? It's an abrupt change from her reeling when Barry gave her a long look at the first official sit-down dinner. Is it just that they're close in age and share some similar beliefs? What we see as overbearing in matters of the heart by Barry, she sees as sweet and caring.

'Thanks, Princess.' He rubs the back of his neck and averts his gaze, suddenly shy.

I'm not an expert on love by any stretch of the imagination, but even I can see sparks flying. Are these two meant to be together? These two who I have spent the last five days judging for their relationship 'mistakes' – Barry a stage-four clinger, and Princess, who has given up on love because of a curse, which really might not be a curse at all but a crisis of confidence after losing the three loves of her life.

I tap Jasper's jean-clad leg and want to DIE when I see how close to his nether regions I'm touching. 'Oh God, I'm sorry, I meant to tap your knee!'

'Sure you did.' He sends me a flirtatious grin that would make my legs buckle if I weren't already sitting down.

'Anyway...' I struggle to remember my cunning plan. Ah! I lean in close, doing my best to ignore how within kissable distance he is. 'What do you make of the Princess and Barry situation?'

'Love hearts for eyes, right? We might have to kick them out of the group if this keeps up.'

'Oh, imagine if they did become part of the Lucky in Love Travel Club! But Princess has sworn off love, you know, in the unlikely case that the man will also leave this mortal coil. Do we need to help this budding romance along?'

A slow smile spreads across his face. Jasper might be a romantic by the look of it. 'Well, normally I'd say let nature take its course, but we're only on the train for a couple more days and then the hotel for three nights. There's not much time, is there? Barry will return to Australia and Princess to one of her many homes abroad, so it's not likely they'll bump into each other.'

'Right. But how do we convince her that he won't keel over and die if she pursues a relationship with him?'

Jasper rubs his chin. 'We have to get the curse reversed.'

My forehead furrows. 'You don't really believe she's cursed, do you?'

'I've heard weirder on my travels, haven't you?' I acknowledge that with a nod. Jasper continues. 'It's more that Princess fully believes in it so in order for her to give her heart away again she has to fully trust that the curse is fixed.'

'You're a genius.' Whether she's cursed or not, we need to take her beliefs seriously. She's got a lot of love to give. Why can't she enjoy time with a companion or partake in a full-blown love affair? 'Between us, I've been doing a little digging into it. And it turns out there is a solution for those who believe they've been cursed.'

Jasper's eyes go wide. 'Really?'

'Really. I found some people online who deal with such a thing. Perhaps I'll reach out to them?'

'Sure. Why not?'

Sabrina returns, hobbling slightly. 'The Christmas dance battle is on in an hour and I hope you don't mind but I registered you as a team.'

I dance about as well as I walk in heels. Badly.

Princess claps her hands, face lighting up. 'A dance battle, you say? Yes, please! What's the prize?'

'Bragging rights. There are Christmas t-shirts to wear. Each table has a design made to match the song you're given.'

'What's our song?' I gulp. Please be something gentle and slow, like 'Away in a Manger'.

Sabrina giggles. 'It's a song that's been slightly amended to "Jingle Ladies". There's, um, tassels on the jingly bits.'

'The jingly bits?' I'm not loving this new development.

She points to her chest.

'Ah.'

'I'm not usually a fan of cheap polyester fabrics but I can make an exception for a dance battle if the prize is bragging rights – that's something that money can't buy, am I right?' Princess is jumping out of her skin while the rest of us are a little more lacklustre with our excitement. 'Am I right?' her guttural tone suggests we better agree with her or else. Tiger Mum is back and we quickly nod, knowing refusal is futile. 'Gather round,' Princess orders while she brings up Beyonce's 'Single Ladies' on YouTube. Oh no, that's not a slow song at all! 'Let's figure out our routine. Jasper, you'll be up front middle.'

'Why me?'

'Because you're gorgeous,' Karen says, rolling her eyes as if he should know why. 'And quite honestly, their eyes will be out on stalks staring at you – is there any gyrating in the routine?' She turns to Princess with a suggestive eyebrow raise.

'There can be.'

'We'll leave that to Jasper,' Karen says decisively.

'I'll only do it if Aubrey does it.'

I gasp. 'Why me?'

'You're also gorgeous, so we're covering all bases. And don't even think of snatching this victory away from Princess.'

I promptly close my mouth against the eleventy-seven protestations that sit on the tip of my tongue. But then it dawns on me – he thinks I'm gorgeous, or is that a lie to get me to take the heat off him? 'I'm really not much of a dancer.'

'Don't make the Tiger Mum roar,' Karen says, challenge flaring in her eyes.

'Fiiiiine.' There's no way in hell I'm gyrating. I'll simply tell them in the heat of the moment it slipped my mind.

19

21 DECEMBER, HAMBURG, GERMANY

After a quick wardrobe change, I head back to meet the group, feeling all sorts of stupid wearing my Jingle Ladies t-shirt with wildly inappropriate tassels over the nip area which jiggle and jangle as I walk, drawing the eye of everyone I pass.

I bet a man designed this.

I find my friends in the lounge carriage. An area has been cordoned off for the 'stage'.

Princess is like a child on Christmas morning, jumping up and down. 'Look at the dance battle arena! Isn't it spectacular?'

'As much as a patch of train carriage carpet can be, yes.'

She groans. 'Ooh, don't be such a stick in the mud, Aubrey! Your tassels really are in a tangle.'

I bite down on a laugh. Her enthusiasm is a little cute. I'm not sure I really want to be front and centre, and no doubt every man and their dog will be recording the performances for posterity, so there's also that to worry about. Not to mention the rather sexy moves Princess insists we do. Twerking? Kill me.

Jasper makes his way down the carriage towards us. With his tassels swishing about, somehow he makes the godawful t-shirt look good. Probably the way his muscles fill out the thin fabric; in fact, said muscles are bulging out all over the place, capturing the attention of many of the so-called loved-up passengers. Should they be overtly staring at him with such hunger, like he's a tasty morsel? I would say not. Cravat man gives his wife a sullen glare and she promptly turns her gaze away from Jasper. Good, she's already spoken for and Jasper is off limits. Well, I mean, he's a free man, with free will and with no ties, but they're meant to be in committed relationships and thus their eyeballs should be firmly directed at their significant others.

'Who are you talking to?' CJ frowns.

Dammit, that weird under-my-breath life commentary I do strikes again. Makes me look crazed. 'Just giving myself a pep talk. I'm not one for the limelight.' Bullet successfully dodged.

'But you said Jasper was off limits. Were you insinuating that I had my eye on Jasper? Because I want to assure you I do not. He hasn't even listened to any K-Pop, like, ever.' CJ wrinkles her nose as if Jasper has really let her down.

'Why is Jasper off limits?' Karen pipes up. 'Ooh... are you two a thing?'

'What's going on?' Princess pushes in between us. Jasper is two steps away from hearing this whole disaster of a chat.

'Nothing! Nothing is going on!'

'But you said—'

'I was talking to my dead husband, Miles. Even though he's gone to the great Ctrl + Alt + Delete in the sky, I still talk to him.' I want to slap my own head, but it does the trick and their suspicious expressions turn soft. I shouldn't use the (faux) grieving widow guilt trip but here we are.

Desperate times call for dead husbands.

Princess rubs my arm. 'Miles will help us win this thing. With him up in heaven and God on our side, anything is possible!'

I can only commit to a tight smile.

'What's up?' Jasper says, dropping his eyes to my... ahem... tassels.

'My eyes are up here, Jasper.' I make finger forks and point. He goes from romantic to ogling my chest, just like that?!

His eyes crinkle at the corners.

'Well?' I demand, expecting a full apology.

'It's just that your tassels have tangled. And I was about to point that out when you accused me of... sneaking a peek.'

'What?' I drop my gaze to the t-shirt. Sure enough, somehow the stupid things have tangled together. 'Oh.'

Princess raises her eyebrows. 'I did tell you that not a moment ago! And besides, Jasper would never objectify women. I'm sure he's a feminist, aren't you, Jasper?'

Here we go. Princess is firmly on the Jasper bandwagon again.

'Are you?' I ask, crossing my arms over my wardrobe malfunction.

He gives a loose shrug. 'All decent men are feminists, aren't they? So yes, I'd consider myself a feminist and believe in equal rights.' Damn it, he appears genuine.

'And he loves his mum. That's how you can always tell the makings of a good man.' Karen speaks as if she has direct proof of this.

I'm not sure why I bristle. It's probably because Jasper has the same effect on me as much as he does on every damn fool who looks his way. We all instantly like the guy because of his mad charisma, and his physical attributes don't hurt either, and is that fair? He's just been hit with the lucky stick of beauty, brains, brawn, and we all fall at his feet in supplication.

'Jasper is one of the good guys,' Karen says. 'It's obvious from the way he comports himself.'

'I didn't know you were a psychologist,' I say stiffly to Karen.

'I – oh.' Her lips twist into a grin as if she knows something I don't. 'I'm clearly not the authority on love, but I do have a rather long list of red flags to look out for. And OK, maybe that list is a little too detailed, considering no man makes it past the first date. But if we don't set standards for ourselves, who will?'

Damn, she's got me there. I admire that in her.

'And Jasper doesn't seem to check any alarm bell box. Wouldn't you agree?'

'I'm right here, guys.' Jasper frowns. 'Why are we even discussing this?'

CJ points to me. 'Ask Aubrey.'

'Jeez, thanks.' Talk about throw me under the bus. 'I'm just as confused as you are, Jasper. Now, are we doing this performance or what?'

'We're just waiting on Barry,' Princess says, craning her neck past gathered groups of passengers to search for the missing Australian. 'Ah, here he comes. Oh, I think his t-shirt might be a little snug. I can see most of his belly. Isn't it cute!'

Barry apologises politely as he pushes through clusters of people and joins us. 'Well jingle bells!' he declares. 'I'm not sure they make these in my size, but heck, it's all part of the performance, so I figured who cares if I flash a little skin, it's only natural, right?'

We all agree that he's rocking the look, even if he's being strangled by the fabric. It's all in good fun and he doesn't seem to mind the fact the t-shirt only comes up to his midriff. It actually suits the silliness of the challenge. The look is completed by a fabric headband he wears around his forehead like he's about to get physical, like Olivia Newton-John did back in the eighties. I love the way he commits to having fun – Princess is similar and up for anything.

'Should our group dance first?' I ask. 'Get it over and done with?'

Jasper nods. 'Yes please. Do you want... a hand untangling your tassels?'

'Leave it with me.' Princess darts away to ask the entertainment coordinator if we can start the dance battle.

'Thanks.'

Jasper steps forward and I make the mistake of looking up into his eyes. Our gazes lock while he holds my tangled tassels, and it all feels too intimate somehow. I gulp. He gulps. Time stops as I wrangle with desire that floods through my turncoat body. Didn't I just despise him a moment ago for being hit with the lucky stick? And now I want to launch myself at him?

'Actually' – I swallow hard – 'I like my tassels tangled. Kind of a metaphor for my life.'

He drops the coloured ribbons. 'Sure, sure.'

Princess returns, thank God, and claps for our attention. 'Right, team! Everyone know their choreography? We're up first!'

'No!' Why did I agree to this?

Jasper swings a supportive arm over my shoulders. 'If all else fails, just look at me, not them.'

Doesn't he know that will make it a hundred times worse? But he's doing his best to put me at ease. I really don't like being the centre of attention but I remind myself, Jasper's one sharp dance move away from his muscles splitting out of the fabric of the thin shirt, so I'm sure all eyes will be trained that way. All I have to focus on is not falling over.

Karen and CJ grin. 'This is so fun!'

Igor approaches me. 'Do you want to give me your phone?'

'I want no such thing.'

He frowns. 'To film your performance.'

'That won't be necessary.' Nerves roil as we make our way to the battle arena. We face off against a group of much younger lovebirds.

'Great,' I hiss. 'They probably know all the moves from TikTok or something.'

'No way,' Barry says with a confident gleam in his eye. 'These young 'uns wouldn't have the first clue about booty poppin'.'

My eyes go wide and I grab Barry's arm. 'I don't have the first clue about booty poppin'!' Why are my team so calm? This is going to be next-level embarrassing. Why couldn't we have a singalong to 'All I Want for Christmas'?

Barry's forehead furrows. 'Shoot. What about the Billy Bounce? You must know that one.'

What is going on! 'What! No, are you making that up?'

He ignores me and gathers the group into a huddle. 'Guys, we have a situation. Aubrey doesn't know how to booty pop and hasn't heard of the Billy Bounce.'

There are audible gasps from the Unlucky in Love Travel Club, and for a second I wonder if this is some elaborate prank, because what else could it be?

Princess covers her face, while Jasper comforts her. CJ takes charge. 'Aubrey, have you lived in a bubble? OK, no time for recriminations, what's done is done. This is a booty pop.' She demonstrates a move that might look simple but clearly isn't, a sort of wide leg lowered stance where she pops her butt forward. 'And the Billy Bounce.' Again, she demonstrates some ridiculous tiptoed bounce move, flapping her legs from side to side. 'Or when it's your turn, just freestyle.'

'What do you mean, when it's my turn?'

She grimaces. 'It's a dance battle, Aubrey. That means we all take the lead at some point and dance on our own.'

'ON OUR OWN! I'm going to kill every last one of you.'

'That's the spirit!' Princess says. 'Edgy, gritty. Use it for inspiration!'

The music starts and I'm barrelled into line next to Jasper. I'm green around the gills, I didn't know that you could actually *feel* green, but I can now confirm it's possible. I steal a quick glance at my club mates, wearing rapt expressions like this is the most fun they've had in ages. I pull my shoulders back and lift my chin. I do happen to know a couple of dance moves that might just blow their socks off. And even if internally I feel like curling up and dying from embarrassment, outwardly I don't have to show that.

A member of the other group goes first, pulling out moves I've never seen before but which are announced by the entertainment director as 'the Floss' and 'Orange Justice'. Whatever it is, it looks pretty tame to me. When it's our turn, Jasper goes first and does some rather risqué Magic Mike moves. He throws himself on the floor and does the… Oh. My. God.

His hips don't lie.

I freeze. And I bet every warm-blooded person in the vicinity does the same. I pull out my collar. Why is it so hot in here? Jasper is doing some sort of caterpillar move but SEXY, like he's an exotic dancer and…

When my soul returns to my body, the noise level hits me. Everyone is screaming, whooping and pointing to the man mountain. I half expect him to rip his shirt open and am relieved when he doesn't. I'm having trouble standing. Must be the adrenaline. The abject fear.

The other team have their turn but the crowd is calling for more from our team. Makes sense, I guess. Maybe it's because we're trying harder? The song nears the end and just as I think I might get away with not having to take the lead, I'm thrust forward.

I make the mistake of looking at the crowd and let out a little mewl.

'You can do it!' Jasper encourages me. I remind myself I'm a fun-loving person with zero baggage and that I also never have to see these people again once the trip is over.

I break out my dance moves. First up, the robot. When that doesn't get the requisite cheers it deserves, I go for the sprinkler. Tough crowd. There are even a few boos. What the hell? These are classic dance techniques that never go out of fashion!

'Bring back the hot guy!'

Jeez, no guesses who they're referring to.

Jasper sidles up close and starts Magic Mike-ing all over me. In the interest of winning the dance battle, I of course allow these provocative, sexy moves to be performed. His body thrusts against mine, and... and my heart is RACING. Probably from the exertion. The heat.

When the music comes to an end, there are thunderous roars, but they all fade away as Jasper leans close, cupping my face. He's a breath away and in the interest of a good show, I pull him in for a long kiss. Fireworks go off inside my brain as the kiss deepens. I'm bereft when it ends and Jasper steps away, confusion in his eyes.

'Sorry,' I say quietly. 'I shouldn't have done that.'

'Yes, it's too soon. I get it.'

'Far too soon. I got caught up in the dance.'

'Same. It was performative more than anything.'

'Yes! Have to win that coveted prize of bragging rights.'

'Yes. Or else Princess will be disappointed.'

At that, Princess perks up. 'Maybe we should ask for do-over? I'd personally like to see that again.'

I let out a laugh that sounds like I've been run over by a cement truck. A gurgling, gasping grunt. 'I don't think so. My legs aren't working.' I stagger to my chair and scull a full glass of wine, grimacing when I taste it's a mix of red and white again.

'What the hell was that?' Sabrina appears, like my fairy godmother, full bottle of champagne in her hand. She pops the cork and liquid ejects itself all over me. It all feels rather explicit somehow.

'I need champagne,' I say with a shaky laugh. 'I'm still processing.'

'You'll need more than this to cool that blood of yours. Wow, that man can move. You better act fast, because he's going to have a line of women after him, married or not.'

'How does he know how to move his body like that?' My mind goes to exotic dancing, strip clubs. To bad places!

'Instinctually, I bet. That or a lot of practice in the bedroom.' She waggles her eyebrows suggestively.

Later my team accept the win in the arena. CJ calls for me to join them, but there's no way my poor body can move without tumbling over. No, it's best if I stay well away. Just me and a bottle of bubbles is the much safer option.

20

22 DECEMBER, COPENHAGEN, DENMARK

I wake up with a screaming headache. Oh God. The bottle of bubbles was a bad idea. Talk about plot twist. Probably dehydrated from all that dancing. Doing the robot sure takes it out of a person. I groan as I stretch, regretting the fact we're arriving in Copenhagen today and I'm going to be running on low battery.

'Good morning, darling!' Princess struts into my cabin in a cloud of floral perfume. The scent doesn't help the banging in my head. 'I knew you'd sleep in. Talk about burning the candle at both ends!'

'Ah – what?'

'You really got the hang of those interesting dance moves last night. Well, you tried, I suppose that's the main thing.'

I cup my face as a memory forms. Jasper teaching me to do that horrifically sexy caterpillar grinding move. Oh. No. No. No. Damn you to hell and back, expensive champagne! 'Yes, well, now I'm an accomplished dancer we can all move on.'

'Morning!' Sabrina enters the fray. At least I think it's Sabrina. She's dressed as a flashing Christmas tree with the addition of green face paint. 'Don't even mention it. My manager insisted I be the test subject for the rest of the Christmas trees.' She rolls her eyes; at least, I get a flash of white eyeball so I presume that's what she's doing. 'And then I get to wash all this off and reapply when you board again this evening.'

'Wow, for a luxury experience they really went... gaudy with the outfits.' Princess shakes her head. 'I thought Aubrey was at risk of self-immolation with all that polyester she's so fond of, but this takes the prize. Is it safe? How does it light up like that?'

Every minute or so the Christmas lights that wrap around change colour and flash and sparkle. It's very impressive, if not slightly jarring with her poor green face that's been decorated with tiny gold stars.

'Battery operated. There's some sort of power pack tied up inside. I've given up asking questions and at this point if I do ignite, well, it would get me out of work for a while.'

'Manager still giving you grief?'

Sabrina jiggles. 'I'm shrugging.'

'Ah.'

'So... Aubrey, anything to report? You and Jasper kissed and I don't even know what to call that carpet-gyrating manoeuvre.' She holds a hand to her heart. 'Teach me to dance, Jasper!'

Princess trills. 'She's mimicking you there, Aubrey.'

'I got that. Thanks. Well, as the person responsible for filling my wine glass, this is on you, Sabrina! I'm not a big drinker, and clearly I was well out of my comfort zone last night and used alcohol as a crutch...'

'Keep telling yourself that!' Sabrina guffaws. 'The man is obsessed with you, even after he saw you dance.'

'What does that mean?'

'The robot. Really?'

I frown. 'It's a classic.'

'Yeah, you mentioned that. A number of times. Anyway, I'm

here as requested. Your personalised wake-up call. Get cracking as your chariot awaits and you, my dear, have plans with the man of the hour.'

'No I don't.' Oh, I do. I made plans to spend the day with Jasper because I am an idiot who drinks like a fish and makes poor choices. 'A Christmas beer tour? Or am I remembering wrong?' More alcohol equals bad idea.

'It's meant to be great, if that's any consolation,' Princess says.

'No, it's not.' I pull the pillow over my head, and Sabrina snatches it back.

'Get moving.'

'You are the worst welcomer ever.'

'I aim to please. The beer might help the banging head.'

There is that. 'Fine. I'll throw myself in the shower and hope that washes away all my sins.'

'Sins. You haven't committed those yet, but the day is young.'

They leave making lewd jokes and giggling like schoolgirls. Once I'm ready, I take a couple of paracetamol and promise myself to hydrate with actual water today. Outside the cabin I run into my thirty-something neighbour, a fur-dressed siren who goes by the name of Georgiana; at least, that's the name I hear her significant other yelling out when they're... indisposed. The walls are a little too thin for my liking, but hey, the alcohol definitely drowns that out most evenings, like last night when I must've fallen into a champagne-infused coma. Not good. Not good at all.

'Hi.'

'Hiya, nice dance moves last night.'

'Oh. Thanks.' I summon a smile but even that hurts. My poor body.

'Lucky you, snagging the hottest guy on the train. Especially after losing your husband to that freak storm. I mean, I've heard lightning can strike twice and all... but I thought it was just a figure of speech.'

Miles got struck by lightning. Twice?

She doesn't wait for a response, instead lets out a frustrated sigh. 'Between us, I'm at my wits' end with Hamilton. The man is insufferable.'

My ears perk up. Could this be our couple on the rocks? 'Oh, why's that?'

'You must have heard him? His snoring rattles the entire train. I haven't got a wink of sleep since we got on.'

'Ah – I've heard this and that.'

'And he leaves his wet towels on the bed. My side of the bed, mind you. It's the little things, isn't it, when you go away with someone? The man can't hang a towel up. Simply can't. He also has trouble putting his clothes away – they cover every surface imaginable whether they need washing or not. He's a man child. A mummy's boy. And don't even get me started on—'

The man himself appears, looking relaxed and decidedly unruffled. Will Georgiana give him a mouthful in front of me? I hate myself for it, but I wait it out so I can report back to the Unlucky in Love Travel Club, but she does no such thing. Instead, she gives him a megawatt smile that comes across as totally genuine. 'Hi, Hamilton,' I say.

'Hi. Loved the robot. Such a classic.'

'Thank you!' Vindication! 'So, enjoying the trip so far?'

'Loving every minute of it, aren't we, baby?' He scoops up Georgiana, who lets out a squeal of delight. I'm a little miffed. Were her earlier protestations just a vent? Sharing a small cabin and being together 24/7 can heighten those petty annoyances, but to flip the switch and act all giggly – well, that's a little strange.

Could Georgiana and Hamilton be the couple careening

towards splitsville? We've only spoken a handful of times, usually a greeting as we pass in the hallway, and yet she's opened up to me, so it's more than likely she's also confided in Sabrina, who pulled the short straw and is often around the cabins, delivering room service or turning down the beds, with George a few steps behind.

Hamilton deposits a flushed-faced Georgiana to her feet. 'Yes, we're really learning a lot about each other. Aren't we?' This time, the smile she pastes on is a little more rigid.

'We are. And today we're going to Tivoli Gardens for the Christmas market and a trip to Rosenborg Castle, if there's time.'

'Nice.' There's a definite tic in Georgiana's jaw, or am I reading too much into it? For her sake, I hope that being off the train gives her some much-needed breathing room. Perhaps those little petty annoyances will be forgiven when they're entrenched in all things festive at the markets. 'Enjoy Copenhagen.'

I give them a wave and go to the dining carriage to share my suspicions with the group.

21

22 DECEMBER, COPENHAGEN, DENMARK

I'm lost in thought about my cabin neighbours potentially being our suspects and what a possible fix might be – do we pull Hamilton aside and give him tips about being courteous when sharing a small cabin? No! Not only is it overstepping, but he'd instantly figure out Georgiana has been talking about him behind his back, which might make things worse.

I'm so distracted that I almost forget about Jasper and our dance 'lessons' last night but when I see the others around the table with a cheeky gleam in their eyes, I know it's probably going to come up in conversation. Dammit.

'There she is!' Karen gets up to give me a hug and CJ follows suit. 'How's the head?'

'Thumping. And you?'

She gives me an apologetic smile. 'Clear as a bell. I drank the alcohol-free stuff.'

Huh. Note to self: be like Karen. 'Clever.'

Princess and Barry are deep in conversation but when she spots me, she jumps up. 'Darling! You look beautiful. Doesn't she, Jasper?'

There he is, the man of the hour, sitting there with a plate of fruit, looking hotter than any man has a right to. 'Yes, beautiful,' he agrees, for the sake of politeness, I'm sure.

Before the conversation can drift back to – gulp – my dancing prowess or lack thereof, I motion for the Unlucky in Love Travel Club to come closer, and I spill the beans on what I've just learned about Georgiana and Hamilton. And, yes, I hope it's enough to distract them from chatting about my dance shenanigans with Jasper.

'Ooh.' Princess's eyes go wide. 'That's interesting. Barry what's your take?'

Barry pats his mouth with a napkin. 'Trouble in paradise.'

CJ pours coffee from the jug and slides it over to me, and I send her a grateful smile. I take a sip and I swear I hear angels sing – maybe the remedy for my godawful hangover is caffeine and lots of it. 'I don't know…' CJ's mouth twists. 'Those kinds of squabbles are normal when you travel, aren't they? My ex-husband used to do all those things too, and yes, I wanted to strangle him from time to time, but it didn't make me want to divorce him or anything.'

'Why did you divorce him?' Princess asks, dropping the question with all the grace of a sledgehammer.

The sporty forty-something sighs. 'Our love story just ended because we grew apart. Sad but true. We were high-school sweethearts who married young, had a family, raised our boys in blissful harmony, or so I thought. But then this insidious thing crept into our relationship when we weren't looking – complacency.'

There are knowing nods around the table.

'Life flashed forward, so fast, like it does when you're running a business together, sports goods stores in case you're wondering, and raising energetic boys that you have to ferry to school and hockey practice. Life was a series of Post-it notes left on the counter for each other, as caring for the kids and work life consumed us. I woke up one day, and it just hit me – we'd become roommates. Best friends, yes, but the passion, the sizzle, had gone. Replaced by ennui.'

Karen gives CJ's shoulder a squeeze. 'Same thing happened to my parents.'

'Yeah, it's common. When I had a chat to my husband that night, he broke down and told me he'd been feeling the same, maybe even for longer, but he didn't have the courage to broach it with me. He'd even had a small flirtation with someone who'd worked for us, but hadn't acted on it.'

My heart breaks for CJ, having been lost in the mire of her life, trying to keep her head above water, that the love they shared suffered because of it.

'Did you try couple's counselling?' I ask.

'Yeah, we tried it but it only lengthened the end of our marriage. We both felt like staying together wasn't the best option for us or the kids. They don't want to see blank-faced parents going through the motions. The spark had died, and nothing we tried would reignite it. We had the most amicable divorce ever and now we split time with the boys fifty-fifty and still run the businesses together. It works for us. He's moved on with a lovely woman who treats my kids well, and that's all I care about.'

'Oh man, who else was hoping this would end differently?' I blurt without thinking.

Jasper raises a hand. 'Me. I hoped some time apart would show them that they were perfect for each other all along.'

CJ laughs. 'That's the thing – we *were* perfect for each other. For that season in our lives. I couldn't have asked for a better husband, a better father to my kids, but that season ended. And I count myself lucky for it. Who gets the fairytale and then a platonic friend for life? It worked out exactly how it was meant to.'

CJ's reasoning hits me hard. I get it. It's presumed we'll behave the way society expects us to. Marriage, house, babies, the 9–5 of work. Staying put, staying together, even if the spark has gone. They could have stayed in the marriage, followed the path of least resistance, but they chose to end it at the right time so that they could remain friends and be the best parents for their boys. They didn't wait until that complacency turned to apathy, or worse, became acrimonious. Maybe CJ's right. Love comes in seasons. Love comes in different packages. Isn't it enough to have loved and been loved? Maybe it's not always forever.

It's like me, close to forty and saying yes to Miles's marriage proposal because after returning home I wondered if perhaps I'd got it all wrong – and life was meant to be lived the regular way. Maybe I should yearn to raise babies alongside Freya. My husband and I could buy a house, host dinner parties for our friends. Settle into domestic harmony.

When he asked for my hand in marriage, it felt a bit like a second chance. Like maybe I hadn't missed that window of time for marriage and babies if I wanted it. Despite those niggling doubts, I went all in, because what if it was my only chance? Marriage was never on my radar, but part of me figured I'd regret not following the crowd, and I loved Miles, so why not risk saying yes to becoming a wife at the very least?

Now I wonder, after hearing CJ's story am I the one who made the mistake, by accepting a proposal and agreeing to a life that doesn't really suit me. A life that might seem perfect from the outside, like when I look at how happy Freya and her family are, but that was never *my* dream. Maybe I'm set to roam alone? And that's OK.

'I love that you recognised what you needed, even if making that choice came at a cost.' There's no question it would have been hard for them. Telling their children. Their friends. Redesigning how life would look for them all.

'The only sad part of it is that I haven't found the next love of my life. Without love, life is a little less sparkly. But I know he's out there, it's just a matter of finding him.'

I hope she finds him soon. She deserves love. All of the Unlucky in Love Travel Club do. Including me. But who do I love next? If Miles came back on the scene, would I give him a chance, tell him that village life isn't actually for me? Somehow, I just don't see it any more. On the morning of the wedding, I'd been fighting with those same emotions but managed to explain it away as nerves, as jitters. If I'm honest with myself, I can admit I was also second-guessing whether it was the right choice for me. It had felt too late, like I couldn't back out of it. But had I wanted to? I still find it hard to make sense of it all.

'You'll find him soon,' Princess assures her. 'What about Hamilton? Do wet towels on the bed bother you?'

'Hamilton?' CJ gasps. 'He's in a relationship!'

Princess steeples her fingers and gives us a sly grin. 'But for how long?'

We burst out laughing at her matchmaking attempts. 'That would be a no. Even if he were an eligible bachelor, he's too polished, too fussy. I want a man who enjoys getting out into the wild, who is up for athletic pursuits, and he must be a fan of K-Pop. I listen to it all the time and I don't want a guy who turns down the volume on me, you know?' It's such a great metaphor for relationships.

It makes perfect sense to me. CJ's at the point of her life where she wants a partner to add to her life, not subtract from it. That's the mindset I should be aiming for.

Someone who doesn't turn down the volume on me...

22

22 DECEMBER, COPENHAGEN, DENMARK

Once we disembark in Copenhagen, our group splits off into various factions. Princess and Barry are off to Nyhavn harbour for a foodie tour and CJ and Karen to the Hans Christian Andersen Christmas market, named in ode to the Danish storyteller. That leaves me and Jasper, and the mood between us is all kinds of awkward after the dance battle fiasco. There's a lot of hands in pockets, pavement-kicking, heads-averted action going on. I cannot look at the man without blushing. My own fault.

Who asks for one-to-one dance lessons with the next Magic Mike? That stupido would be me. Lesson learned. Heat rushes me when my mind does return to last night's shenanigans. Let's just say, I remember the feel of his body and all its accoutrements a little too well. In my drunken haze, I'd been certain we fit together perfectly, like a jigsaw. Although, from what I remember of the intensity of his gaze, I swear he felt the same. Probably all part of the performance. I see that now.

Almost every red-blooded woman from the train has stopped to compliment him, the jezebels. OK, that's maybe going too far, but it's hard not to be leery of these women when they fuss and fawn over him in an overly flirtatious manner. Like how many men do they need? Leave some for the rest of us! It's not much to ask.

The silence between us unnerves me. 'So, should we go to the rendezvous spot for the beer tour?'

'Sure, but before we go,' he says, gazing directly into my eyes making heat rush to my face, 'I should apologise. Last night was wild and I really enjoyed it, but perhaps I went too far with the whole dancing thing.'

'Why do you say that?' I'm curious if he means his own dance moves or more specifically dancing with me.

He scrubs his face while he dithers. What's going on here? Jasper is not the dithering sort. 'I enjoyed it. A little too much. And you've made it abundantly clear that you're in no means ready, and I totally understand that – I mean, who wouldn't? You've just lost your husband, and here's me sliding up and down your body. I'm sorry, it was disrespectful.'

Oh God, why did he have to paint that picture? Desire floods me, and I cough and clear my throat to appear anything but ruffled when I'm really rather ruffled by him. 'Disrespectful because of the dead husband thing?' I just want it to be abundantly clear what I'm dealing with here.

His mouth falls open. 'Ah – yeah.'

'Right.' What does one say to that? Do I want Jasper to slide up and down me? Yes. Should I want that? Not sure. 'I'm sure my dearly departed is fine with it.' There. He can stop worrying. 'He'd want me to be happy.'

He cocks his head. 'So, you're saying...?'

I'm not really sure what I'm saying, but part of me wants to encourage Jasper and the other part is screaming in protest because it's not a good idea. 'I'm saying I'm not going to worry any more.' Why can't I be more like Rox, who would shrug off the past and already have moved on with the next hottie that walked her way? But that's Rox's MO – act first, think later. I've got to worry and obsess and potentially scare Jasper away, all because I have loyalty to Miles, even though he doesn't deserve it.

Confusion sparkles in his eyes. 'Last night you mentioned that it was too soon, is all.'

'What is?'

'Moving on.'

'Ah.' Drunk me is all over the place! 'It does feel a little soon. I have a bit of a process with this kind of thing, but if you're talking about us, specifically, then we were only dancing, right?'

'Right. We did share a kiss. Twice.'

How could I forget? It's not even possible. 'What are you asking, Jasper?' I'm sending mixed messages and he's conflicted too, and I'm just too poorly to deal with this today.

He waits a beat. 'Nothing, nothing.' His expression clears, as if he's made up his mind about something. 'You're in a fragile place and I respect that.'

'Yeah, this hangover is a doozy.'

He laughs. 'OK, let's forget the official group tour, eh, and go drink some festive beer by ourselves?'

I want to throw myself into his arms, but refrain. 'Yes! A more casual day sounds just like what the doctor ordered.'

We go on the hunt for juleøl. 'Can you believe there's an actual word dedicated to Christmas beer?' I ask.

'Beer is big business here. I read up about it this morning. Apparently in the early 2000s there was a craft beer revolution in Copenhagen. Craft beer breweries popped up all over the city with a focus on producing high-quality beer.'

I groan. 'More alcohol though…'

'Why don't we try a couple for posterity's sake and then head for the Christmas markets?'

'That sounds like a much better idea.'

We visit some Danish dive bars, which are called bodegas, and sample some delicious fruity juleøl. These relaxed cosy bars are full of hygge-like atmosphere with the moody lighting and low ceilings and warm wood panelling. There are plenty of hipper places that sell it too, but we're quite taken by the charm of the more down-at-heel bars that feel more welcoming somehow. The bodega is full of a diverse crowd and it's not long before Jasper is challenged to a Danish Viking game of Meier, played with dice. It's a game about lying and I'm thrilled to bits when he loses. Not a good liar is good in my book.

We share a plate of smørrbrød: crusty slices of rye bread layered with various toppings like roasted beef, pickles, cucumber and remoulade, and a heaped plate of Frikadeller: meatballs, because you can't come to Copenhagen and not have meatballs, a beloved national dish. As we eat, we fall into an easy conversation about our favourite places around the world that we'd like to revisit someday.

'Next favourite place?' I tap my chin contemplating. 'Tasmania would be in my top five, for sure.'

'Would you move to Tasmania if you could?' Jasper asks as he points to a slice of smørrbrød layered with pickled herring, beetroot, egg slices, capers, and fresh sprigs of dill.

I move the slice to my plate. 'No, but I would love to visit there again. It's got the most beautiful coastlines. You can take a hike up any mountain and be rewarded with the most stunning view of the ocean and not see a soul. That solitude, up high like that, made me feel like I was the only person left in the world.'

'Not lonely at all.'

I laugh. 'Depends if you're in a solitary mood or not, I

suppose. What about you? Where's your next favourite?' So far, we've worked down a long list of places we've loved.

He takes a sip of beer as he considers it. 'Next favourite would have to be Venice. The floating city. So much charm and history.'

I smile. 'Venice is gorgeous. Shame about the sinking factor.'

'That's why I went. I did a story about it.'

'I'd love to read it. Do you ever see yourself writing a novel one day? Or a travel memoir?'

He grins. 'Maybe one day when I've got something fun to write about. Like upping sticks and living in a rainforest or sailing around the world on a yacht.'

'Rainforest spiders though.' I shudder. 'They're terrifyingly big and hairy.'

He laughs. 'I'm doing the Camino de Santiago pilgrimage walk in March, have you heard of it?'

I gasp. 'I've always wanted to do the Camino! Are you going from St-Jean-Pied-de-Port?' There are many different routes you can walk to get to Santiago de Compostella. Originally it was a religious pilgrimage, but these days people do the month-long walk for many different reasons – religious and spiritual, recreational, or sometimes more for the physical and mental challenge it presents.

'Yes, I'm doing the Camino Frances.' It's also known as the French Way because it starts in Saint-Jean-Pied-de-Port before pilgrims cross into Spain over the Pyrenees and it's the most well-known and popular route. 'I'm doing a story on the auberges as I go.'

The auberges are the hostels along the route, humble dorm rooms for pilgrims walking the Camino. The owners are well known for their hospitality and support. 'Are you kidding? Seriously! Doing the Camino Frances has been a dream of mine for the longest time. I've read far too many memoirs about it. I'd love to do it someday.' What an experience it would be. It's not just about pushing your body to the limits walking all eight hundred miles over thirty-five or so days, it's the pilgrims you meet along the way, the stories shared by people from all corners of the globe, all walking for different reasons.

'Why don't you join me?'

I go to protest and catch myself. What's stopping me? There is Wi-Fi in the towns, or I could cut right back on work for that month. A chance like this doesn't come along very often. Doing the Camino with a friend, rather than alone, appeals and would put my mum more at ease, knowing I had someone with me.

'Just say yes.'

'Yes.' I let out a shriek, excited by the prospect of ticking a very big item off the bucket list. You can do the Camino on all budgets, including mine – tiny. The humble auberges charge a nominal amount and food is cheap but plentiful. There's enough time between now and then to fill up the coffers and ready myself to pare back work for March to be able to give the pilgrimage the attention it deserves. This is why I love the flexibility of my job. This is why I do what I do. A rush of goosebumps breaks out over my arms, and I have this strange sense that I'm coming back to myself – back to my true happiness, the freedom to follow a travel whim that makes my soul happy. It's like a cloud has lifted and I can see clearly again, and it's blue skies for days.

'I'd better start my training.' I'll have to train to be able to walk ten to fifteen miles per day, and let's be honest, I'm not the sporty sort but this trip feels so much bigger than exercise. It's about connection. And conversely about being alone with your thoughts for much of the day.

Jasper smirks. 'Maybe after the Winter Wonderland Express.'

'Yes, it's not as if there's a gym on board.' Wait, have I just agreed to go on a month-long walk with Jasper? Maybe I need to do the unthinkable and ask my sister her view on this, simply because she'll remind me of all the good that might come of it...

'Actually, I'll, ah – think about it. I'll have to check my work schedule and a few other things.' Guilt blossoms about my sudden backtrack, but it's a big decision when I don't even know where I'm going to go after this holiday. Not back to the village for long, that's for sure, except to cuddle Freya's baby when he arrives and to get my things and say my goodbyes.

But it's not like I haven't made spontaneous plans with other people I've met on my travels, is it? Am I overthinking this just because it's Jasper?

Is that disappointment in his eyes? He quickly rearranges his expression to one of understanding. 'Totally get it. It's a big trip. We barely know one another and here I am asking you to spend an entire month with me. But something tells me we'd have the time of our lives, Aubrey.'

Damn it. Something tells me that too.

I can't control my big goofy smile.

* * *

Later that evening, we meet the Unlucky in Love Travel Club at Tivoli Gardens. It's a popular theme park and lush gardens with something for everyone. It's rumoured to be the magical place that gave Walt Disney his inspiration for Walt Disney World. During the festive season, the park sparkles under thousands of twinkling fairy lights, making the place feel like something truly out of a fairytale.

'There they are.' I point to our friends huddling together, steaming mugs of hot drinks in their hands. The scent of pine trees fills the air as we make our way to them.

'Did you know,' Princess says, 'Tivoli has over one thousand Christmas trees? You're not the only guidebook nerds, you know.'

I laugh. 'You want to be a guidebook nerd too?'

'Yes, I hate missing out.'

Jasper grins. 'Of course. It's all part of our club.'

'Shall we check out the stalls?' Karen asks. 'I've been told I can't leave Copenhagen without trying Æbleskiver, a deep-fried dessert with a crust which has the texture of a pancake, and the inside is like a donut, and you dip them in jam and then icing sugar.'

'Count me in,' I say.

'Best served with gløgg,' Princess adds.

'I love all the different names for mulled wine we've encountered along the way,' CJ says.

We meander along, cosy in our little group of six, checking out the carnival rides and the happy smiles of the people riding them. It's like a dream being here, with people who I now consider friends. This kind of bond doesn't come along very often and so I enjoy the glimmer of happiness at how lucky we are to have met and bonded over our shared singledom. Though by the way Barry has his palm hovering at Princess's lower back, some of us aren't going to be single for long. At least I hope so.

Soft snow seesaws lazily from the starry sky. 'Are you cold?' Jasper asks as I hold out a gloved hand to catch a snowflake.

I'm not cold – I'm layered to the hilt – but I say, 'A little.'

'Let me warm you up.' He swings an arm over my shoulder and pulls me in tight. 'Is that OK?'

'Much better.'

'Who wants to ride on the Elf Train?' Princess asks.

We giggle at the idea of riding a far cutesier train than the one we're staying on, but we duly comply, grabbing our seats and munching on candied almonds as we're driven around the park with a view of snowcapped mountains in the distance. After the train, we take a ride on the Forest carousel with the sound of tinny Christmas carols playing loudly from speakers above. Princess jumps from her horse to take photos of us. It's one of those magical evenings and I wish I could stop time, so it never ends.

Later we find a spot sheltered by a fir tree that's swathed in twinkling fairy lights to watch the fireworks explode across the sky, and it feels as if I'm exactly where I'm meant to be. Jasper and I exchange a glance. Does he feel it too?

23

22 DECEMBER, COPENHAGEN, DENMARK

Jasper walks me back to my cabin, as if we've been out on a real date and he's escorting me safely back home. It's sweet, in a gentlemanly way. 'Thanks for today,' I say. 'I had the best time.'

'It was great.' He leans against the door frame, doing that manly deep stare-down thing that sends my heart close to cardiac arrest. How does such a simple gaze hold so much weight? Silence hangs between us, charged, tense, and I hate myself for dithering in these stolen patches of time while I fight the urge to grab the man by his collar and pull him into my room. That's not me. I need to obsess over all the ways this is not a good idea before I even think about a tumble in the bedroom, yet here I am, on the cusp of doing such a wild thing.

While I enjoy bursts of glimmers, tiny explosions of happiness, my mind spins with reasons why I should act on these urges. I haven't heard from Miles, and I'm not a doormat. If I want to throw myself into this experience, what's stopping me? I deserve happiness just as much as the next person, and if this turns out to be nothing more than a festive fling, is that so bad?

Maybe Jasper will be the bridge that I have to cross to get to the next phase of my life.

I rise up on tiptoes as Jasper's head lowers to meet mine.

'Evening all!'

Jasper jumps back as if he's been zapped, and not in a good way. I could cheerfully kill my neighbour. Like, can't he read the room?

'Hamilton.' I give him a nod. 'Where's Georgiana?'

He waves into the middle distance. 'Oh, I left her at the bar with Princess.' He rubs the back of his neck. 'I've got some making up to do. We had a chat this morning and it seems I've been rather letting her down. I've been a bit of a bad roommate. I asked her to move in with me after this trip and she said yes, with a caveat – picking up after myself.' He blushes. 'I'd die for that woman. Oh, how dramatic do I sound? I'm just glad she was honest with me so it didn't become a divide between us. I best show her that I'm a tidy housemate.'

He's so animated and clearly very in love with Georgiana. I'm glad she spoke up and that he took it on board. 'Congratulations on moving in together.' I'm genuinely happy for them.

'Thank you.' His phone trills. 'Business calls. Enjoy the evening.' Hamilton lets himself into his cabin and Jasper and I are alone again, but the moment between us is lost.

'They're not our mystery couple, then,' Jasper says.

I shake my head. 'Nope. Not them. But they get their happy ever after, which is great. Meet you later for dinner?'

Jasper nods and gives me a wave, heading off back to his cabin. As I watch him stride away, I fight a pang of loneliness. How does it feel so right, so easy with Jasper? As if the world is suddenly full of colour, full of sound. Vibrant. As soon as he's gone, it pales again. Dulls. If I didn't know better, I'd say this was love at first sight. But how can that be? Isn't that just fodder for romantic comedies? I run a fingertip over my bottom lip, the memory of Jasper's mouth so tantalisingly close to mine before we were interrupted. But... what if it's real? And this is my one chance to act? What's the worst than can happen if I allow myself to dive into the unknown?

It's too much, the idea it could be serious consumes me, so I let it go. Tell myself to find a distraction.

I take a moment to send Freya some travel pictures and ask how she is. She texts back:

> Wow, stunning! I'm craving watermelon, is that weird?

I smile.

> It would be weird not to crave watermelon! Get James on to it! x

* * *

Distraction is hard so I flop on my bed and do the unthinkable and video-call Rox for advice. When the train is stationed, the view out the window is the busy platform, other trains whizzing in and out, passengers disembarking, trundling heavy suitcases as they leave to explore the city. The Winter Wonderland Express takes a slow drive to each new destination during the night as we sleep, so we have woken up each morning to our next station and city of call.

'Aubrey, are you being held against your will?'
'What? No.'
'Have you been kidnapped?'
'Isn't that the same thing?'

'Not quite. To what do I owe the pleasure of this call, seemingly not done under duress?'

Tonight, Rox's hair is spiked up, punk-rocker style. Only Rox could get away with such a style and pull it off. 'I'm... I'm confused.' I go on to explain about Jasper and him inviting me to walk the Camino, which I readily accepted with no thoughts of ulterior motives, not even the fact that I find him incredibly alluring, and some of those auberges are a little remote where anything could happen. And then backtracked on my decision and told him I'd think about it.

'Oh my God, he suggested the Camino? Does he know it's like your lifelong dream?'

'I know, isn't it crazy! He's doing a story on it and it just came up in conversation.'

'Golly, it's like you're two peas in a pod. You've bent my ear about doing that walk for ages.' A frown mars her brow. 'So, what's the issue here? You've always travelled like that, being invited here and there on the fly and rolling with it, because you can work anywhere with internet. And so what if you feel something for him – isn't that reason enough to explore this thing? See where it leads?'

'Yeah. When you put it like that it sounds simple. It's just the walk is four weeks long. Imagine if a week into it, it goes pear-shaped.'

'Then you part ways. You let him get a day ahead of you on the route and you complete the Camino under your own steam. Get your pilgrim passport stamped and there's another bucket list item checked off. You have to do this, and honestly, at the risk of sounding like Mum, I'll feel better knowing you've got a friend on the road with you.'

'Thanks, Rox. I'm not sure why I'm so conflicted. The Miles situation has really knocked my confidence. It's like I'm afraid to make any moves in case it's the wrong one again. Jasper is lovely, too lovely, and I'm afraid that if I do give in to whatever feelings I have – the same thing will eventually happen. I don't think I can take any more rejection because it does start to feel like maybe I'm the problem. What is the fatal flaw that stops any relationship of mine going the distance?'

Rox takes a moment to untangle the question. 'Well, if you want me to list your flaws, of which there are many, I can. But in terms of love, I don't think you do anything wrong per se, do you? True love doesn't come easy, and you might have to admit to yourself that Miles wasn't the one, not even close. You felt, for many reasons, a bit panicked and rushed into the idea of matrimony. Mum liked the idea of you having a travel buddy to keep you safe. Dad liked the idea of you being home again. Freya wanted you to have a million babies so you could do whatever they do at those hideous mothers' groups with you by her side. And on and on. Even I probably had a hand in your decision – I also liked the idea of my big sister being in the same time zone. But that's the thing, Aubrey. All those things are what we wanted, not what you wanted.'

I've suspected this all along but couldn't admit it to myself, not really, because who makes big life decisions in such a flippant way just to go with the flow! 'Yeah. And I guess trying to fit into that mould was never going to work. Not long term anyway.' It's like Jasper asked when we first met, was I truly looking to settle down or was I just settling? For second best. For a life I would eventually find mediocre, all because I felt that pressure to follow the crowd. Pressure I'd never felt before until I made that trip home and fell for my high-school crush and thought what if...?

'What's wrong with living for the moment like you've always

done? You don't normally think ten steps ahead, so why start now?'

There's a lot of truth in that. My only concerns are usually about safety precautions and budgeting for my stay. 'You're right. And fine, I'll admit it, Rox. You are very good at this whole life advice thing.'

'Damn it, why didn't I screen record that? Say it again!'

I laugh. 'Not likely.'

'I hate to ask, but I will anyway. Still no word from Miles?'

I shake my head. 'None, and to be honest, his silence says it all. I'd wanted to give him the benefit of the doubt, hear him out, but now, I think a clean break is best. I feel...' How do I feel about Miles? Really? 'Like we both rushed into this, with the idea of a belated happy ever after, mimicking what our friends had, but that wasn't us, was it? I'm happy exploring and maybe Miles is happy—'

She guffaws then yells, 'With himself!'

'I was going to say living the bachelor lifestyle.' I shake my head. 'And I have to respect that. We thought we'd be the missing piece of the puzzle for each other, but it turns out we were two completely different puzzles all along.'

'So will you go on the Camino pilgrimage?'

'Why not? I'll crunch some numbers and see what the budget is doing, but wouldn't it be kind of perfect? Spending those long days walking, ruminating? Feels like just the tonic.'

'You and your tonics. Less ruminating and more—'

'Don't you even say it!'

* * *

After a quick shower I'm dressed and ready for dinner with the Unlucky in Love Travel Club. Tonight's theme is 'Cosy Christmas'. Pyjamas, fluffy slippers – we're encouraged to don whatever we feel most comfortable in. I've opted for a pair of Grinch PJs and Ugg boots. If only we could dress like this every evening, although I bet Princess won't be impressed by the thought of dressing so casually. I lock my cabin door and make my way down the hallway to the dining carriage.

Sabrina pops out, startling me with her green face. 'Nice PJs!'

'Thank you. Wow, that Christmas tree costume is somehow even more... vibrant.' I give her a wide smile. Her costume flashes and pulses to the music as if the festive Christmas lights share the same beat. Was it only this morning she showed us her practice run in it? Feels like light years ago. The days and nights are deliciously slow on the Winter Wonderland Express.

Her lips purse in disapproval. 'I can't wait to get this monstrosity off. Gift-box shoes should be outlawed, and that sleazy guy Silas from table three keeps squeezing my baubles and yelling ho, ho, ho.'

I pull a face. 'Eww. What makes him think that's acceptable?' The mention of him reminds me that I forgot to tell the Unlucky in Love Travel Club that he might be in contention for our splitsville mystery... and if so, I can see bloody well why. He's the letch who won the ugly Christmas jumper competition and gave every woman the winky face.

Sabrina shakes her head; at least, that's what I think she's doing. It's hard to tell with her costume hiding the bulk of her frame. 'He's actually a pig. And strangely he's coupled up with that statuesque blonde Gigi, the supermodel type with the cool gaze. Like, in what universe does a man like him get the love of a woman like her? He is punching well above his weight.'

Silas and Gigi haven't been as blatant with their PDAs as the other passengers; if anything, the tall cool blonde has been a little cold and I can see why if he's being inappropriate with other women.

'Why do women settle for men like him? She's lovely and he's... not.'

Sabrina lifts her tinsel-wrapped arms. 'It's a mystery.'

I decide not to wait to confer with the group. I have to know now. 'It's got to be them. The couple heading for splitsville?'

Sabrina shakes her head. 'Unfortunately not. She's stuck by him as far as I know.'

I deflate at the thought. 'Well, at least that means Silas won't be joining our table, I couldn't cope with that.'

'Somehow I can't see Jasper putting up with a guy being handsy around you.'

I stop short. 'What do you mean?'

'Haven't you noticed how protective of you he is?'

Have I? A few times he's put an arm around me, like in the Louvre to stop me from being jostled forward, or that time in Hamburg he grabbed my hand to guide me through a horde of tourists. 'That's just Jasper being Jasper.'

'Oh, you poor lovesick fool. Why is the love interest always the last to know?'

'The love interest? Me?'

'You must have blinkers on, Aubrey. The man is smitten with you. Smitten. He can't take his eyes off you. Even when you were doing the robot and everyone else was gasping at how bad you were, he had this look on his face that I can only describe as wonderment, and that's really saying something. If a man can find the way you dance cute, then the sky is the limit.'

'I'm trying not to take offence as I untangle that, Sabrina. How can the robot dance be bad? It's the robot. It's meant to be robotic.'

'Your robot short-circuited! There was a system failure and a malfunction in the motherboard.'

'Wow.' I promptly dissolve into giggles. 'You paint a tragic picture of my skills, Sabrina. Was I really that bad?' I mean, it tracks. I absolutely hate being in the spotlight, and that hatred is magnified when you add a dance battle into the mix.

'Worse. And despite that, the man stared at you like you were a goddess come to life.'

Did he? 'And he joined in with my dance, what – to save me from further mortification?' I remember the crowd calling for Jasper, wolf-whistling, so I'd just presumed he wanted more of the limelight.

'To save you and to be close to you.'

'Oooh, maybe I do see it now.' Jasper has been looking out for me this whole time. It's in the little things he does. He's considerate, aware. The type of guy that's always on your side. I'm not used to a man like that, so much so that I didn't even recognise it in him until now and that's only because Sabrina's pointed it out. Could I really let myself fall for Jasper though? Risk it all again, so soon?

Sabrina blanches when she spots another staff member coming our way. 'Oh shoot, there's my manager. I'm supposed to guide you to the Elfie-Selfie Station and encourage you to pose for an "elfie" that you can share on social media.'

I keep my face neutral when the sucked-lemon-faced manager swings her gaze to us, and I say quietly, 'They're really big on photos around here.'

'It's the way of the world, is it not? If you don't take a photo, did it even happen?'

I laugh. 'True. Are you allowed to come and get an "elfie" with me?'

'Sure, as we're supposed to be encouraging shares to social media!'

As the manager walks past, she shoots Sabrina a dark look and says to me, 'I hope Sabrina is assisting you with whatever you need?'

I give her a wide smile. 'She is, in fact, and has ever since I stepped on board. I commend you on hiring such friendly staff, such as Sabrina, who has gone above and beyond for us passengers and truly made this trip unforgettable. You're lucky to have her.'

The manager's jaw unhinges before she quickly collects herself. 'Thank you. That's lovely to hear.'

When she leaves, Sabrina screeches. 'Oh, that was priceless! Thank you, Aubrey.'

'I meant every word.'

We find the Elfie-Selfie Station and pose, pulling silly faces. 'I'm going to miss you all at the end of this journey,' Sabrina says when we finish, handing our props to the next passengers.

'I'm going to miss you too. I guess it's an ongoing stream of goodbyes for you in this line of work?'

Sabrina smiles. 'It is. Some are harder than others. It's always surprising how close you can grow to a group over a short amount of time. Being together like this, in a bubble almost, fast tracks those friendships. And then the dreaded goodbyes come and, as much as you plan to catch up again one day, that day never comes. You must find that too the way you live?'

It's a little soul crushing to think I'll never see Sabrina or the rest of the group again. She's right – we've grown close over such a short time, aided by the fact we're confined to the train for half the day. It's a wonderful way to travel, in that respect. 'Yes, I find goodbyes difficult too when I travel, but someone is always leaving for the next adventure, and then I find myself with itchy feet, inspired to explore further. I'm not sure where to next, though. Maybe Paris? Maybe I'll work my way down France...' I can then meet Jasper for the Camino in March.

'Sounds bloody good to me.'

'What about you? Do you plan to stay on the Winter Wonderland Express long term?'

'It was the plan, but now I'm not sure. I love the train but my manager has it in for me. You saw the way she looked at me. According to her, I can't do anything right. I've been offered a job crewing on a yacht in the Maldives, so I might go for that. I'm just... not sure. You ever feel like that? At a crossroads, let down by people and just meh?' It's a big change from Sabrina wanting to get her boyfriend a job on board to suddenly wanting to leave. I'm sorry that her manager is dulling her shine. It's not right.

I give her shoulder a squeeze. 'Yeah, hard relate.'

'You better head to dinner so you don't miss out. All I have to do is protect my baubles from being squeezed and all will be well. If I knock any more wine off the table, I might actually get fired, so wish me luck.'

I smile. 'Princess would never allow that, there'd be mutiny on board.'

Sabrina grins. 'God love her. Have fun at dinner, I'll be along later.'

At the table, I sit with the group who are gossiping hard behind their hands.

'What have I missed?' I ask Jasper, wrinkling my forehead. It must be good because even Princess has lowered her voice.

CJ leans close, brackets her hand around her mouth, and whispers, 'Do you know the couple who call each other Jellybean and Gummy Bear?'

I bite down on my lip to stem laughter. I mean, it's cute and all but really? 'No, I don't know them. Which ones are they?'

'They always wear the matching couples' outfits, you can't miss them.'

I nod. 'Ooh, the ones from Hawaii? The young couple.'

'Yeah. Well, apparently the girl—'

'Is she Gummy Bear?'

'No, she's Jellybean.'

We exchange a grin. 'I'm going to have to make notes to keep track.'

'Actually, this is Jasper's story to tell…' CJ motions her head to Jasper, who covers his face with his hands. I none-too-gently pry them away for him. I need answers, not another delay in what looks to be a juicy story.

'So tell it, Jasper.'

'It's really nothing. Jellybean…' he starts and promptly stops.

'What? Don't leave me hanging. What did Jellybean do?' My mind spins with ideas. Maybe she followed Jasper into his cabin and propositioned him! Maybe she threw herself at him and kissed him!

'I'm not sure why we're even discussing this. It's nothing. Jellybean asked me if I… if I…' Poor Jasper looks uncomfortable in his own skin, and how can that be?

'Oh God, can someone please fill me in because at this rate we're going to arrive in Lapland before I find out.'

Karen waves me close, darting a glance at the passengers at the tables close by who are doing that pretend-to-read-the-menu thing again but whose eyes are trained on us. 'Jellybean asked Jasper if he wanted to try a festive fling!'

'SHE WHAT!' I see red. Probably because of the sanctity of her own relationship. How dare she try and steal another man when she's got one of her own! Greedy much? 'I've got half a mind to go over there and have it out with her.'

The Unlucky in Love Travel Club goes completely silent. Deathly silent, even. What? Am I overreacting? Aren't they as incensed as I am? Best to play it down, maybe? I lock a natural smile into place, one that shows my teeth.

Princess grimaces and gives me a quick shake of the head and points to her own genial smile. I relax my facial muscles as best I can and say in a low voice, 'Because... um... don't we think that's a little offensive, considering she's in a relationship with Gummy Bear?'

'That's what we're considering,' Karen says, taking a hearty sip of wine. 'As in... what if Jellybean was speaking on behalf of Gummy Bear too?'

I gasp. 'A ménage à trois?' Could this get any worse? Now I've got to fight off men and women?! I catch myself, Firstly, Jasper isn't mine. Secondly, I'm not the jealous sort. But all of a sudden I am, and why is that? Train politics, probably. Being stuck with couples who act like they're smitten with one another then try their luck with a side piece? I'm incensed!

CJ lifts her palms and Jasper all but slides down his chair as if he wants to slip away to avoid this conversation. 'It could be, but we don't have enough details to know for sure.'

'Jasper?' I ask. 'What do you think?'

'I took it as a joke. I didn't think anything of it.'

'Then why tell the group?'

'Ooh, that was me who told the group,' Princess says, a smug smile lifting the corners of her mouth. 'I overheard Jellybean and then extricated our pure-of-heart boy and then reported my findings. That woman was practically salivating over poor Jasper here. And if she's going around propositioning men, then I think we have our suspects, don't we?'

Jasper's complexion pinkens further. Honestly, isn't he used to being approached by flirtatious women? Especially after a dance performance that steamed up the train carriage, so much so that we were all a little hot under the collar. He can't really be that aloof to it, surely? Either he is, or it's more that he doesn't like the attention. Could that be it? And he only danced so well, determined to win the battle for Princess?

'I'm in agreement with Princess. I'm sure they're the couple who've called it quits. Didn't Sabrina originally say the reason for the impending split is because of a suspected cheating scandal?' Barry says, his eyebrows knitting. 'And Jellybean has shown form with Jasper.'

'Ooh.' I think back to Sabrina's comments. 'Yes, she did say that! But didn't she also say it was the guy who went rogue?'

Karen hits the table with a palm. 'Yes! That's right. I'd forgotten that. So either Jellybean is getting payback for Gummy Bear already cheating, or else they're in an open relationship or just love adding a third person when the mood strikes.'

'Golly,' I say, a little scandalised. Rox is always calling me a prude, so there is that to consider too.

Jasper shakes his head. 'If you'd have seen Jellybean's face, it was all tongue-in-cheek. If Princess hadn't ripped me away by the ear, I'm sure there would have been some kind of explanation.'

Thank God she'd been there to rescue him.

'You are so naïve,' Princess says. 'That girl was undressing you with her eyes.'

He frowns but stays silent.

Sabrina enters the fray and Princess fills her in on the latest. 'Oh.' Sabrina laughs. 'No, she didn't mean an actual fling. In the bar, the cocktail special this evening is called a Festive Fling! It sounds like she was simply asking if you'd like to try a Festive Fling cocktail...'

Jasper lets out a belly laugh. 'I told you it was nothing.'

It's my turn to blush. 'Poor Jellybean. We misjudged her so badly.' Jasper crosses his arms and gives me the 'I told you so' stare-down. I screw up my nose. 'Sorry.'

'I'm sorry too,' Princess says, bowing her head. 'I may have grabbed your ear a little too hard trying to extricate you from her clutches.'

'It's still ringing.'

'I can't help but think I played a part in this whole charade too,' Karen admits. 'Sorry, Jasper. You're looking at the queen of snap judgements here and I'm beginning to see it might be the thing that holds me back from finding love myself.'

'What do you mean, snap judgements?' I ask. If anything, Karen's been the opposite in most conversations, listens intently and then makes informed comments.

'Oh, you know, fifty first dates and not one of them made it to a second. I've got this defective part of me that can't seem to look past an ick. The guy could say he was into playing poker and I'd be out of there in a flash – imagining our future, card-game nights with his buddies, me relegated to the bedroom. No thanks. That's what my brain tells me, that I'm always going to be shoved aside for whatever reason.'

'Ah, so you reject them on the first date before they can potentially reject you?' Jasper asks with a sad smile.

'Wow, yeah, I guess that's exactly what I'm doing. Isn't that crazy?' Karen lets out a surprised laugh. 'I hadn't quite made that connection, Jasper, but that makes perfect sense. I'm getting in first, rejecting them over the silliest things, so they don't get to reject me first. For example, my last date mentioned that he wasn't a fan of spicy food, so I ended the date right then and there, despite having felt a spark between us. I regret that, but what I told myself was to think of all the spicy food I'd miss out on for the rest of my life. When really, it was about rejecting him first before he could reject me.'

'You were protecting your heart,' I say. 'And now you've recognised that you're self-sabotaging, you can easily fix that without lowering your standards or changing who you are.'

'Huh. That makes so much sense.'

CJ drums her fingers on the table. 'Do you still have his number? You could reach out to the guy, right? But don't explain, don't apologise, just say you're ready for the second date whenever he is.'

'But what about the spicy food thing?' Princess's face is a picture, as if she's mourning the loss of spicy food too.

'Maybe he's never tried the right kind of spicy food?' Barry says. 'He might be open to trying it. I would be, if that was a deal breaker for my beloved.' He gives Princess a longing look.

'Oh no, it's too late,' Karen says, dropping her head. 'He's probably chalked that date up as a disaster.'

'You're doing it again,' CJ says gently, patting the top of Karen's hand. 'Making excuses as to why it won't work. Be vulnerable, just this once, and see what happens.'

I hold my breath, hoping that Karen agrees.

There's a full minute of silence as if we're all too afraid to talk and interrupt her contemplation. Finally, she blurts, 'What have I got to lose? I'll text him now.'

We shriek and clap for our friend.

'And if he turns me down, well, at least I'm more aware of my dating foibles now, so that's progress.'

'Right!'

Princess claps her hands together. 'Karen, you're a fox, and don't you forget it. Who's up for the staff Christmas pantomime held in the library in an hour?'

'Me!' I say. 'And you, Jasper? We can have a drink in the bar beforehand.'

'If you're up for a Festive Fling, I am too.' The sizzling look he shoots my way just about stops my heart right then and there.

'I – ah – eee – k.' Great. I can only squeak.

24

23 DECEMBER, STOCKHOLM, SWEDEN

We're sitting around the breakfast table, discussing last night's pantomime, *The Snow Queen*, after having arrived in Stockholm in the early hours of the morning. Princess is missing, so I'm only half listening to the chatter, wondering if I should go and check on her.

When there's a break in the conversation, I ask, 'Where's Princess?'

'In her cabin, I presume,' Karen says, buttering a slice of sourdough. 'She and Barry were up late. When I left the bar, the karaoke machine had just come out, and wow that woman has certainly got a set of lungs on her. What she lacks in talent she makes up for with her energy.'

I smother a laugh, imagining it without any trouble at all. 'Is she OK?' I face Barry's way.

He fumbles with his napkin, averting his gaze. Huh. 'Yeah, love. Just a late one. Princess belted out a number of bangers. Quite the fan of karaoke.'

I contemplate it. 'Princess has more stamina than all of us put together though. Belting out bangers is one thing, but she's never missed a breakfast, not one.' There is the fact she's seventy-five; have all the late nights finally caught up with her? But no, I remember her saying she'd never miss breakfast in the dining carriage because it was a chance to eavesdrop on gossip and ogle handsome men. Maybe she was joking and just trying to get me to leave my cabin that day.

I fold up my napkin and push my chair back. 'I'll go check on her. What's her room number?'

'Number one.' Barry blushes. 'Or so I've heard.'

Only the best for our very own Princess. 'Of course.' Leaving the group, I ask sweet George where cabin number one is and am surprised to find it's past the library carriage, in another area I haven't explored before. These must be the super-deluxe suites that cost more than I care to imagine.

I knock at the door and hear a faint 'I'm not here right now.'

'Princess, it's me, Aubrey. Open up.'

A loud groan greets me. 'I can't.'

'Why? Are you sick? Do I need to call the medic?'

'No.'

'Then what is it?' I lean my head on the door, barely able to make out her voice.

'You'll ask me tough questions and I don't have the heart to lie.'

What would Princess do if the situation was reversed? She'd simply ignore me and storm into my cabin all guns blazing, so that's what I do.

'Wow.' I'm momentarily distracted by the beauty of her cabin. It's about four times the size of mine. Stunning artwork hangs on walls. There's a dressing room with a full-length mirror. Princess lies prone in a king-size bed that's as regal as she is. She's hiding her face behind a satin eye mask.

I make my way through a small a lounge area with antique-style furniture. Off to the side there's a small library and an actual bar! I whistle my appreciation. 'This is next level. No wonder you don't want to leave!'

Princess pulls the eye mask down. 'Tell the group I died. Tell them I slipped off in my sleep and it was all very peaceful.'

'What? Why?'

'It's the only way. Just tell them, will you? That I love them all and I'll be waiting for them at the pearly gates when their time comes.'

'Not going to happen.' Only one of us can fake a death around here, and I've already claimed that for missing Miles. 'I'll do no such thing,' I reply firmly. 'What's all this about then?'

'Fine. Just tell them I got off the train early this morning.'

'Princess.'

She sighs. Without her make-up and glamorous clothes, she seems so much more fragile. Vulnerable. Lovable. Ooh. I get it.

'Is this about Barry?'

Her bottom lip wobbles.

'You've fallen for him?'

Princess takes a shuddery breath and gives me an infinitesimal nod. 'But I can't take it any further than flirtation, I really can't.' She slips her eye mask back on as if the conversation is closed.

'Princess, how do you know that?'

'I know it.'

Is it time to pull out my trump card? I've been doing a little work behind the scenes but I'm just not sure how this will land. Seeing her like this, avoiding the group, forlorn and lonely, it's not right. She's a firecracker of a human and all she's missing is love. 'What if there was a way to reverse the curse?'

This time, she pushes the silken eye mask atop her head. Her eyes are wide – with hope? 'How?'

Here we go. Make or break. 'I did a little digging online, and please correct me if I'm wrong, but I researched curses and found that an albularyo might be able to help.'

'A Filipino witch doctor?'

'Yeah.'

'You found one?'

I hope I haven't culturally overstepped, having no idea about what exactly Princess believes or even if I have the right, but simply wanting to help my friend who is clearly carrying the weight of trauma from her losses.

I nod. 'I found one. And I might have crossed the line, but I told her that you've been cursed by a jealous rival – I hope that's OK?'

Princess grins. 'It's not exactly a secret, is it? I tell everyone because it's best they know. Men do fall in love with me at an alarming rate, so it's mostly to manage their expectations.'

I swallow a smile. 'Right. Well, I told her about your case and she's confident that she can help. She educated me a little about how our physical health is entwined with emotional and spiritual health and it made sense to me that what you're suffering is quite complex. There are many elements at play here.'

'And the rival?'

'The albularyo agreed there very well could be a curse, or it could be that you're afraid to love again because you've already suffered so much loss. She's prepared to video-call with you until you can get to Manila to meet her in person.'

'Hm. And did this albularyo come highly recommended? How do you know she's legitimate?' She narrows her eyes as if she's not quite sure yet whether to trust in this new development.

'She wasn't recommended, and I don't know if she's legitimate, but what I do know is she was very understanding about your plight, sensitive to your needs and seemed to have plenty of ideas about possible fixes, not only for love but for letting go.'

Princess gasps. 'Letting go?!'

I sit at the end of the bed. 'Letting go,' I confirm. 'Princess, do you blame yourself for their deaths?'

Her composure breaks. 'Yes.'

'Why?'

'I wasn't there for them like I should have been. Not really. I'd been so obsessed by my work. Driven by making money. It's all well and good for men to be like that, they get called ambitious, but when women do the same, they're called money hungry, but still, it's what gave me life. I wanted to be the best property developer in the world. And I strove hard for that. My husbands enjoyed life on the back of my toil. But in turn, it ruined them. Ricky drank too much, Arturo smoked too much, and Miguel couldn't outrun his age and his love for sweets like halo-halo.'

'But none of that is your fault.'

'You say that, but if I'd been more present, I could have hidden the whiskey, thrown the cigarettes away, demanded they look after themselves better.'

'They were all fully grown adults, quite capable of making their own choices. By the sounds of it, your marriages were all happy ones.'

Her eyes crinkle at the corners. 'Very happy. We travelled and had a lot of fun together. The love was real.'

'Isn't that enough? They got the girl, they lived in the fast lane – what if that's all they ever wanted?'

She double-blinks. 'I've never thought about it that way before.'

'You've been so focused on blaming yourself, that's why.'

'Huh.'

'They weren't young men when they died. They lived rich and full and happy lives.'

'But what if it happens again?'

'What if it doesn't?'

She exhales a long breath, as if she's still not quite convinced.

'Princess, you can deny yourself love for the rest of your life, but then you'll have missed out in what are essentially the best years of your life now that you're retired. The Princess I've come to know and adore has a lot of love to give and it would be a crying shame not to share that.'

'I hate it when you make sense, Aubrey.'

25

23 DECEMBER, STOCKHOLM, SWEDEN

I leave Princess with the albularyo's phone number and hope she gets in touch. I find the group, who are sitting in the lounge carriage waiting to depart the train for a day in Stockholm. 'Is she OK?' Barry asks, concern marring his brow.

I smile. 'Yes, she's going to have a lie in and meet up with us later.'

'It'll feel weird going out and about without her, won't it?' Karen says, swiping on her signature scarlet lipstick.

'Maybe I should stick around?' Barry asks, running a hand through his thinning hair. 'Keep an eye on her, without intruding too often. Karen's read me the riot act about all that stuff.'

Karen shrugs. 'What would I know? Princess seems to like the attention, so don't listen to me.'

He's waiting for permission from us, which I find inordinately sweet. Princess really didn't give much of an indication what her plans were, but I have a feeling that she's hoping Barry will visit her cabin for a chat. 'That's a nice idea, Barry. Why don't you send her a text and tell her you're staying on board for a bit?'

'Good idea, love. Then she can call me as needed, if needed.

Although she hasn't had breakfast, so perhaps I could take her a tray… or I could wait and we could share lunch. Or afternoon tea? I don't want to be overbearing.'

'Send the text, Barry.'

He trundles off in the direction of his cabin, like a man on a mission. It's sweet seeing love bloom between two people who have stumbled in the past.

'Against my better judgement, CJ's roped me into going to the ice rink on kungsträdgården. Did you and Jasper want to come with us? I might need his muscles if I take a tumble…' Karen says with a smile. 'Although CJ is pretty strong from all that hiking, so maybe she could heft my weight if needed.'

CJ bumps her with a hip. 'I'm quite capable of performing first aid when required. Don't forget, I've got teen boys; there have been an alarming amount of breakages. But I don't plan on playing nurse today, because you're going to remain upright, even if I have to hold you upright.' It's sweet to see these two have formed a strong friendship, teasing each other in a sisterly way – well, not how my sister does, but regular sisters.

'Oh thanks for the invite,' I say. 'But there's absolutely no way I'm going to go ice skating. I struggle walking on solid ground as it is. And seriously, I do not need any more videos of me circulating. According to Sabrina, the Winter Wonderland Express is trending on Insta after someone uploaded a video of the dance battle. No doubt it's because of Jasper's erotic dancing, but surely my robot moves are second to that. Told you that style never goes out of fashion.'

'Ah, yeah, I'm sure you're second in views because of your robot talent and for no other reason,' Karen says and does some rather sketchy side eye in CJ's direction. Is she being sarcastic? Hard to tell.

'Jasper might be keen on the idea?' I say.

'No, I'll stick with you, Aubrey. Apart from anything, we've got to find you another ugly Christmas mug, eh?'

I laugh. 'Sure. Princess offered the use of her private car, so why don't you girls take it?'

'Fab. Text us if you want to meet up later and maybe Princess and Barry will be around then too?'

'Sure.'

Jasper and I head out into the snowy day and catch a ride share to ArkDes museum to visit the gingerbread house exhibition. When we arrive, we're assailed with the heavenly scent of gingerbread. It conjures Christmas for me and always makes me smile. As soon as December first hits each year, Mum would have mixing bowls out and we'd help make gingerbread man biscuits, and the countdown for Christmas started that very day. Rox would decapitate her men – the writing has always been on the wall with her – and Mum would try not to scold her and ruin the mood. In the end she just let her dismember them however she wanted. You can tell a lot about a person by how they bake.

Of course, our cooking attempts with Mum at the helm were always a disaster, but it wasn't about that; it was about enjoying the ceremony of it together. The spicy ginger scent brings to the fore all those shared moments in Mum's cosy kitchen and makes me homesick for my family. Right now, Mum will be preparing for the big feast to come, making as much ahead of time as she can and dashing to the shops to buy more Christmas festive cushions, because you can never have enough, and Dad will be up on the roof fixing Christmas lights and musing that his inflatable Santa is missing his Mrs Clause, and Mum will be outlawing any more money spent on decorations, and then they'll get into it over the new cushions before drinking eggnog made with too much brandy and will both fall asleep holding hands together in front of the fire. Good times.

'I've lost you. You're off doing Pythagoras theorem again, aren't you?'

I laugh. 'I'm hopeless at maths. More of a word person, actually.'

His slow smile is enough to stop my heart. 'We haven't even finished our discussion about favourite books yet,' says he, as if we've got our whole lives to chat about the things we love. And if I were truly untethered, I could throw myself at this, couldn't I?

'We really need hot chocolate and the warmth of a roaring fire for that.'

'I live in a little cabin in Connecticut with a log fire and bookshelves along one wall.'

Oh God. How to kidnap me 101: tell me there's a log fire and books. 'Are you the kind of guy who likes spending all day in bed with a book?' Please say yes! My mind goes off on a tangent picturing Jasper twisted in sheets, book in hand, hot-guy-reading fantasy. I shake my head to dislodge the vision, but it's stuck.

'When I come back from work trips, I often spend all day in bed with a book, and it's even better if it's cold outside, or you can hear rain drumming on the roof. I would happily spend a whole weekend like that.'

'Reading snacks?'

He rubs his jawline. 'Chocolate truffles. You?'

'Dark chocolate truffles.'

'Do you read in the bath?' His lips twist into a grin.

'Yes, for my sins.'

He lifts a brow. 'Dog ear the pages?'

'I'm not sure I know you well enough to answer that one.' I make a show of being coy. It's a sin in literati-land and causes quite the stir among bibliophiles. Books are meant to be enjoyed, to bend with the reader, take shape under my hands; so what if I fold the page? But I don't tell anyone that!

'That means yes!'

I grimace. 'Fine, yes. But in my defence, I mostly buy from second-hand bookshops so the novels are usually pretty well loved by that stage anyway…'

He waves me away as if to stop the excuses pouring from my mouth. 'I do too, and I highlight passages I want to reflect on.'

'You monster.'

'Guilty.'

'We better check out the gingerbread houses before you share any more secrets.'

The museum is full of gingerbread creations made by professional chefs and amateur bakers. We explore each section of the museum and buy some gingerbread on the way out.

My phone beeps. 'It's Princess. They want to meet up at the Stortorget's Christmas market in a couple of hours.'

* * *

We meet the Unlucky in Love Travel Club at the Stortorget's Christmas market, which has been trading since 1837 and is located in Old Town. It's the oldest festive market in all of Sweden. We wander around the cute cabin-like stalls with offerings such as handcrafted ceramics and knitwear. There's a stall selling fresh spices, and another with a range of hard cheeses, chutneys and relishes. We come to the hot food stalls. On display are big, fat, juicy sausages, which of course make me think of Princess, who spots them at the same time, her eyes lighting up. I drag her away before she can make any lewd jokes.

We wander along, snow crunching underfoot. There's a stall selling pepparkaka, ginger biscuits, so I buy some for the Unlucky in Love Travel Club to eat later. We stop to warm our hands by an open barrel fire and listen to a children's choir sing a beautiful rendition of Stilla Natt, which even I can recognise is Silent Night. With their long white gowns and sweet pure voices they're like little Christmas angels. When the Christmas carol ends, we clap for the choir and make way for other market goers to warm their hands by the fire. Princess ambles beside me. From what I can gather, she's back to her bubbly self. The others peruse a stall selling lussekatter or Saint Lucia buns, saffron brioche named for the patron Saint of light. Princess takes the opportunity to pull me aside, her face is bright with happiness. 'I spoke to the albularyo. You're right, she's knowledgeable. My mother always trusted in healers, more so than conventional doctors. If my mother was alive, she'd have insisted on me consulting with an albularyo ages ago. In fact, she'd have marched me there, despite any protests on my behalf. I grew up with a life very different to the one I have now, and that's all down to my mother believing in me, showing me the way. And so you've brought her alive again, reminded me that perhaps I'm being unfair to myself, taking all the blame, punishing myself the way I have.'

'So... you don't think there's a curse?'

She shakes her head sadly. 'The albularyo helped me understand what a real curse would look like, and it's not this. What ails me is different. It's a broken heart that never quite healed and then broke again twice more. Putting the blame on myself stopped my heart from healing over and didn't allow me to let that love go. I'll always love my husbands, but life is for living and, by holding on to the past, I'm allowing grief to win, blame to darken my days. I've finally retired but instead of enjoying myself with a companion, I've been denying myself that gift. And look how many men I've left in a puddle of tears because I said "no, sorry, you'll die this horrible early death if you so much as kiss me!" Well, no more! I've got a whole life to cram into the next twenty-five years. I'm not going to say no any more.'

'I'm happy for you, Princess. You deserve to enjoy your retirement with someone who loves you for you. Have you... met that certain someone, do you think?' I slide my gaze in Barry's direction.

Princess follows my gaze and smiles. 'I've made a great friend, that much I'm sure of, and friendship is a good start. And what about you?' Her eyes land on Jasper. 'You also seem to have found a friend amid your sadness.' We watch Jasper, who has his head thrown back and is laughing at a story CJ is recounting.

'Yeah, I have, I've found six wonderful friends in all of you.' Princess cocks her head, purses her lips, but doesn't call me out on it. 'And I'm going to walk the Camino with Jasper in March. Why not?'

'And what about the in between time?'

I lock eyes with Jasper and my breath catches. 'No plan as yet, but I'm sure I'll figure it out, eventually.' I have to do a bit of research but I haven't wanted to spend time locked away in my cabin when I can spend it with my new friends. Every moment we share is precious and I want to enjoy all our time together. It's not often seven people, if you include me, gel the way we have. It's one of those magical travel marvels that make you wish that the time together will never run out, but maybe the beauty of it is that our time together is limited and that's why it is so special. We've all cast aside those masks everyone wears when you first meet and peeled back those layers to get to know one another on a deeper level, fast. But then there's me, who hasn't been truthful, despite trying umpteen times.

I'll have to come clean. But not now, not while they're all smiling and laughing and enjoying the festivities.

'I hope we can all meet again,' Princess murmurs. 'But life sure is a wily beast, so I know to take it one day at a time.'

26

23 DECEMBER, STOCKHOLM, SWEDEN

We're all squashed together in a booth at the bar on the Winter Wonderland Express, while the staff sing Christmas carols. When it's Sabrina's solo, we all hush. She belts out the lyrics for 'Little Drummer Boy' and it's enough to bring a tear to the eye; her voice is mellifluous and soulful.

'Wow,' CJ says. 'Who knew she could sing like that?'

Even Princess, our resident karaoke queen, is stunned. 'Sabrina has the voice of an angel. Her talents are being wasted.'

When Sabrina's song is over, she gives us a fluttery little wave as if she hasn't just captivated the crowd and goes behind the bar to help.

The next singer pales in comparison so we get back to our conversation and chatter about our plans for Lapland, including meeting up for Christmas Eve dinner at the lodge. 'What about Sabrina, though?' Karen asks. 'She and her boyfriend are staying in a hostel close by, aren't they? It would be great to celebrate with them too.'

'Definitely,' Princess says. 'We'll ask her what their plans are.'

The staff finish their carolling. We stand and clap, thanking them as they pass to resume their duties.

'Music requests?' Sabrina calls from behind the bar, gesturing to the sound system.

'What about "Last Christmas"?' Princess announces, holding out her hand to Barry. 'May I have this dance?'

Barry blushes and fumbles. 'I'd love nothing more.'

Princess gives me a not-so-subtle kick as she edges past me. There's absolutely no way I'm asking Jasper to dance, if that's what she's thinking. Princess tries her laser-like stare at me, but I duly ignore it. Instead, I study my nails like they're endlessly fascinating.

Jasper lets out a surprised gasp, which I take to mean she kicked him on the way past too. The minx.

'Ah – Aubrey, would you like to dance?' he asks, darting a glance at Princess, as if to ask why she has to resort to under-the-table kicks. She's as subtle as a sledgehammer, that woman.

'You're not asking under duress or anything, are you?'

He laughs. 'Absolutely not! I'm sure you didn't receive a nudge to the shins, either?'

I take his hand and we make our way to the small area used for entertainment. When Jasper pulls me tight against his body, everything melts away, except him and his intense gaze, which burns so hot I have to look away. He's like a real-life romance novel hero come to life and I just want to delight in that. It feels natural, being in his arms, feeling the beat of his heart as I press up against him. It takes me a moment to work up the courage to stare into the unfathomable depths of his eyes, because that's where I get lost, looking for signs that this is where I'm meant to be. That he is the one I want.

'Aubrey,' he says, his voice husky.

I keep my gaze on his. 'Yes?'

So much remains unsaid but sometimes words are just words. I don't need assurances, I just need to feel his lips on mine. Maybe that's all I need to do, listen to my body for once.

I slowly rise on my tiptoes as he brings his mouth to meet mine. Stars collide as we kiss tenderly, softly. Desire flames in my heart and my soul. All at once I'm sure I've never felt like this before, and how can that be?

'What the hell? Aubrey...'

The voice breaks my reverie. It's so familiar. Jasper pulls his lips from mine but keeps me in his arms.

'I – I didn't expect to see that.' The once missing groom nervously runs a hand through his thick dark locks.

Oh God, Miles is here. I'm frozen to the spot, unsure of how to react, while my lips are still tingling from Jasper's kiss.

'What – what are you doing here?' Seeing his face, his expression layered in anxiety, his vulnerabilities playing out, somehow reminds me of the love we shared. Or the love I felt, at any rate. Those dreams I had for my future bounce right back to the fore – the soft satin of my wedding dress as it slipped over my body, the excitement and trepidation I felt about the idea of walking down the aisle to meet my handsome groom. Who stands before me now, with a hint of devastation in his eyes that he tries hard to mask. 'Oh – ah God. I'm sorry, Miles, but you being here, well, it's a bit of a shock.'

There are audible gasps from the Unlucky in Love Travel Club. Jasper's face falls, and he drops his arms, stepping away from me. His sudden distance feels almost like a betrayal. As if I'm left marooned, alone in a sea of startled faces. By the dark angry gleam in Jasper's eye, he's the one who feels betrayed.

This is my worst nightmare. I tried to tell them but clearly I didn't try hard enough. And now he's here and they're confused. Hurt. Jasper's hands are fisted by his side.

'Miles is alive?' Princess says under her breath.

'I came to fix things, Aubrey. Fix us. But it looks like I'm too late.' His Adam's apple bobs up and down as if he's swallowing shock. I feel like a horrible human.

The carriage falls silent and all eyes are on me. I'm exposed as a fraud. Time slows to a crawl and for the life of me, I can't think of a response. Miles's face reddens the longer I leave the silence hanging.

I don't dare look at Jasper, but steal glances at the rest of the Unlucky in Love Travel Club, for help, for guidance, for courage maybe. CJ's mouth is a perfect O. Karen's eyes are comically wide and Barry is blinking away like he's trying to process it all. Behind the bar, Sabrina bites down on her lip and shakes her head. Do they feel deceived by my lies too? Princess steps forward, her expression neutral, impossible to read.

'Excuse me,' she says to Miles with a gentle smile. 'I believe this is a conversation best taken in private...'

27

23 DECEMBER, STOCKHOLM, SWEDEN

Back in my cabin, I sit on the edge of the bed and Miles slumps in the chair near the writing desk.

While I feel guilty, I shrug that sense off. Miles left me. He's got some explaining to do. 'What happened, Miles? What made you decide that abandoning me ten minutes before the wedding was a good idea?'

He covers his face with his hands. 'I'm sorry, Aubrey. I really am. I had a panic attack. A bad one. Everyone in the church witnessed it.'

'I'm sure they all understood, it's a big day, nerves are high and—'

'No, it's more than that, Aubrey. I'm prone to them but I've managed to hide it from you so far, from everyone, which upon reflection wasn't a smart move. I didn't want you to think less of me.'

'I'd never think less of you for something like that, you know that, right?' Why would he try to hide that from me? 'You sharing your vulnerabilities would have only brought us closer together.'

'Yeah, that's what Leo said too. It's just... I'd almost had a handle on them of late, and then with the wedding creeping up, I had a cluster of them. Funnily enough, it's the thought of travelling that mostly brings them on.'

And he never told me that? 'And yet you're here.' Did he battle his travel demons for me?

'I'm here because I love you and I'd do anything for you. I made a huge mistake, running like that and leaving you to deal with the fallout.'

'Why didn't you call me? I had no idea how you felt or what happened between us. It hurt, Miles, being discarded and then absolute radio silence.'

His face twists in embarrassment and I see the toll this has taken on him. Miles is all about how he's perceived by others, so I start to piece together how he must've felt in that moment waiting for me at the church.

'I wanted to have a chat face to face, not via text or video call, and maybe a small part of me was afraid too, afraid that I'd made a big mistake that couldn't be fixed. I should have had this conversation with you before the wedding, then I was going to have it with you after, but I got violently ill. I'm not saying your sister is at fault but I have my suspicions – but anyway, I did have some worries about us, silly things, like you'd bankrupt us with all your travelling, or insist I go away all the time when really I'm most comfortable at home. But we can both make compromises, I see that now.'

'Bankrupt you? I have never spent a penny of your money, nor would I.' Early on, I insisted we keep our finances separate. I like being in control of what I earn and budgeting accordingly.

He has the grace to blush. 'Yeah, but I thought things might change once we were married.'

I keep my expression neutral. 'I wish you'd reached out to let me know the love we shared was real. Apparently you thought you'd rushed into the relationship and it had all moved too fast – that didn't feel good, Miles, especially when it was you doing the rushing. There I was sitting out at the front of the church, hearing that news. It broke my heart.'

Can this be fixed? Can we go back to dreaming about our future together? I picture the cottage I had my eye on, with its garden full of fragrant wild roses. The holidays I'd hoped we'd take – with or without children. We'd know when the time was right, wouldn't we, if the time was ever right? The cosy movie nights. The candlelit dinners I'd burn. Lazy Sundays, coffee and croissants in bed together, if Miles would agree carbs were OK sometimes and put the gym off for just one day. And what would I need to give up – sorry, compromise – to make Miles's vision a reality?

'I'm sorry, Aubrey. I've handed this all wrong, I know that. I love you so much, do you feel me?' He stands up and moves towards me. When he's close, he drops on one knee. 'Will you marry me, Aubrey? We'll have the sweet intimate wedding that you wanted and we'll honeymoon in a little B&B in Devon...'

Isn't this what I wanted? Honesty? A solid future with a man who loves me? And that's exactly what Miles is offering, a safe, secure future. I have the beautiful dress, an open heart... and without question I know it beats only for one man.

28

23 DECEMBER, STOCKHOLM, SWEDEN

I return to the Unlucky in Love Travel Club. They need a truthful explanation too. My mind is firmly on Jasper and what he's going to make of what I have to say. Back in the bar carriage they're still sitting in the booth, eyes bright as if the speculation has run wild. I don't blame them. A man has come back from the dead; it must be a shock.

'Can I have a word, Jasper?' His mouth is a tight line but he nods. We go to the relative quiet of the library carriage.

'I'm sorry I lied,' I say bluntly.

His eyes are ablaze. 'I might have downplayed how I felt about the end of my marriage, Aubrey, but I don't like being lied to. Maybe I should have been more honest about that. Trust is a really big deal to me.'

I take his hand and lead him to a sofa. He quickly unlatches his palm from mine. 'I know you downplayed it; I could still see the hurt in your eyes. But you see, I sort of did the same thing. I didn't want to be known as the jilted bride and I made up a story to save face and, well, it snowballed. Dramatically. And for that, I am truly apologetic.'

'I'm hurt you kept it from me. It's such a big thing to keep hidden.'

'Well, at first, you were just another passenger, Jasper. I didn't know things were going to evolve the way they have. Miles made the choice on the wedding day to leave – and I know now that it was the right choice. Whatever you decide, you have to know I can't go back to him, and not because Miles made the choice to leave the church, or because he and I fundamentally want different things, but also because now... well, I've met you. And how can I be with him when *you* exist in this world? Even if you don't want to be with me... I can't be with anyone else. I've never felt this way before. Whatever this is, I want to give myself up to it, explore what might be, which might sound mad after a handful of days – but a day on the Winter Wonderland Express feels like a week – and that's what's in my heart. Our paths crossed for a reason, Jasper, so I'll leave it up to you.' My heart bongoes hard against my ribs but I'm glad I said my piece, said my truth. It's not like me to be so open with my feelings this early on, but if I don't speak up, I will lose Jasper. I might lose him anyway.

I wait for him to tell me no. That I'm rushing things. That I'm imagining this mad off-the-chain chemistry between us. And he doesn't say a word. Instead, he gently cups my face and kisses me. The kind of kiss that lights up my heart and makes me long for more.

'I've never felt like this before either. I swear my heart broke when I heard you utter his name – I had that overwhelming feeling that I'd lost you before we'd even begun. And all I know is, this... relationship might be in its infancy, but I already know I don't want to let you go, Aubrey.'

* * *

When we return to the bar, I'm surprised to find Miles is relaxing among the Unlucky in Love Travel Club after he'd asked me to give him some time alone in the cabin when I told him it was over between us.

He's usually so standoffish around people he doesn't know. Maybe that's a testament to the group and how friendly they are, or in Princess's case, downright nosy. 'And then what happened?'

'Then I'm sure her sister, Rox, tried to poison me!'

Big yikes.

'Wait, it was her sister who laced your meal with death cap mushrooms?' Princess looks to me for confirmation. I quickly shake my head.

Miles frowns. 'Mushrooms?'

'There was no sinkhole?' CJ asks.

'He didn't plummet to his death down the gap?' pipes up Sabrina, who is pretending to work behind the bar while listening in.

Igor, who sits at the booth behind, turns around and says, 'You weren't struck by lightning. Twice?'

'What?' Miles asks, face flushed.

I manage to stem giggles, but I have some explaining to do. 'No, Miles didn't fall down the gap like I told you, Sabrina. I'm sorry I lied. I just... felt put on the spot. I blurted that and then his fictional death took on a life of its own. I did try and tell you all he wasn't really dead but that backfired too.'

'She did. Many times,' Karen says, giving me a supportive smile.

'So why lie?' CJ asks.

'The truth is...' I go on to explain what happened, and Miles jumps in and shares his side of things, opening up about how his panic attacks have hampered him and that he then escaped and hoped it would all go away if he hid out long enough.

Miles averts his gaze. 'I... I was an idiot. But like Aubrey has reminded me, I'm a homebody and she is not. Aubrey's the sort of person who's happiest when she's learning a few words in another language, and I break out in a cold sweat even holding my passport.' He's handling the official break-up rather well, which only convinces me that we weren't right for each other except as friends. Sometimes the old high-school crush should remain just that – a crush.

Jasper steps forward, eye to eye with Miles. 'I can't believe you left her there.' There's a fragility to Jasper's voice that breaks my heart. As if he's able to put himself in my shoes that terrible day and understand how truly awful it felt. How humiliating. 'And then you cut contact.'

Miles blushes. 'I'll regret my actions that day for the rest of my life, probably. I didn't handle it well – and Aubrey suffered for it. I truly am sorry.'

'I'm sorry too.' I give him a half smile. There's no question I feel lighter, as if I've made the right choice – now, at any rate. And if not for Miles having panicked and run, I'd have gone through with the wedding when deep down I knew it wasn't right.

It's sweet to see Jasper's protective instinct is alive and well. The man has a deep well of empathy that feels so very special. Even as he gives Miles a bit of a telling off for ghosting me, it's done in a non-threatening way, that even my former flame admits he was in the wrong. But honestly, it was both of us feeling unsure but not wanting to hurt the other.

Miles clears his throat. 'Well, I might be unlucky in love, but staying on board will be far too awkward. I should be able to get a last-minute flight home and spend Christmas with Leo, who is a bit over me at the moment too.'

'I'm sure he'll be happy to have you back.' The bachelor pad will stay just that, and it's probably what was meant to happen all along. 'I appreciate you coming all this way to have the chat face to face.'

Miles says his goodbyes to the group, and I walk with him out to the platform, appreciating his efforts in flying to Stockholm now that he's admitted he despises travelling.

'Miles, I want to thank you for having the courage to leave that day. Having had this space, this distance, our differences are glaringly obvious, and they're not the kind of differences that we can compromise on.'

Miles swallows hard, like he's struggling to control his emotions. 'Yeah, part of me always hoped you'd change, be the way I wanted you to be,' he eventually says, his voice low, inflected with sadness. 'Which is unfair.'

'Yeah.' I give his hand a squeeze. 'You knew it wasn't right, or you'd have stayed at the church.'

Miles gives me a sad smile, like he agrees. 'And that guy?' He jerks a thumb in Jasper's direction.

'We met on board. But Miles, when I first saw Jasper, I felt a spark. Like, a literal spark, as if he'd shocked me back to life. How can you feel that way about someone else unless it's real? It emphasised to me that you and I were playacting at being soulmates. And I'm not saying that to hurt you. I'm saying it so you can be free too.'

Miles gives a slow nod of his head, as if in confirmation. 'Yeah, I think that maybe – maybe you're right? How did we not see it sooner?' An awkward laugh escapes him. 'I'd been so conflicted, because I didn't want to hurt you. I couldn't make sense of the confusion. The pressure was unreal. I tried to push myself into it, insisting on making the guest list bigger and all the plans grander. Like that would make it more valid. Prove to the world that what we had was real. But when I got to the church, I just knew I couldn't go through with it. Do you feel me?' His favourite catch phrase is lobbed into conversation once more.

It's a relief, a weight off my mind that Miles has come to the same conclusion. 'I'm glad you acted on that impulse, I really am. And what jilted bride can honestly say that?' I let out a volley of laughter. Miles isn't a bad guy, and I'm thankful now that it's all ended this way.

'Safe travels, Aubrey.'

I give Miles a goodbye hug and wish him all the best for the future. There's a sparkle in his eyes, as if he too knows this is for the best.

Back inside, I rejoin my friends, feeling at once happy and a little sad. It's bittersweet, the ending of things, but there's no question I made the right choice. Jasper sends me a sultry smile and I just about melt onto the carpet.

'I don't suppose he likes K-Pop?' Karen asks, watching Miles make his way slowly down the platform outside. CJ gasps, giving her friend a good-natured shove.

'Umm – Karen, that goes against girl code.' CJ shoves her back.

'Sorry, I figured why not ask the question when love is blooming on this train and there's still time to pull him back from the platform.'

'No, thanks.' CJ shakes her head, smiling. 'Looks like it's just us two singletons now, Karen. We've lost these two to Cupid's arrow.' She motions to Jasper and me sitting side by side, holding hands.

The apples of Karen's cheeks pinken.

'What's that blush about?' CJ twirls a finger at Karen's complexion before inhaling sharply. 'The no-spicy-food guy texted back, didn't he?'

Karen bites down on her lip and averts her gaze. 'Uh – yeah, he did. We've been messaging like a lot. We're going to meet up for dinner in the new year. I told him that I catastrophised about never being able to eat spicy food for the rest of my natural born life, and he got a kick out of that.'

'What do you mean?' I ask.

'On our first date, I told him I find sushi appalling, which is his favourite food, and he said that was almost a deal breaker for him too, so we got to talking about silly ick lists and how easy it is to discard a first date in these modern times when the next person is only a right swipe away and so maybe we need to be more open minded. Sushi isn't that bad, as long as I don't have to eat it.'

'Ah. I love that. It's so true. We're so quick to dismiss people.'

'And for me and him, well...' Karen muses. 'It's such a basic fix. We both realised that perhaps our ick list isn't really an ick list, more of a protective barrier. The Unlucky in Love Travel Club helped me see that.'

'So I really am the only singleton left in the Unlucky in Love Travel Club?' CJ makes a show of pouting.

'Ah, but the holiday isn't over yet,' Princess says, lifting her brow. 'Even if I have to send for a K-Pop fan, then send I will.'

We fall into easy laughter at Princess's efforts to always find a solution, even if that means paying for it.

Sabrina wanders over. 'Miles, eh? What a plot twist! The gap didn't claim him after all. I'm glad, in a way. I've been very careful walking on and off the train ever since then, let me tell you.'

'Me too!' Jasper laughs. 'I had my suspicions about your story, the way you told it so matter of fact, but your tears the day Igor proposed made me believe that you were grieving, and now I see you were grieving in a way – the loss of that day, what you thought your future should be if only you'd settle.'

'And that's the thing, settling isn't for me.'

'Thank God. So is the grieving period officially over?'

I laugh and pull him closer to me. 'It is.'

'And we're doing the Camino in March.'

'We are.' But where do we go from here?

* * *

Later that evening I fall into bed, mind spinning at the way everything has unfolded. Just as I'm about to switch my bedside light off, my phone rings. It can only be one person calling this late.

'Rox, it's late, even for you.'

Her pinched face appears on screen. 'Word is, Miles is on his way to you! You're not going to be taken in by whatever excuses he makes, are you?'

'Too late. He's already been here.'

'Already?'

'Yeah, been and gone.'

'Just like that? You didn't take him back?'

I give her a wide smile and explain how it all went down.

'Wow, Aubrey, and so you and Jasper are a thing now? It's not like you.'

My eyebrows shoot up. 'One minute you're telling me to fall into bed with him, the next you're questioning my feelings for the guy?'

'Well, I mean, I hardly know him. You didn't send me his details for the deep dive. What if he's as bad as Miles? What if he's a serial killer? How well do we know him, really?'

'It's early days, Rox. We've stolen a few kisses and we'll see what happens.'

'This is all so fast.'

'You are up and down like a yo-yo!'

She laughs. 'I only want the best for you, but I'd feel better if I saw this man in the flesh, you know?'

'And let you scare him off? No thanks.'

'So, are you coming home after the trip?'

I consider it. 'Maybe for a bit. I'll pack up my room, snuggle Freya's baby when he makes an appearance, and then head off again. I want to explore France.'

'You don't need to pack up your room here.'

'Thanks, Rox. When you're not committing crimes, you're not a half bad person.'

'Well, Roan ruined most of your clothes, but that's not on me, that's on her.'

I roll my eyes. 'How does a cat manage that?'

'Mostly with her claws. Between us, sometimes she scares me. She gives me this look, like she's plotting my downfall.'

'You get the cat you deserve, Rox!'

'Not that again!'

29

24 DECEMBER, LAPLAND, FINLAND

Christmas Eve

At our very last breakfast on the Winter Wonderland Express, Princess leans across the table and says, 'I can't help but feel like we're huge failures when it comes to solving our break-up mystery.'

I'm only half listening, distracted by the view outside, a snowy wonderland with whitecapped mountains in the distance. It's postcard perfect. I can't wait to explore Lapland.

'Did you hear me, Aubrey?' Princess asks.

I swing my gaze back to her. 'The break-up, ah – yes.'

'We're absolutely hopeless detectives. Agatha Christie would be turning in her grave.' Karen grimaces. 'So far I have personally witnessed two couples get engaged and one announce they're renewing their vows. You have to ask yourself, is it all the wine they're consuming? Why is everyone so happy?' She herself grins and is lit up from within, so different from the woman with the severe winged eyeliner and sad eyes that I met at the dinner table at the start of our journey. Love is all around. Or at least the hope of it is on the horizon.

'Well... I have a theory,' I say, all at once unsure if I should voice it. What if I'm wrong? But the Unlucky in Love Travel Club are the nurturing type and if I'm correct then this person could really use a little support right now.

'Do tell,' CJ says, munching on a freshly made buttery croissant. I'm certainly going to miss the five-star breakfasts when this holiday is over.

'I don't think it's a couple on board at all.'

Barry frowns. 'But... how can that be? Sabrina can't expect us to guess if it's someone we have no contact with.'

Jasper gives me a knowing nod. 'Ah, I see where you're going with this.'

'Please share the details,' Princess says, taking an unladylike swig of her breakfast mimosa. 'Put the rest of us out of our misery.'

'I think it's Sabrina.'

'Oooh.' Karen's mouth falls open. 'What makes you say that?'

'I have this feeling that Sabrina doesn't usually fail at attention to detail, like she has on this trip. Five-star service is a tough industry to get into, because of the impossibly high standards they set, so I'm certain she is more than capable of handling this job. The way she mixed the wines up, and her level of distraction, leads me to believe that she's the one who is suffering a heartbreak.'

'Yes,' Jasper agrees. 'And obviously management has pulled her aside and warned her about her performance, which has only made it worse.'

I've had my suspicions for a while. 'And she mentioned a suspected cheating scandal, the guy going rogue, so I wonder if she found out after we boarded the train. She was bright and bubbly early on, showing everyone photos of her boyfriend, hoping he'd get approval from his boss for time off, and then she stopped mentioning him altogether. She said she was tired and looked more listless than usual, which I put down to the intensely busy days that staff work – and that's when she told us about the couple heading for splitsville.'

'Ooh, the clues point that way for sure.' CJ's croissant is forgotten as she cups her chin. 'How sad, if it's true. She's such a sweetheart. And he's a fool if he did cheat.'

We lapse into silence.

'Let me guess, another fiancé died? Why the long faces?' Sabrina appears, coffee pot in hand.

'Oh, ah.'

'No!'

'We're sorry!'

'Are you OK?'

'You're beautiful, too beautiful for him!'

Sabrina tilts her head to the side. 'What? What's all this?'

Another silence hits, gazes are dropped, cutlery examined. It looks like I'll be the one to broach this most sensitive of subjects.

I take her hand in mine and give it a comforting squeeze. 'We think we've figured out the mystery you set for us. We hope we're wrong, but something tells me we're right.'

She arches a brow.

'Is it you?'

She does a remarkable job of holding on to her composure; the only slip is the slight wobble of her bottom lip. 'Yes.'

'Who is he?' Princess growls. 'I'll have him killed.'

The situation might not call for it, but we erupt in laughter. Tiger Mum is back.

Sabrina laughs too, her eyes glassy with tears. 'The love of my life, or so I thought. We met a couple of years ago. We both work in the travel industry. He's a chef, so there's a lot of time apart as we both take different jobs around the world, you know how it is, Aubrey. Living the dream of seeing as much of the planet as possible, while still trying to navigate love. We had plans to work like that for a few more years, save the deposit for a house and then find regular nine-to-five jobs. It made the long-distance thing easier, knowing that we had a goal, a dream and that these separations wouldn't be forever.'

'So what happened?' Barry asks softly.

'I left for Calais and he stayed in the Caribbean. When I pushed for him to book his flight to Lapland, he kept making excuses. Eventually, after many video calls, he admitted that he'd taken up with someone else while I've been away. Out of sight, out of mind, I guess. And now I'm back to square one, alone and probably about to lose my job because I've been so caught up in my heartbreak.'

'You're not alone,' Princess says. 'You have us. You always will.' She stands and gives Sabrina a quick hug. When she pulls away, she says, 'And there's no chance you'll lose your job.'

'Oh, there is, Princess. I just got my second warning for chatting to George. We were stocking up the coffee station, so it's not like we weren't working, but apparently, we shouldn't have been doing that. One more warning and I'm done.'

'Not going to happen.' Princess takes the coffee pot from Sabrina's hand. 'Sit down, darling. Have some breakfast.'

Sabrina's eyes go wide. 'No way, Princess! If she—'

'I insist.' Princess won't let it go and pushes Sabrina into the chair. 'I'm one of the owners of this train, the majority shareholder, actually, and I decide who stays and goes. And right now, I'd like you to enjoy breakfast with me and after that I'm going to have a little chat with your manager, OK?'

Princess is the majority shareholder of the Winter Wonderland Express! What! We're all stunned before laughter gets the better of us.

When we're composed, Sabrina says, 'Umm, OK, wow, I did not see that coming. Sure, I'll sit down, and I'll bloody well enjoy it too!'

'Good.' Princess smiles.

'One other thing,' Sabrina asks. 'Does this mean I officially get to join the Unlucky in Love Travel Club?' She gives us a watery smile.

'We'd be honoured,' Karen says. 'You dodged a bullet with that guy, Sabrina.'

'Yeah, I sure did. And you never know, maybe it was all for the best.' George walks by. The six-foot tall cutie pie gives Sabrina a shy smile and doesn't seem the least bit curious as to why she's sitting down with us.

'Oooh,' Princess catches the look Sabrina and George share and grins. 'The thing about our club is that love blooms in the unlikeliest of places.'

Sabrina shrugs and leans forward to whisper, 'George is just the sweetest. He's got that golden retriever energy, and after dating the cliché alpha male, I'm done with those egomaniac types.'

'Love those cinnamon roll heroes,' I say. 'Can't get much sweeter than that.'

Sabrina stands up and grabs the coffee pot again, as if she can't relax even though Princess has insisted on it. 'I better get back to work or it's not fair on the others. More coffee, Aubrey?' She doesn't wait for an answer and pours coffee into my tea, but I don't mention it. She's got enough on her plate, though something tells me her heartbreak will soon be a thing of the past.

30

24 DECEMBER, LAPLAND, FINLAND

The last stop

I find myself a little teary as I pack my belongings, ready to disembark at the last stop for the Winter Wonderland Express. It's been one of the best experiences of my life and I'm happy the holiday is not quite over yet. Glancing around the cabin once more, I make a mental note of how it's laid out and how I'll package the idea for my clients. Jasper's writing an article about the train for a prestigious online newspaper – which I'll be sharing on my website in the hopes it inspires future travellers. I take one last look around, hoping that one day I get to ride the Winter Wonderland Express again, although there's a big chance it won't be as special as this trip was because it's been all about the friends I've made and the time we've spent together.

We meet on the platform. Sabrina is dressed up in a one-piece candy-cane costume, and I can't help but laugh.

'They saved the best for last.' She gestures to her red and white striped ensemble.

George stands beside her. 'I did offer to swap but she said no, and thank God for that. I'm not sure I could pull off all that Lycra like Sabrina can.' George is wearing a more sedate Nutcracker ensemble.

'It doesn't leave much to the imagination, George, does it?' Sabrina giggles.

He bites down on his lip as colour rushes his cheeks. 'Ah... I... uh, hadn't noticed.'

We're standing in a huddle as everyone checks they've got all their belongings when Gigi, the tall blonde with the cool smile, steps down from the train and turns, throwing a gold wedding band at Silas.

'Gigi, wait! I'm sorry.'

She spins on her heel and walks away with all the grace and poise of a supermodel. It's so cool, it's like something out of a movie. The Unlucky in Love Travel Club exchange glances, but none of us dare speak – probably because it wouldn't be polite to cheer a break-up, but that's what I feel like doing. Silas slinks off, head down, trundling his suitcase behind.

'Told you there'd be some casualties.' Sabrina's gaze lingers on Silas's retreating form. 'Thank God Gigi saw the light. That bauble-grabbing buzzard doesn't deserve her.'

'Let's hope he goes home with his tail between his legs and not to the igloo stays.'

'He's not getting on the bus.' Princess motions to a taxi Silas has hailed. 'So that's a good sign.'

I turn back to Sabrina, who wears a hint of sadness on her face – for the impending goodbyes? It feels like an ending, this kind of farewell, even though we'll see her again once she finishes work. The air is heavy with the weight of it. 'Thanks for the best winter wonderland holiday I've ever had,' I say. 'I'll never forget it.'

She grins, and it lights up her pretty face. 'You're welcome, Aubrey. I hope we'll see you back on board one day.'

'I hope so too.'

'I'll see you at the lodge this evening.'

'I can't wait!'

'You and me both!'

Once the Winter Wonderland Express is empty, the staff clean and prepare for the next load of passengers as they make the trip back in reverse. Luckily, Sabrina has a few days off after she finishes work this evening.

'Group photo or it didn't happen!' Karen yells, and we all squish in together in front of the train. Then there's much hugging and fanfare, almost like none of us want to leave. That's the sign of a great holiday – the lingering.

I give Sabrina and George a wave and take one last look at the Winter Wonderland Express before following the group to the bus that will take us to the igloos that will be our home for the next three days.

On the bus, spirits are high as guests are excited for the next leg of the journey. The Unlucky in Love Travel Club choose seats together and soon we fall into conversation about all the sights we want to see in Lapland.

CJ's keen for all those high-octane pursuits she's been dreaming of, which Karen has reluctantly agreed to join in with. 'But I refuse, absolutely refuse, to go naked in the sauna.'

My eyebrows shoot up. 'You have to go naked?'

CJ shrugs. 'It's a personal choice but in Finland, it's a cultural norm to sauna naked, allowing your body to breathe, soak up the steam. You can wear a towel or bathing suit though; your choice will be respected too.'

Princess smiles. 'Karen, you have to try it naked! What's stopping you? It's not like if you were naked on the beach. Yeah, sure, that would get everyone's attention. Here it's more about relaxation. No one will be ogling you, and if they do, they'll soon be removed from the sauna.'

'Oh God, you're all going to peer-pressure me and next minute I'll have no body-image issues and then what? No, it's best if I at least wear a towel. That I can do.'

'What about you, Princess?' I ask. 'Are you going to do the ice swimming and sauna bathing?'

'Absolutely! CJ says it keeps you young, and I have got a lot of living to do.' With that she gives Barry a peck on the cheek, and his complexion soon pinkens.

'I better try it out too then,' he says, still blushing like a schoolkid.

'Look,' CJ says. 'I hope you lot don't mind but I've managed to book the husky sled lesson. Only issue is, I have to go now or I'll miss out. The bus driver is happy to drop us there on the way and pick us up again later. What do you say?' CJ gives us a tentative smile. 'We can check in to the igloos after that. Warm up with some valhalla, Finnish herbal schnaps.'

'Why not?' Princess says. 'We'll happily watch you pursue one of your dreams. I'm sure there's a nice little log cabin where we can warm up with some schnaps.'

* * *

'We're all going to die!' What might be my very last words are whipped away by momentum as we scream across the icy forest with CJ at the helm of our husky-led sled. There's no time to appreciate the beauty of the panting blue-eyed huskies or the view because it turns out I can't appreciate those things and panic at the same time.

Karen frowns at me and then yelps when a heap of snow falls

from an overhead branch. She coughs and splutters, being thrown this way and that, when CJ abruptly changes course. 'Far out, maybe you're right!'

White-knuckling it, we hold on for dear life, torn between wanting to support our friend's dream of roaring through the forest... and staying alive. CJ is only a provisional husky sled driver after all, and when I say provisional, she's had all of an hour of training.

'Whooo!' Princess practically yodels. 'This is the most fun I've ever had!'

Barry grits his teeth and makes agreeable grunts that don't quite belie the fear written all over his face as we bump and slide across the snowy ground. Got to love a partner who's supportive even in the face of sheer terror.

Jasper curls a protective arm around me as his hair blows back, making him even more attractive, if that's even possible. 'On the off chance we do die, it's probably best if we share one last kiss.'

'When you put it that way, how can I refuse?'

His lips barely brush mine, but it's enough to make my synapses fizzle and crackle like an electric current.

Jasper pulls me tight into his body, seemingly unfazed about the danger we face, so I relax into his embrace and think supportive thoughts for CJ ticking off an item on her bucket list and not about our imminent deaths.

'Are you OK?' Jasper, ever the caring soul, asks.

With a stuttering jaw, I manage, 'Uh-huh.'

'Don't worry, I've got you.' And he has. Hook, line and sinker.

'What?' His lips curl into a questioning smile.

I'm doing that dopey lovesick goggle-eyed expression that I have no control over again. 'Nothing. It's – uh, nothing.' Just me here, planning my rosy future, mind skipping off to fantasyland where Jasper is the main character in my story. 'It's just…' Fine, why not tell him? He can't exactly escape from the sled, not at these speeds. But then I chicken out. 'I'm really looking forward to our Christmas feast.'

He cocks his head as if he's waiting for the punchline, but he doesn't call me on it. 'I'm looking forward to spending Christmas with you.'

31

24 DECEMBER, LAPLAND, FINLAND

We arrive at the lodge for check-in. It's the grandest hotel I've ever seen, with a sweeping view of snow-capped mountains in the distance. It's like a log cabin but on steroids. The interior is sumptuously decorated but still has a certain rustic charm to it, with a crackling fire in the centre surrounded by wrinkled leather sofas layered with tartan throw rugs and fluffy cushions.

We queue at the counter and wait our turn. From the striking full-length picture window, the igloos are visible, spread along the snow-covered expanse. I cannot wait to investigate them further.

'I feel like a kid at Christmas!' Princess screeches. As soon as the front desk staff recognise Princess, she's moved to the front of the queue. 'Don't mind me,' she says to the people in front who send her dark looks. 'I'm an old lady who needs to put her feet up.' I love that she doesn't blurt out that she also owns the lodge. She hasn't explicitly admitted it, but I get the feeling from the way the staff behave around her, fluttery and nervous, that she does.

Princess is given her key and doesn't worry about anything so boring as paperwork like the rest of us will need to do. The check-in staff hurry to assure Princess that her igloo has been stocked with champagne. 'Wonderful. Meet you for Christmas Eve dinner, darlings.' She air-kisses us and briskly walks away before she stops short. 'Barry? Are you coming or not?'

Barry's eyes go wide, before he mutters, 'Oh, right, yes, yes. Can I take your suitcase for you, Princess, so you don't need to wait for the porter?'

'That would be lovely, Barry.'

When I get my key, I'm delighted to find my igloo is right beside Jasper's. 'I'll show you mine if you show me yours,' I tease, leaving my suitcase against the door.

'You move fast, Aubrey, but I'm keen if you are.' I laugh and grab his hand as we make our way into the warmth.

Inside, the igloo is surprisingly cosy. The domed thermal glass itself is heated, not only to warm the room but also to keep the view clear and free of snow in the freezing temperatures. A fire crackles in the hearth and I swear there's underfloor heating as warmth creeps up my body. 'Oh my God, how will we ever leave?'

The king-size bed sits in the centre of the room and will be the cosiest place to curl up when darkness falls and watch the spectacular display of the Northern Lights across the night sky. The room is well appointed with a bookshelf of paperbacks, a mini bar, and a plush sofa and armchairs. There's a large en suite – imagine showering with that view, although to maintain privacy, the sides of the wall are blacked out so no one can see in.

'We don't leave. We lock the door on the world and we stay here forever.' Jasper takes me into his arms, and it just feels so right. Like I've found my place, and how can I be so sure, so soon? But somehow I am. They do say when you know, you know.

'Yes, please,' I say with a nod. 'Maybe they'll forget we're here.'

'I hope so.'

My breathing quickens as Jasper cups my face and leans down to kiss me. Sparks fly, igniting my heart. My own Northern Lights, as I light up from the inside at his touch. When we pull apart, I'm love drunk, giddy and hazy with it. 'Should we check out the hot tub?' I ask with a mischievous grin.

'You got the hot tub room!'

'I did!'

'What are we standing here for?' Within seconds he's slipped off his jacket and jumper, his t-shirt pulls up to expose tanned, rippled abs, and oh my, I'm going to die of lust. I double-blink and try to regain my equilibrium. *Play it cool, Aubrey. Don't act like some sex-starved fool*, but it's too late. My mouth is agape and I'm probably doing that under-breath life-narration thing because it bloody well can't be helped. The man is a sex god, no two ways about it.

'Aubrey?'

He frowns.

'Aubrey?'

I snap back to the here and now. 'Yes?'

'Sorry, is the hot tub thing too soon? I can wear my t-shirt...'

My gaze drops to his torso, which is now unclothed. He stands in a pair of denim jeans that hug him in all the right places. How can a body be so earth shattering, knocking all sense from my brain? Still, it's best to downplay the effect he's having on me. 'No, you don't need to wear a T-shirt. I'll change into my bathing suit and meet you in the hot tub.'

* * *

After I'm changed, I check my reflection in the mirror and give myself a pep talk. He's just Jasper; hot, yes, but intelligent too.

The situation calls for alcohol, no two ways about it. In the mini bar fridge, I find a bottle of champagne with a note:

For the lovebirds, from Princess. It's not just a name, it's a way of life.

I smile. God, I love her.

I join Jasper, who's in the tub, arms outstretched, gazing out towards the snowcapped mountains. He gives me a slow once over, his lips curving as if he likes what he sees but is too polite to say. Well, that's a good thing.

'Bubbles, from Princess.'

He takes the champagne flutes from my hand while I open the bottle. Once our glasses are poured, I sit beside him, nestling into him, trying my darndest not to think of what he's wearing on the bottom half.

'How lucky are we,' he says, 'to be here experiencing this?'

'It's incredible. I'm going to have the holiday blues after, that's for sure. What can ever live up to this?' And I don't mean just the stunning vista before me.

'Does it need to end? That's the question.'

'Ah?'

'This might sound massively cheesy, but when I first spotted you on the platform, I felt an instant spark, like love at first sight.' He blushes and covers it by taking a deep sip of champagne.

Love at first sight! But hadn't I felt the very same about Jasper that day on the platform? Shocked back to life? 'Really?'

'Really.' He lets out a self-conscious laugh. 'I've always wanted to find someone who shares the same interests as me, someone who wants to explore the world. Sure, I like my cosy little cabin in Connecticut, but it's just a base. What I'm trying to say, Aubrey, is that I don't want this holiday to end, inasmuch as I don't want to let you go. At the risk of coming across like a stage-four clinger, do you want to keep the holiday going?'

'By holiday, you mean us?'

'I do.'

I bite down on a goofy grin. 'Well, I've been thinking.' I look up at him, my heart stuttering at the sight of him. 'After Lapland, I was considering renting a campervan for my next adventure.' Van life is a popular cost-effective way to travel and I'm keen to give it a try and see if I enjoy living out of a tiny home on wheels. I'm used to travelling light anyway, so it's no real hardship, but living out of a van gives me a lot more freedom when it comes to exploring.

'I love that idea.'

'Yeah? That's good because I had this crazy thought...'

'I'm listening.'

'Would you like to be my travel buddy? I'm sure I can find a van big enough for the two of us.'

'I'd love to be your travel buddy. I'll head home to Connecticut so I can pack what I need for our road trip and the Camino...'

'I'll go back to the village and do the same. Spend some time with Freya and the baby, who will arrive earthside any day... and then meet you in Paris?'

'Under the Eiffel Tower.'

'At night, when it's sparkling.'

'I can't wait for all the adventures we're going to have together, Aubrey.'

He kisses me deep and full on the mouth. The view of the mountain blurs, and all I can see is him and our exciting future of travels together.

32

24 DECEMBER, LAPLAND, FINLAND

Christmas Eve

I'm dressing for dinner in a hurry because I have become one half of those kissy-wissy pairs who spend all their time canoodling and whispering sweet nothings. Jasper's gone back to his igloo to get changed and it's like he's taken the air in the room with him.

My phone buzzes as I clip on a plastic snowflake earring that will no doubt catch Princess's eye.

When I see the name on the display, my heart rate speeds up. It's got to be go time!

'Freya! Is it—'

It's not Freya's face I see; it's James, her husband. 'Hi, Aubrey. There's someone we want you to meet.' He pans the camera to a little baby swaddled and peacefully asleep.

'Awww! He's so beautiful! Look at those chubby cheeks and all that hair!'

'Yeah, he's a big boy, bigger than expected, and he didn't want to bother with a long delivery. He arrived about an hour after we got to the hospital so there was no time to call and tell you Freya was in labour.'

'Well, I'm not a childbirth expert by any means, but fast is... good, I hope?'

'Yeah, Freya thinks so too.'

'How is she?'

'She's doing really well. Hang on, here she is.'

My beautiful friend's face is flushed but satisfied. As if all the hard work has been done and now she can rest with her new baby swaddled up beside her. 'Hello, you! Baby's got a right mop of hair, hasn't he?'

She lets out a quiet laugh. 'Hasn't he just? He looks just like his dad.'

'What's his name then? I can't wait to cuddle him.'

Freya sends a loving smile his way. 'Well, that's the thing, Aubrey, we need your vote. I love the name Bear and James likes the name Noah, and we simply can't agree. Which do you prefer?'

'Ooh, that's easy. Bear!'

'Ha!' She grins and turns the camera on James, who is cupping his face.

'Really, Aubrey? Bear?'

'It's strong yet soft and utterly perfect.'

'Bear it is.'

We spend the next hour chatting before Freya's slow blinks make it obvious that the mumma bear needs rest. I'm woefully late by the time I make it to dinner but have the perfect excuse when I show them pictures that James sent of the cutest little baby bear who ever did live.

33

24 DECEMBER, LAPLAND, FINLAND

Christmas Eve Dinner

'Merry Christmas Eve to one and all!' Princess says as we sit together in the lodge for our Christmas feast. In most parts of Europe, Christmas is celebrated on the 24th, so we've followed this tradition. The dining room of the lodge is packed with guests. Igor and Katya are accosting poor Santa, who was simply ho-ho-ho-ing and trying to jingle his bells when they launched at him for photos. I can only laugh and silently wish Santa well.

From this vantage point high up in the lodge, the igloos are lit up with festive lights that shine brightly under the dark sky. Gorgeous fawn-coloured reindeer mosey past the window and stop to gaze in, their almost human-like doe eyes captivated by the goings on in the lodge.

Princess stands and calls for our attention. 'I have a little surprise for each of you, and before you go blustering about not getting me anything, save it.' She hands us all a small box.

'Go ahead, open it!'

Inside are gold passport charms. On the passport cover is the tiniest engraving: *The Lucky in Love Travel Club*. It's enough to make me well up. Such a sweet, thoughtful gift and one I'll treasure. I take it from the box and loop it through my necklace.

'How did you—'

'Where—'

Princess waves us to sit down. 'I found the charms in Copenhagen, and they offered an engraving service.' Sabrina and George enter the dining room... holding hands.

'Merry Christmas!' I hug Sabrina and everyone follows suit. There's much chatter as we sit back down and enjoy our Christmas feast, looking out over the snowy landscape.

Princess has sorted an igloo for them for the evening, so they're led away by a staff member to check in. Sabrina's face is a picture of pure bliss at the extravagance. 'That was nice of you,' I whisper.

'Least I could do. She's a real asset to the Winter Wonderland Express. And she doesn't know it yet, but she's going to be promoted to Guest Relations Manager. Her talents are wasted turning down beds and pouring coffee, so even though I'm retired I made a couple of calls. She'll be fabulous in her new role with her bubbly personality and care for passengers' needs.'

'That role is perfect for her.' We fall quiet when Sabrina returns gushing about the igloo. It's impossible not to be swept along in her joy.

'Isn't it strange to think there will be an entirely new load of passengers on the train? Sleeping in our cabins, sitting at our table, or in our spot in the library?' CJ says with a bittersweet smile.

'So strange,' I agree. 'I only hope they enjoy it as much as we did.'

'Let's cheers to that,' Jasper says, raising his glass. 'May they make friendship the way we have.' There's the clink of champagne flutes and smiles all round. You don't often make such solid friendships on travels like this, so I vow to hold on to them all and not let time or distance dull this incredible bond.

'So…' Princess raises a brow. 'It might be too soon but what are everyone's plans for the summer? I happen to own a cruise ship that sails around the Cyclades, that stunning archipelago of islands with all that blue of the Aegean Sea…'

'I'm in,' Barry says with a lopsided grin.

'I mean, I only ever travel at Christmas but I'm sure allowances can be made,' Karen says with a wink.

'It's a hell yes from me.' CJ grins.

Jasper clasps my hand, and I give him a nod. 'We'd love to join you all there!'

'Woohoo! Season two of the Unlucky in Love Travel Club. Destination: the Cyclades.'

Who knew that being unlucky in love would lead to this? What the future will bring is anyone's guess. What I do know is Jasper is up for anything, and it might be nice to have a sidekick on my travels, one who sees the same beauty as I do.

As the group chatter away, excitedly making plans for the summer, I lead Jasper to the picture window under the pretence of taking a closer look at the reindeer, when really, I just need to feel his arms around me once more. To feel the warmth of him.

'You read my mind,' he says with a seductive grin and leans down to kiss me, lighting up my heart and my soul. Have I found my perfect match? A man who says yes to adventure? A man who lives life on his own terms, just like I do. A soul mate? Because that's what this feels like, destiny. Like I'm the heroine in a romance movie who finally understands that all paths were leading her here, to this very moment.

* * *

After dinner we're all wrapped in fur blankets as we sit on the deck of the lodge, even though we all have perfectly warm igloos to hang out in. There's a crispness to the air that feels like a tincture when I inhale.

'We're out of champagne.' Karen wiggles the empty bottle. 'I'm not sure whether to call it a night or not.'

The Northern Lights haven't made an appearance as yet but that doesn't stop us craning our necks hoping to see the pinky-greeny-hued swirl.

'Let's have one more drink,' CJ says. 'And then we can call it quits for the night.'

Everyone agrees so CJ heads inside to the bar.

We chatter away about plans for Christmas Day, which consists of sauna bathing and Arctic swimming. How I got myself roped into this I do not know. I blame peer pressure.

'What's taking CJ so long?' Princess asks. 'My mouth is like the Sahara over here.'

I laugh. 'Let me go find out.'

The heat of the lodge is a shock coming in from the cold. As I step inside and make my way to the bar, there's no sign of CJ. It's nice to defrost for a bit – maybe CJ is warming herself by the fire. Not there either. I walk up a couple of steps to the lounge when I hear her laugh. I follow the sound to a staff area. I peek in and a slow smile settles on my face.

There's a bank of security cameras and next to those is a laptop with a music video playing. I'm no expert on K-Pop but even I can recognise the familiar faces of the BTS band on screen. CJ sits next to a security guard with a fit physique as they sing along to the music with eyes only for each other. Has she found her K-Pop fan? I leave them to it and go back to the bar.

34

25 DECEMBER, LAPLAND, FINLAND

'Argh!' A scream escapes because, well, I'm throwing myself into an Arctic lake when there's a cosy heated igloo with my name on it. The cold plunge takes my breath away and shocks me silent until my endorphins kick in. Wow, what a rush. CJ just might be onto something with all these high-octane adrenaline-filled pursuits.

Jasper leaps in and swims over to me, casual as anything, as if he always throws his buff bod into icy pools of water.

'You're shivering.' He wraps me in his arms and pulls my body against his. 'I suppose that's stating the obvious.'

My teeth chatter too much for me to form words and instead they come out garbled. Eventually I manage to control my shivering enough to say, 'How long am I supposed to stay in the water for maximum benefits?' I've never felt cold like it before, but it's somehow invigorating, and heightens the natural world around me. The vista in front of me is all white ice, with the exception of the carved-out section of lake. I must be mad!

'As long as you can handle it.'

Princess swims by doing a gentle breaststroke, with Barry

trailing in her wake, not quite as graceful a swimmer. Karen remains on the edge, holding onto the ladder for dear life, while CJ tries to convince her that she will not become an ice block.

'Get in, Karen!' I encourage her.

'YOLO, right?' Karen throws herself into the water with a scream, while CJ dives in just after. A few seconds later they pop up next to me.

Karen's expression is one of awe. 'OK, yes, it's both awful and wonderful at the very same time. How is that possible?'

We laugh, as much as our lung capacity allows us to at any rate. Princess swims back, merry as anything. 'Isn't this a refreshing way to spend Christmas Day?'

'It's definitely going to be a core memory,' Jasper says.

Sabrina and George are off to the side, chatting away like they're the best of friends. When he splashes her, all bets are off, and she soon dunks his head under water.

CJ pops up near me. 'Sooo,' I say subtly as anything. 'Am I wrong or did I see an impromptu K-Pop concert for two last night with you and a rather handsome security guard?'

The Canadian woman grins. 'Spying, were you?'

I laugh, it comes out breathless from cold. 'Yep.'

'Details!' Princess yelps. 'Name, age, net worth.'

CJ shakes her head. 'His name is Eeli, and he's thirty-five. Not sure about his net worth, but I am sure he loves K-Pop and Korean pop culture. And he's into extreme sports!'

'More extreme than this?' I ask.

'Much more! We're meeting later to go ice climbing!' CJ explains the terrifying technique involved in ice climbing, where essentially an ice axe and crampons are used to climb an ice fall. 'I'm a beginner obviously so we're starting small. And who knows, I just might have found the next great love of my life, or just a really fun buddy to join me on outdoor pursuits.'

'And yet you risk the development of that love or friendship by climbing an ice fall...' Princess says. 'I will never understand adrenaline junkies.'

CJ laughs. 'Carpe Diem!'

We all join in yelling Carpe Diem, even though I have no intention of seizing the day if it means partaking in an activity that is so scary, it makes even my bones shiver. Speaking of shivering, Barry's complexion has a slight blue tinge to it and his stare is vacant.

Being Australian, Barry is definitely not acclimatised to cold like this but is doing his best but his smile seems frozen in place almost like rigor mortis has set in. It's rather unsettling. 'Are you... OK, Barry?' I ask.

'Oh my God, I've killed him! Haven't I?' Princess yells in a panic. 'Is he dead? The curse is real and I've only gone and killed yet another man.' She covers her face with her hands and lets out an anguished cry.

I give Barry's shoulder a shake. He might look like a corpse, but I'm sure he's still alive. Isn't he? My pulse races as I fear I might have a real death on my hands this time. I'm the one who encouraged Princess to love again. 'Barry! BARRY!' I yell.

'Is he just... a bit frozen, do you think?' Sabrina asks, surveying him up close. 'He blinked! He's alive!'

'Barry?' Princess launches herself at him. 'You poor man. He's never encountered temperatures this cold, let along plunging his body into the icy depths like this. I'd better get him out.'

She helps him back up the ladder and wraps him in a towel, admonishing him for scaring her witless. I let out a relieved breath.

Once the panic is over, we resume swimming. CJ is ducking and diving and having a whale of a time while Karen's teeth chatter so much it's like she's having a one-way conversation with herself. 'I'm – g – g – going to...'

'Get out?'

'Y – y – yes.'

'Me too,' I say.

'Sauna?' Jasper asks.

I nod and let him lead me out. We quickly dry ourselves with a towel and robe up, slip on shoes and jog to the wooden hut. I practically catapult myself into the heat of the sauna. Princess and Barry are already inside, their cheeks rosy from the warmth. Barry makes jokes about his Aussie blood freezing over and Princess puts her head on his shoulder. 'We'll have to holiday in sunnier climes for you, my dear man.'

When my body finally recognises it's not dying and the blood resumes flowing, I say, 'That was crazy!'

Jasper laughs. 'Crazy fun, right?'

'Right. I do think, however, I'm going to give the snowshoeing a miss.'

'Yeah?'

'Yeah.'

'Any other ideas?'

'Hot tub?'

'Hot tub.'

We say our goodbyes to the group and take the courtesy car back to the igloo.

* * *

After a lengthy and rather steamy – in every sense of the word – hot tub session with Jasper, he returns to his own igloo to make some notes about ice swimming and sauna bathing for his article. I shower and dress in fluffy Christmas PJs and call Freya.

'Aubrey! Good timing, he's awake.' The camera pans towards little Bear, who has such a wise face even though he's only a day old.

'Merry Christmas, Bear!' He frowns like an old man, which makes me laugh. 'How are you feeling, Freya?'

She brings the phone back to her face. 'I'm a little tired but that's to be expected, probably for the next eighteen years or so.'

'Probably.'

'What happened with Miles? I heard he boarded the Winter Wonderland Express?'

I go into great detail about how it all played out and what's happened since with Jasper.

'Golly – I look away for one minute…'

'Yeah, but it's all worked out for the best. But maybe James could drop in on Miles and check how he's doing once you're all settled in back home?'

'I'll make sure he does. You know, I sort of feel like I had a hand in all of this. I pushed you towards Miles and really put the pressure on. Upon reflection, I shouldn't have done that, Aubrey. Tried to sway you in such a way.'

'You only wanted me home, and it's not like you forced me to date him, you just vouched for the guy, that he'd in fact matured after high school, unlike most of his friends. The rest happened naturally.'

'Yeah, but I did kind of push you. It's just I had this vision of us, raising babies, babies you don't even want, and growing old in houses with white picket fences… Since having this little fellow, I've sat here snuggling him and contemplating what kind of life he'll have, and wonder what if he's like you? A person who loves adventure and wants to follow the sunshine and have endless summers – I would be in awe of him for living out his dreams in a true free-spirited fashion. And yet here I am trying my utmost to get you to stay in Kent, so I can selfishly have my best friend with me.'

Her sentiments bring a tear to my eye. 'Aw, Freya, honestly, it isn't selfish of you, and a very big part of me was tempted to stay in the village for all those reasons too. I miss you like crazy when I'm away, and at times an ocean might separate us, but that doesn't dim our friendship and it never will.'

'I know, but thank you for being so understanding. When Bear is a little bigger, maybe we can meet you somewhere in the world for a family holiday.'

'Well, Princess is talking up summer in the Cyclades...'

35

25 DECEMBER, LAPLAND, FINLAND

Princess clinks her champagne glass for attention. All eyes turn to her. 'Merry Christmas, all. I'd like to give my thanks to Aubrey.' Her eyes go glassy with tears. It's not often Princess loses her composure. I wait for her to continue, unsure of how to help. 'I know, I know, but if you can't cry at Christmas, when can you. Anyway, without Aubrey's intervention I'd have remained alone for the rest of my life, convinced I'd been cursed, because how unlucky in love can one woman be?'

There are murmurs of support around the table as Princess takes a tissue from Barry and wipes the mascara smudges from under her eyes.

'But that's just the thing, I haven't been unlucky at all! In fact, I've been just the opposite, I've been lucky to have given my heart to three good men, and now, if Barry plays his cards right, possibly a fourth.' There are titters around the table and Barry grins. 'And I'm not just saying this because I have a vested interest in the Winter Wonderland Express, but because I truly believe magic happened on that train ride, not only in the friendships that were formed between us, but also the potential of love in the air...' She gazes at me with a fond smile. 'And that makes this a Christmas to remember. Thank you to all of you. My world got so much bigger with you in it.'

We stand and take turns hugging and soon dinner is served. We share yet another huge meal of Finnish festive fare. There's roast meat with a rich and luscious blackcurrant sauce, delicate white fish topped with a juniper berry remoulade. Ham coated in Nordic mustard. And so much more my eyes bulge.

With the roaring fire crackling in the background, Santa peeping around the corner in his attempts to hide from Igor and Katya, reindeer meandering past the window without a care in the world, jaunty Christmas carols playing from speakers above, and Jasper's hand resting on my leg, this Christmas is going to be impossible to beat.

* * *

Jasper and I are snuggled in my igloo, lying sprawled on the king-size bed, food coma activated. He's brushing a lock of hair from my face and I'm staring intently into his eyes, sure I'll never get tired of plumbing the striking unfathomable depths of them.

'Aubrey, what do you dream about?' Jasper's small talk is always big talk. I love that about him.

'You mean in the future?'

'Yeah.'

'Living in the moment. Long road trips staying in soggy tents. Finding cheap flights to Bali and visiting temples. Eating street food at hawkers' markets. Watching sunsets in places I don't speak the language. Surprising my family with a visit home for Christmas where Rox decapitates her gingerbread men as she shapes them and Mum will bake them until they're burnt anyway. Buying this guy I like magnets and souvenir spoons for his secret collection. Walks on a white sandy beach, with you. What do you dream about?'

He strokes my face with a gentle fingertip, his touch sending sparks through me. 'I dream about a little white van, with a bit of character-building rust and a few golf-ball-like dents. The vehicle sputters and backfires like it's got something to say. We have an old-school road map, because isn't it more fun to get lost that way? I see fresh-baked baguettes with lashings of thick butter as we eat greedily, parked on the side of a road we don't know the name of with a view of the vineyard somewhere in the south of France. At night rain drums on the roof of the van as we snuggle on a thin mattress that we're both too polite to admit is making our backs ache. And I dream about a lot of kissing and a lot of canoodling.'

'Sounds perfect.'

The map of our lives, where all those roads before led us to each other.

'It does.'

'France, then Spain, then…?'

'Anywhere you go, I'll follow.'

His lips are a breath away from mine, so I bridge the gap and go to kiss him, just as a flash of colour catches my eye. Above the dome of the igloo, the Northern Lights flash a spectacular show, but eh, they're just the Northern Lights and this is Jasper. I close my eyes and press my lips against Jasper's, certain that I've never felt this kind of love before and never will again. We'll have road trips and wrinkled road maps. Passports full of stamps. Stolen kisses under foreign skies. Stories told around a campfire. Lazy Sundays in bed with our books. And a whole world to explore, while he writes about far flung destinations, and I curate holidays for those with wanderlust in their veins. As our kiss ends, the heavens above explode in colour.

* * *

MORE FROM REBECCA RAISIN

Another book from Rebecca Raisin, *The Paris Bookshop for the Broken-Hearted*, is available to order now here:
https://mybook.to/ParisBackAd

ABOUT THE AUTHOR

Rebecca Raisin writes heartwarming romance from her home in sunny Perth, Australia. Her heroines tend to be on the quirky side and her books are usually set in exotic locations so her readers can armchair travel any day of the week. The only downfall about writing about gorgeous heroes who have brains as well as brawn, is falling in love with them–just as well they're fictional. Rebecca aims to write characters you can see yourself being friends with, people with big hearts who care about relationships and believe in true, once-in-a-life time love.

Sign up to Rebecca Raisin's mailing list for news, competitions and updates on future books.

Follow Rebecca on social media here:

- facebook.com/RebeccaRaisinAuthor
- x.com/jaxandwillsmum
- instagram.com/rebeccaraisinwrites2
- bookbub.com/authors/rebecca-raisin
- tiktok.com/@rebeccaraisinwrites

ALSO BY REBECCA RAISIN

A Love Letter to Paris

Christmas at the Little Paris Hotel

The Paris Bookshop for the Broken-Hearted

Last Stop on the Winter Wonderland Express

BECOME A MEMBER OF
THE SHELF CARE CLUB

The home of Boldwood's book club reads.

Find uplifting reads, sunny escapes, cosy romances, family dramas and more!

Sign up to the newsletter
https://bit.ly/theshelfcareclub

Boldwood

Boldwood Books is an award-winning fiction publishing company seeking out the best stories from around the world.

Find out more at www.boldwoodbooks.com

Join our reader community for brilliant books, competitions and offers!

Follow us
@BoldwoodBooks
@TheBoldBookClub

Sign up to our weekly deals newsletter

https://bit.ly/BoldwoodBNewsletter

Printed in Dunstable, United Kingdom